Praise for Beth Cornelison

"Steady pacing and a solid plot, complete with a dramatic, passionate ending, are all hallmarks of one terrific romance."
—*RT Book Reviews* on *Colton Cowboy Protector*

"Cornelison has written a page turner that is truly enjoyable from beginning to end."
—*Fresh Fiction* on *Cowboy's Texas Rescue*

"A tough, protective hero is at the center of this suspenseful story. Good pacing, expert storytelling and sweet chemistry makes this story a page-turner."
—*RT Book Reviews* on *Protecting Her Royal Baby*

Praise for Karen Whiddon

"Strong writing, plenty of action, solid characters and sizzling chemistry will keep readers turning the pages."
—*RT Book Reviews* on *The Rancher's Return*

"Action-packed with a lot of twists and turns that lead the reader on an amazing ride."
—*Fresh Fiction* on *The Lost Wolf's Destiny*

"An exciting blend of a tension-filled plot, terrific secondary characters and a pair you can't help but root for. It all makes for a wonderfully satisfying read."
—*RT Book Reviews* on *The Perfect Soldier*

* * *

**If you're on Twitter, tell us what you think of Harlequin Romantic Suspense!
#harlequinromsuspense**

Beth Cornelison began working in public relations before pursuing her love of writing romance. She has won numerous honors for her work, including a nomination for the RWA RITA® Award for *The Christmas Stranger*. She enjoys featuring her cats (or friends' pets) in her stories and always has another book in the pipeline! She currently lives in Louisiana with her husband, one son and three spoiled cats. Contact her via her website, bethcornelison.com.

Karen Whiddon started weaving fanciful tales for her younger brothers at eleven. Amid the Catskill Mountains, then the Rocky Mountains, she fueled her imagination with the natural beauty surrounding her. Karen lives in north Texas and shares her life with her hero of a husband and three doting dogs. You can email Karen at KWhiddon1@aol.com or write to her at PO Box 820807, Fort Worth, TX 76182. Fans can also check out her website, karenwhiddon.com.

Visit the Author Profile pages at Harlequin.com.

ROCK-A-BYE RESCUE

Beth Cornelison
Karen Whiddon

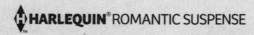

HARLEQUIN® ROMANTIC SUSPENSE

ISBN-13: 978-0-373-27976-0

Rock-a-Bye Rescue

Copyright © 2016 by Harlequin Books S.A.

The publisher acknowledges the copyright holders of the individual works as follows:

Guarding Eve
Copyright © 2016 by Beth Cornelison

Claiming Caleb
Copyright © 2016 by Karen Whiddon

Recycling programs for this product may not exist in your area.

Printed in U.S.A.

CONTENTS

Dear Reader,

One of the best parts of my job is the camaraderie I have with other writers. One such writer friend, Liz Talley, sat down with me on a Saturday last April over a yummy lunch of fire-roasted pimento cheese and helped me plot out the premise for this two-in-one story. The saying goes two heads are better than one, and that is most certainly true when bouncing ideas around for a new book, new characters and the right setting.

Liz was especially helpful in creating Dean Hamilton. She waxed poetically at lunch that day about a warrior with mad fighting skills and a bad boy persona who is really loyal and gentle under his gruff exterior. Hmm, that does sound like a great hero!

Lila, an artist and tenderhearted foster mother, seemed a perfect counterpoint to Dean. Add an ice storm to strand the two together with a vulnerable baby. Check! Send danger their way in the form of an escaped cult leader. Check! Before we knew it we'd cooked up a plot as delicious as the diner's special pimento cheese. Thanks for the plotting help, Liz!

And when asked by my editor who I thought should write the other story on the two-in-one, the talented Karen Whiddon topped my list. I'm so glad she had room in her schedule to join me on this project!

Whether it is frigid where you are this month or heading into spring, I hope Dean and Lila's story adds some sizzle and excitement to your day!

Happy reading,

Beth Cornelison

GUARDING EVE

Beth Cornelison

To Amy Talley—a sweet friend and awesome writer who helped me plot this story (Dean is for you!), and to Karen Whiddon, my partner in (written) crime on this project. Best wishes to you both!

Prologue

The Enemy was at his door. A whole army of government minions were, even now, breaching the sanctity of his compound, seeking to destroy him. The voices had told him they would come. He'd heard the warning about The Enemy soldiers screaming in his head at dawn that morning. And he'd prepared.

He'd gathered his wives, his children, his brothers and servants. He'd assembled them all in his bunker, armed the men with blades and called on them to defend their family, their leader, their freedom even unto death. Better to die in a battle for The Truth, he'd warned his family, than to be taken a prisoner in The Enemy's realm.

He was ready.

"Kent Pitts!" The Enemy bellowed through a bullhorn at his gate. "This is Max Dunn of the FBI. I have a warrant for your arrest on charges of kidnapping, rape and weapons violations."

A gasp of horror whispered through his people. One of his wives began softly sobbing.

"Be strong, my family," he shouted. "Fear is a tool of the government." In his chest, his heart pounded like the drums of war.

"You need to open the gate and come out with your hands over your head."

Kent clenched his teeth, felt the eyes of his soldiers turn to him for guidance. "Stand firm, brothers."

"I have the ATF and local police with me, and we are prepared to enter by force if you don't surrender peacefully," The Enemy's minion shouted.

"Master Pitts," one of his men said, "maybe we should just—"

"Silence!" his younger brother, Wayne, barked. "Our leader has spoken. Through him, The Truth has spoken! We will stand and fight. This is our home, our private compound! We will defend it, defend our leader against *anyone* who interferes with our mission!" Wayne looked to him, his face seeking approval, and Kent jerked a nod.

A tense silence fell over his people. Only the sound of his newest son, Caleb, mewling hungrily to his young mother and his six-month-old daughter Eve's restless whines could be heard as his people held their collective breath...and waited.

"Mr. Pitts, this is your last warning to come out peacefully before I give the order to breach the gate!" The Enemy called again. "Don't make us do this the hard way."

Slowly, methodically, Kent began lining his wives up, oldest to youngest, and turning them to face the door.

They looked like angels, wearing their matching blue dresses that marked them as his brides, and all with their hair worn in a single braid down their backs. When The Enemy's men entered the bunker's meeting hall, the first thing they'd see would be the women, the girls, their babies. "We face a dark hour, my friends, but I am confident of our victory. The Enemy may enter our doors, but I, your leader, will not let him take your freedom!"

A loud boom sounded just beyond the doors of the sanctuary.

A few of the women screamed, and Caleb's mother, Lydia, began crying, hugging her baby to her chest. Though his wife had just turned eighteen, had only been brought into the family a year ago, her lack of trust and cooperation irritated him. He moved his gaze to the girl next to Lydia. "Rachel, come here."

His youngest wife hesitated, glancing up at him with wide eyes, then handed baby Eve to another woman. Head bowed, she obediently stepped forward.

"Bring Lydia with you."

Rachel and Lydia exchanged a look, then joined hands and crept forward together, heads down. Another echoing blast sounded outside, and the girls flinched.

Kent walked to the podium, where two ceremonial long swords were displayed with blades crossed. He took them both down and handed one to Wayne. As he walked back toward his young wives, Lydia's eyes rounded.

"Rachel, hold the baby. Lydia, lift your skirt and bend over." When the girls were slow to act, he slapped the sword against the podium. The sound echoed through the sanctuary, as loud and ominous as the explosions outside, where The Enemy's minions entered the compound. "Now!"

Baby Caleb squawked as Rachel scooped him from Lydia's arms. Lydia turned and exposed her undergarment-covered backside with trembling hands.

Stepping up to her, Kent raised the sword and intoned, "Let it be known that any act of disobedience, lack of faith or show of rebellion shall be dealt with swiftly and severely! On behalf of The Truth and on the authority bestowed upon me by this family, I reprimand you!"

Kent swung the flat side of the blade against Lydia's bottom.

She cried out in pain as he lashed her. From the corner of his eye, he saw Garrett Ware, one of his newest men, an unproven soldier of The Sword, step closer to the podium, his body tense.

"Be still, Mr. Ware. Do not interfere."

Ware sent him a glare but stood down, his hands restless at his sides. Garrett Ware could be a problem. Kent was unconvinced of his loyalty to the family.

Lifting the sword again, Kent struck Lydia again. "By my hand, I will strike down The Enemy and cut out the heart of tyranny and deception!"

As he raised the blade for a third strike, a loud crash announced the government's army had arrived, and the locked door at the back of the meeting hall rattled on its hinges. Once. Twice.

Rachel rushed over to huddle with Lydia, the young girls holding each other, Caleb between them.

Kent grabbed Rachel by the braid and yanked her away from her friend, positioning her in front of him.

The door smashed open under the power of the battering ram the black-clad men wielded. The women gasped, and those who scuttled backward in fear met the resistance of his servants, his army of faithful men who stood ready for battle.

"Kent Pitts, you are surrounded. Surrender peacefully and order your followers to stand down!" The Enemy's minion called from his bullhorn.

"Better that I sacrifice my followers, my wives and children and release them to The Truth than leave them to be cast into the realm of The Enemy!" Kent shouted. With that, he drove the long blade into Rachel's lower back and let her slump to the floor. Lydia screamed, and Kent seized her by the arm.

"No!" she cried, clutching her baby to her chest as tears streamed down her face.

Kent nodded to Wayne, who surged forward to meet the swarming ATF and FBI agents, his sword raised for battle.

Gas canisters were lobbed to the front of the sanctuary, and noxious gases spewed forth. Poisons, just like the voices had told him.

Chaos erupted as his faithless followers tried to escape the stinging gas rather than defend their leader. Only Garrett Wade moved against the surge of the family going toward the exits. His newest recruit shoved past the other men and was heading for the podium. Toward Rachel's fallen body.

Seeing his people scatter, Kent seethed, and he squeezed harder on Lydia's arm when she tugged against his hold, trying to break free.

He drew back the ceremonial blade, still wet with Rachel's blood, and plunged it into Lydia's side, piercing her heart.

"No!" Garrett Wade bellowed, rushing forward to snatch Caleb from Lydia's arms as she crumpled. His new recruit held the baby close and snarled at Kent over the din of the family's destruction. "Damn it, you murdering bastard! *Why?* She was an innocent girl!"

He aimed the tip of the long sword at Wade. "Either turn and fight The Enemy's soldiers or die by my hand!"

The next instant a tiny dart-like probe hit Kent in the throat and volts of agony flooded his body. Like the hounds of hell, the men in gas masks and flak jackets descended on him and took him captive. As darkness overtook him, the voices spoke one last time in Kent's ear.

The Enemy may have won this battle, but do not surrender the war. Fight on, mighty leader, fight on!

And fight he would. For his freedom, for his children. But most of all, for vengeance.

Chapter 1

"'Teens slain during raid on compound,'" Lila Greene said, reading the news story headline on her laptop screen, horror twisting through her.

As if answering, her brown-and-black tabby, Chloe, meowed loudly.

"I know! Horrible, right?" Lila said to the cat, her only companion in her parents' isolated mountain cabin. She'd moved to the family's remote vacation home for the privacy, for the inspiring views it provided for her work…and for the peacefulness it afforded her broken heart. As an artist, she preferred plenty of uninterrupted time by herself to experiment with different mediums and bring her commissioned oil paintings to life. As a casualty of her ex-fiancé's cheating, theft and lies, she considered the location an escape as she healed from her deep wounds of betrayal.

She'd been hard at work on an oil painting of the West Virginia landscape near her cabin when she heard the first pings on her window of the predicted ice pellets. She, along with the rest of the populace of Collins Ridge, West Virginia, had been glued to weather forecasts as the wintry mix moved in from the northwest. The headline about the raid on the nearby cult compound had snagged her attention as she'd logged on to the internet to check the current weather update.

Now, sidetracked by the tragic news story, Lila clicked the video associated with the headline and watched the sound bite that included footage of the raid conducted by the FBI and ATF just a handful of miles from her cabin.

"Pitts, the self-proclaimed leader of The Sword, a radical and militaristic cult, stabbed the teenaged girls, whom he claimed were two of his nine wives," the reporter said while standing in front of a fleet of law enforcement vehicles that flashed red-and-blue emergency lights. "The slain teens are believed to have been kidnapped, and each had borne a child to Pitts."

Lila gasped, shocked—and, sadly, not so shocked—by the story unfolding in the report. She'd come to expect the worst of people based on personal experience with her ex, Carl, and the all-too-common circumstances that necessitated her second career as a foster mother for the local courts.

"The identity of the murdered girls is being withheld by authorities while their next of kin are located and notified. The girls' infants will be placed in foster homes during the search for the babies' families."

Lila cut a glance to her hall closet, where she kept a stock of baby supplies so she'd be ready at a moment's notice to receive an infant to care for. "Well, Chloe, we may be getting company soon."

Chloe hopped up in her lap and butted her head on Lila's hand, demanding a cheek scratch. Lila complied as she used her free hand to navigate her laptop to the local weather website. The radar showed a significant winter storm making its way toward her cabin. "If they want to bring me one of the babies, they'd better hurry. In a couple hours, the roads up here will be impassable."

Chloe only purred and continued bumping her hand every time Lila stopped patting the cat's head, but her landline phone, as if intentionally fulfilling her prediction, rang seconds later. She lifted Chloe from her lap and hurried to answer the call.

"Lila, it's Miriam Webber," the coordinator of foster services in her area said. "If you've been watching the news, you probably know why I'm calling."

"Yes," she said, brushing cat hair from her clothes. "I just saw something about an ATF and FBI raid on a cult, if that's what you mean. Can I assume this call means you need me to take one of the babies rescued in the raid?"

"You assume correctly. Are you available? We'd like to get Eve placed before the ice and sleet get much worse."

Lila pulled the sheer curtains back from her front window and peered out at the pale gray sky. Sleet plinked on the dead leaves covering the forest floor, and the first shimmers of icy accumulation glimmered in the muted daylight. "I'm happy to take in one of the babies. How old will my charge be? Will I need formula? What size diapers?"

"We'll be bringing you Eve. She's five months old. Almost six months."

Lila smiled. All babies were precious, and every month of an infant's first year was marked with developmental achievements and new skills, but little Eve was at Lila's favorite age. At around five to six months, an infant begins laughing and smiling, can sit up alone and eat solid food.

"All right. I'll be waiting. Do you have access to a vehicle with four-wheel drive or snow tires? It's already looking icy up here."

"I'm sure the sheriff's department does. I'll be riding with them. See you in about thirty minutes."

Lila disconnected and faced her living room. She'd allowed it to get a bit cluttered. Okay, a lot cluttered, but weren't all creative people a little messy? She started to pick up magazines and fold laundry but quit after a minute or two. While straightening clutter might spare her a little embarrassment for her poor housekeeping, a tidy living room wasn't as important as preparing the crib for the baby—Eve, Miriam had called her—and mixing up a bottle of formula.

"Come on, Chloe. Let's get the nursery ready for our guest." Moving to the spare bedroom, Lila began prepping the crib for her little charge. When she shook out the sheet, Chloe hopped into the crib and pounced on the flapping bedding. "Oh, no, you don't. We need to keep this bed kitty-hair free."

The tabby stalked out of the room as if pouting, and Lila chuckled. "Sorry, Chloe."

As she tucked the crib sheet around the mattress, the images she'd seen in the news report replayed in her head. The raid had been a violent and emotionally charged event. Eve's mother had been murdered. Lila's gut twisted with sympathy and concern. Poor little lamb, losing her mother at such a young age. Little Eve would undoubtedly need plenty of TLC, and Lila's heart swelled with affection for the infant she'd not met yet. She had an abundance of love to share with the motherless baby girl. She understood the pain of losing someone you loved, and she'd make it her mission to smooth the transition between homes for Eve.

Wayne Pitts sat on the hard seat in the back of the police department's transport van and kept a watchful eye on Kent. He was ready to act on Kent's signal.

His older brother's eyes stayed locked in a lethal glare on the US marshal who rode with them to the holding facility. From that jail cell, they'd await a preliminary hearing—or some such government crap. Assuming they got that far. Kent wouldn't let things progress that far. He'd show them the way forward. He always had.

Wayne's body was growing stiff and sore from sitting with his hands cuffed behind him, and he chalked up his discomfort to The Enemy. The government's lackeys had no right to take him or any of The Sword family from their compound. No one had authority over another man, except to whom he chose to give his loyalty.

For Wayne, Kent had every bit of his loyalty. His big brother had been looking out for him since they'd been old enough to hide together in the linen closet when their father went on one of his drunken rages. Kent had taken care of Wayne after their father killed their mother, and they'd slipped out the back window while their father was passed out. They'd survived on the street thanks to Kent's smarts and his good sense not to trust the government. After the cop had caught them living in an abandoned building, the government had tried to separate the brothers, but Kent would have none of it. He'd rescued Wayne from that horrible foster home and vowed to keep Wayne safe.

Kent had moved them to the farm outside of town, and the brothers had begun building their own family. Kent took a wife, then another, and had led them all toward a greater Truth. He'd had the vision of The Truth in a dream. He'd seen the manipulation of the government and freed his family from the tyranny of Uncle Sam. The Sword represented strength, freedom, Truth… at all costs. The Enemy would not prevail. Wayne was certain. So he waited. Watched.

Kent was working on a plan. Kent would see them freed.

"How do you live with yourself?" Kent said in a low tone.

Wayne was roused from his thoughts to follow his brother's lead.

The marshal returned a placid, bored look. "You were read your rights. That one about remaining silent? I'd use it if I were you."

"You have no say in my rights. I alone determine my rights."

The marshal said nothing, only curled his lip in a dismissive sneer that sent fire through Wayne's veins. "Don't you dare disrespect Master Pitts!"

"Master Pitts, is it?" the marshal asked with a mocking edge to his voice.

"Wayne." Kent's calm, stern tone silenced Wayne, even without taking his eyes from the marshal.

"Where did you take my children?" Kent asked, his stare as icy as his voice.

"They're safe."

"Where? Foster homes?" For the first time, Wayne heard a note of emotion in his brother's tone. A hatred for the abhorrent foster family that had taken Wayne in was one of many bonds he shared with Kent.

Their guard gave Master Pitts a withering glance. "They're safe."

"Not as long as they are in The Enemy's hands," Wayne said, unable to keep his peace.

"They will be freed," Kent said with only a slight side-glance to Wayne. "My family will find them. All of my wives and children will be found and sent to a better place."

The marshal took out a pad and started making notes. "You know all of this can be used against you. You've been warned."

"I will find my children, the innocents first, then my wives. And I will free them from the bonds of earth and man's dominion."

The Enemy's minion pulled a face that said he thought Kent was crazy.

Wayne gritted his teeth, wanting to strike out at the impudent man. If not for the shackles binding his hands behind him and looped around the steel bar on the side of the paddy wagon, he'd dispense the kind of beating his father used to dole out.

With a ragged breath, Wayne shoved down his rage. Wayne knew The Truth. Kent kept his word. Kent would do what he vowed, no matter the cost.

"Could be kinda hard from behind bars," the marshal mocked with a sloppy grin.

Kent arched a dark eyebrow. "I wouldn't—"

The van shifted suddenly, slinging the men in the back from side to side as the vehicle fishtailed.

Wayne and the other members of The Sword gathered themselves, grunting in pain where the shackles had jerked against their wrists. The marshal tapped on the small window between the front seat and the transport bay. "Everything all right up there, Stan?"

"Black ice. Sorry. It's getting dicey out here, so I'll probably get off these side roads and try the highway. They're more likely to have been salted," was the muted reply from the front seat.

"Radio the staties and ask which—"

The van jerked again. Pitched hard left, then right. Rolled. Men and metal were tossed, crumpled, broken.

When the world stopped spinning, Wayne blinked at the opposite side of the van, which was now above him. He lay on his back, and his arms ached, having been yanked in a tug-of-war between momentum and the handcuffs as they had flipped. His head throbbed, but he was conscious, in one piece.

He searched the space around him quickly. Found Kent struggling against the metal shackles.

The marshal groaned and rolled onto his side. His head was bleeding. His leg lay at a funny, unnatural angle. The other members of The Sword—Jimmy, Oscar, George and Burt—were in various states of injury. All of them were moaning and moving slowly.

The scrape of metal drew his attention back to Kent. "Help me, Wayne. The bar is loose."

Sure enough, the steel bar their handcuffs had been looped around for transport had been dislodged as the van wall crumpled. Kent had slid his shackles to the loose end of the bar and tugged to free the final bolts from the twisted metal.

"We have to act fast. We don't have much time." Kent worked his handcuffs free of the bar and hauled himself to his feet. He stepped over the handcuffs to bring his arms in front of him and quickly snatched the keys from the marshal's belt. With key in hand, Kent turned and sent Wayne a hard look. "You know what has to be done."

Energized with a new mission and fresh resolve, Wayne gave a terse nod. "I do, Master Pitts."

Miriam and a sheriff's deputy arrived at Lila's twenty minutes later with Eve. They brought a small supply of baby clothes, Eve's blanket, favorite toys and a few jars of baby food.

Miriam wrote both her number and the contact number for FBI Special Agent Dunn on a notepad as a precaution. "But you shouldn't need either," Miriam reassured her with a smile. "The cult members are in custody, and it's only a matter of time before Eve's grandparents are located. We should have her resettled in a day or two."

After signing some legal documents and getting the usual procedural instructions from Miriam, Lila was left alone with her foster baby to get acquainted and settle in. Eve was understandably fussy. The events of the morning had to have been frightening and confusing to the little girl. Eve had lost her mother, had been bustled from one strange environment to another, and had been roused from her morning nap when they'd arrived at Lila's cabin.

Eve released a mournful wail, and Lila lifted her from

the baby carrier. Cuddling the infant on her shoulder, she paced the cabin, rubbing Eve's back and cooing to her. According to Miriam, the baby wasn't due for another feeding for almost two hours. Sleep was the priority, so Lila walked the floor, sang lullabies and murmured sweet nothings to calm the cranky baby.

Chloe, who'd hidden while the social worker and cop were delivering Eve, crept out from the back of the house and cast a wary eye to the noisy little creature that had invaded her house. She sniffed the baby's things and sent Lila a disdainful glare.

"It's just for a little while, Chloe. We've had babies here before. You know the routine. Don't pretend you don't."

With a loud meow, Chloe traipsed over to the door to her screened porch and stared at the door handle.

Lila chuckled. "It's thirty-three degrees and dropping, Chloe. Trust me. You don't want to go out there."

Chloe meowed again, more emphatically, and Eve raised her head from Lila's shoulder to glance at the cat. Her cries calmed a bit as she studied the feline with a curious wrinkle on her button nose.

"You like that kitty? Her name's Chloe. Nice kitty."

Eve gave a loud squawk and waved a chubby hand toward the cat. Chloe merely regarded the baby balefully then trotted down the hall, presumably to hide again. With the cat out of sight, Eve's whines tuned up again, and Lila resumed her pacing and back patting. "I know, sweet girl. You miss your mommy."

Lila shuddered as the news story replayed in her mind. A teenage girl, a young mother murdered by her kidnapper. Horrible!

Finally, Eve settled down when Lila rocked her in

the nursery glider, and the infant drifted off to a restless sleep. Lila transferred the baby to the crib, turned on the nursery monitor and tiptoed out of the room.

"Me-row!" Chloe chirped from the hall.

"Shh!" Lila pressed a finger to her lips and lifted her cat in her arms as she headed to the kitchen, whispering, "Don't you dare wake Eve up!"

After setting Chloe on the couch with a last head scratch, Lila contemplated her painting. She ought to squeeze in a little more work on the landscape before Eve woke up. Or perhaps she should fix her own lunch, she thought when her stomach growled. She needed to get back in the routine of attending to her own needs while her foster baby was asleep or safely occupied with toys.

She opened her refrigerator and took out a cup of yogurt and a container of leftover Chinese takeout. Giving the sweet-and-sour chicken a sniff, she decided it had become more sour than sweet, and she carried it to the kitchen sink. After dumping the spoiled Chinese food down the garbage disposal, she peeled the top off the yogurt and started eating it as she crept back to the nursery door to peek at Eve again.

The little girl had stolen her heart at first glimpse. With round rosy cheeks, large dark eyes and a dusting of brown curls, Eve was a living doll. Her heart-shaped lips were parted as she slept, and she snuffled slightly with a stuffy nose. *Angelic.* Eve slept with her rump in the air and her blankie squeezed tight in her hand.

Lila's chest ached again, thinking of the tragedy that had befallen Eve's young mother. Such a precious baby, born from such a terrible crime. After finishing her yogurt, Lila didn't linger any longer, though she could have spent hours staring at the girl's sweet face.

As she returned to the kitchen to throw away her trash, a movement outside her window caught Lila's attention. Stepping closer to the sink to peer outside, Lila scanned her yard. Ice had quickly built up in the trees and ice-burdened branches hung low. In the past several minutes, the sleet and freezing rain had become mixed with snow, and a thin accumulation had dusted every surface.

The swirling snow amid the zinging ice pellets created a peaceful scene. She saw nothing unusual outside except for the fluttering flakes and thickening layers of ice. Maybe what she'd seen had been a falling branch. A woodland animal?

Maybe she'd imagined—

Lila's breath snagged in midthought as a large man, clad in a dark coat, jeans and a knit hat, emerged from behind her shed...carrying an ax.

Chapter 2

Jamming her feet in boots, Lila grabbed her father's hunting shotgun from over the fireplace and rushed outside. "Hey!"

The man in the dark coat jerked his head around.

She raised the shotgun and aimed at him. In an angry voice, she shouted, "You'll be putting that ax down now, then getting the hell off my property."

The man didn't move, only stared at her with dark eyes. He sported a couple of days' growth of facial hair, and though the beard was trimmed and neat, the look still gave him a rugged edge. When he only glared at her for long seconds, her pulse picked up an increasingly ragged cadence.

Rather than backing down, the man seemed to grow larger, his body bowing up as he slowly squared his shoulders and moved into a defensive position.

"Put the gun down." His voice grated like steel on flint.

Lila tightened her grip, and a chill rippled through her. He still clutched the ax with one hand, and his free hand balled and flexed aggressively.

She'd thought the shotgun would be enough to scare off a casual thief. She forced enough spit into her dry mouth to swallow. "I said put the ax down and get the hell off—"

"Lila?" His voice was still deep and gruff, but now full of intrigue.

A prickle chased down her spine. He knew her name? "Wh-who are you?"

He took a couple steps closer, the ice and crust of snow crunching under his boots. "Is that you, Lila?"

She re-aimed the shotgun even as she stepped back from him. "Who *are* you? What do you want?"

He angled his head toward her and narrowed his eyes even more. "You put that shotgun away, and we'll talk. Otherwise, I'll have to take it from you the hard way."

Something in his stance, his size and the lethal look in his eyes told her he could easily get the shotgun from her if he wanted. Assuming she couldn't get a shot off first. Her father had taken her hunting, taught her to shoot. But it had been years since she'd fired a weapon, and she wasn't sure she had the nerve to shoot a man if she had to. Mistake number one. She could hear her father telling her, "Never pick up a weapon you don't have the skill and will to use."

A tremble raced through her, one she felt sure he saw.

A muscle in his tense jaw twitched. He raised his free hand and uncurled his fingers. "Come on, Lila. Hand it to me."

"No." She forced starch into her stance and lifted her chin. "Tell me who you are. How do you know my name?"

He seemed a bit deflated by the notion she didn't recognize him. "We spent summers together, our families. My parents' cabin, my cabin now, is on the other side of the ridge." He motioned to the steep hillside behind him.

The only other cabin in the area when she was a teenager had belonged to the Hamiltons. She had, indeed, spent summers with the family. With the Hamiltons' son. A memory tickled her brain. A schoolgirl crush. A boy with a wickedly handsome face and devilish grin. The police showing up at their summer's-end cookout to arrest the boy.

Her stomach swooped, and her breath stuck in her throat.

"Dean?" she rasped.

He lowered his head in a slight nod, his eyes still vigilant.

Now she scrutinized him, looking for any resemblance to the troubled and reckless teenager she'd known years ago. The inky hair and dark eyes were the same, but the sinewy body had been transformed. His shoulders were broader, and through the gap in his open coat, she could see the evidence of a tautly muscled torso. Even his hands were large, strong...*virile*.

She gave her head a quick shake as if to banish the inappropriate response from her mind. She may have had a youthful crush on him as a teenager, but Dean Hamilton had proven himself the wrong sort of guy. His frequent scrapes with the law had landed him in a juvenile boot camp. She had no interest in getting entangled with another man like her ex, a man with no integrity.

"So...you do remember me." He arched one black eyebrow, and Lila's pulse fluttered.

"So...you're still a thief," she countered.

Now his brow furrowed in a deep, angry V. "Thief?"

She indicated the ax with the barrel of the shotgun. That split second of diverted attention was all he needed to surge forward, startling her, and seize her weapon.

When she skittered back from him, her foot slipped on the ice. Lila gasped as she lost her balance, and just as quickly as he'd disarmed her, he whipped a hand around her back and caught her under her arm, keeping her on her feet. With a firm tug, he hauled her up against his body, anchoring her until she could get her feet under her again.

The rapid transition from armed defender to vulnerable captive left her breathless. Lila shivered and raised wary eyes. "I-I'm okay. You can let g-go now."

The corner of his mouth twitched. "Maybe I'm not ready to let you go."

His dark gaze roamed over her face, then down toward her chest. A gleam she could only call predatory shimmered in his eyes. "It's been a long time since I held a woman this close. Especially one as pretty as you."

Pressed against him as she was, she'd bet he could feel the heavy drubbing of her heart against her ribs. "I'd guess not. Not a lot of female company in prison," she gibed, then immediately regretted it.

His grip tightened, and his eyes grew even darker and more threatening. "I wouldn't know, seeing as how I've spent the last ten years with the Army's Special Forces defending our country."

She blinked her momentary confusion and doubt. "Defending... You were in the military?"

"Is that really so hard to believe?"

"I—" Staring at him, with his solidly muscled body and grim countenance and with her ax in one hand and her shotgun in his other, he did indeed have a bellicose appearance. "No. I just thought—"

"That I could have only ended up in prison."

She huffed defensively. "Well, can you blame me? When I knew you, you were on that track! The last I heard of you, you'd been sentenced to juvenile boot camp for stealing a car."

"Borrowing."

"What?"

"I was only borrowing the car. I'd have brought it back if I hadn't been stopped by the cop and dragged into jail."

"Your kind of borrowing was still illegal. You earned your time at the boot camp." She realized he still held her against his body, and while she appreciated the warmth, having stormed outside without a coat, his proximity did strange things to her ability to think straight and calm her jittery pulse. She planted her hands on his chest and shoved away from him. He released her with such force that she stumbled again, her feet sliding a little before she found her balance.

"True enough. And in hindsight, I have no regrets about my time at the juvie camp. It set me on the right path." He held out the shotgun, but when she tried to take it from him, he didn't let go. "Don't ever point a gun at someone you aren't truly willing to shoot, or you might find that you're the one who ends up dead."

She stiffened. Her father had warned the same thing, but from Dean it sounded ominous. "Are you trying to scare me?"

He lifted an insouciant shoulder. "If that's what it takes to drill some gun sense into you."

"I know how to handle a weapon." But even she heard a shade of doubt in her tone.

He slanted a dubious look at her as he released the gun and stepped back. "I need to use your ax. I have a large tree limb about to fall on my cabin. It would also take out my power lines if I don't remove it before it breaks free."

"So you were going to *borrow* my ax without asking?" She braced a hand on one hip, squeezing the shotgun barrel in her other.

"I'd rather borrow a saw," he said, clearly ignoring her sarcasm. "That'd be the proper tool for the job, but your shed was locked, and all I found by your woodpile was the ax." When she rolled her eyes in frustration, he added, "For what it's worth, I'd been told no one lived here anymore. I didn't know there was anyone home to ask. I'd heard your parents were in Florida now or something."

"They are. I moved here a couple months ago after—"

"Shh!" His chin jerked up, his expression shifting abruptly to one of alarm and confusion as he scanned the area and zeroed in on a window of her cabin. "Do you have a baby?"

"No," she said automatically before remembering her charge. "I mean, I'm caring for one. I—" Then she heard the shrill cry over the ping of sleet and crackling of icy branches in the woods. "That's... Eve is awake. I have to—" She pointed toward her front door as she backed away, distracted by the baby's cries.

Dean's face was still tense as he jerked a nod. "Go on."

She started toward the cabin, walking as fast as she

dared on the slippery ice. She heard the crunch of a second set of footsteps and thought for a moment Dean was leaving. But as she neared her porch, she realized he was right behind her. Wheeling around to face him, she shot him a glare. "What are you doing? Why are you following me?"

He paused on the bottom step to her porch and angled his head slightly. "I thought I'd wait inside, out of the cold, while you tended to the baby and got the key to the shed." He gave her a sardonic half grin. "But that seems to be a neighborly kindness you don't want to offer me."

Eve's crying grew louder, once again dividing her attention. "Fine," she grumbled, "come in. You can wait in the kitchen while I check on Eve."

She turned and hustled inside, leaving him to see himself in. Eve was sitting in the crib, her hand in her mouth, slobber and tears soaking her face as she wailed. "Poor girl. Don't cry, sweetheart. I know you're scared."

Lifting the infant into her arms, Lila noticed her muscles were tight with stress, and she moved with a jerky stiffness. Eve was sure to pick up on her tension, so she inhaled slowly and blew out a cleansing breath. She found a clean burp cloth and used it to dry Eve's face.

Dean Hamilton was in her kitchen. Dean, who was not a lanky trouble-making teenager anymore, but a man with a warrior's body and a stern countenance. A man with dark, watchful eyes, whose piercing gaze sent sensual tingles through her blood.

She had to get rid of him. A bad boy, and former crush, was not the kind of man she needed to get involved with, even peripherally. She would loan him the saw— heck, *give* him the saw—if it meant getting him out of her house and out of her life. She rubbed Eve's back, and the girl's shrieks calmed to whimpers. Holding the baby on her shoulder, she headed out to deal with Dean.

"Are you remodeling?" he asked as soon as she reappeared in the hallway.

"No. The cabin still belongs to my parents. I haven't changed anything." She tipped her head to the side. "Why?"

"I smell paint."

She flashed a quick half grin. "That's from my canvas. The landscape I'm doing."

Lila carried Eve into the living room and directed his attention to the back window, where her easel was set up. She was so used to the scent of paint, she didn't notice it anymore.

Dean stepped into the living room from her kitchen and peered at her work space, a corner of the living room by the window that provided the best natural light. His gaze narrowed on her work in progress, and after studying it a moment, his brow lifted. "You did this?"

She pulled a face. "No. Eve did."

He shot her a withering glance and added, "I just mean...this is *good*."

She chuckled wryly. "You sound surprised."

Dean lifted a shoulder as he faced her painting again. "I am. I didn't know you were an artist."

With a grunt, she carried Eve into the kitchen and started opening cabinet drawers. His heavy footsteps on her hardwood floor told her he'd followed, confirming her inner prickle of awareness. She shot a look over her shoulder. "There's a lot you don't know about me. Eleven years' worth."

"Likewise."

She inclined her head in a silent *touché*.

Patting Eve's back, she continued searching the kitchen. Where was that damn key? "Look, you can borrow the saw or…whatever you need. Just…" *Go.*

When she cut a quick glance toward him, his expression said the unspoken dismissal was understood well enough. Guilt pinched her. She was being terribly unneighborly, as he'd accused, and he had said he'd served in the military. For his service to the country alone, he deserved the benefit of the doubt. A chance to prove he'd changed. He'd—

"Ow!" she yelped in surprise when she felt a dull pain at her shoulder. She glanced down at Eve and laughed. "Did you just bite me?"

"That's how I saw it," Dean volunteered as he strode closer. "How old is she? Six, seven months?"

Lila rubbed the damp sore spot near her neck and eyed Dean as he approached. "Yes. Almost six months."

"I'm guessing her mood and her biting means she's cutting a tooth or two?" He moved all the way up to her, and for the first time, she smelled the clean aroma of soap and a hint of wood smoke on him. Such ordinary scents, and yet he made them…sexy.

Lila swallowed hard and mentally shoved aside her hyperawareness of him. Forget the inky beard shading the sharp angles of his face and his bister-colored eyes. She'd only noticed these details about him because she was an artist, not because his face had a manly beauty that enthralled her and begged to be captured in paint.

She shrank back a step when he raised a hand toward her.

Undeterred, Dean closed the distance and reached for Eve. With a gentleness she wouldn't have imagined his large calloused hand could have, he cradled Eve's chin in his hand and poked his thumb in the girl's mouth to feel her gums. His expression softened as he looked into Eve's eyes. "Your mouth hurts, doesn't it? I feel that tooth coming in," he said to the infant in an adult tone.

Eve chomped down on his finger in response, earning a lopsided grin from the man who'd been as gruff as a bear with a sore paw to Lila earlier. *Maybe because you pointed a gun at him and were snarly yourself?*

His dark brown eyes shifted to hers, and Lila experienced another prickling in her veins like an electric current.

"Get this kid a cold rag to gnaw on or something."

Lila shook herself from her daze and glanced around for the diaper bag of supplies Miriam had left. "She probably has a teething toy."

"You don't know?"

"She's only been here a couple of hours. I'm fostering her over the weekend until her extended biological family is contacted." She craned her neck to look past Dean. "Do you see her bag on the stool over there?"

Eve tuned up again when Dean moved away. Clearly the little girl was as intrigued by him as the big girl was. Lila kissed Eve's head and swayed in a way intended to soothe the baby. "It's okay, sweetie. We'll get something for those sore gums." Then to Dean, who had located the diaper bag, she said, "I'll take it." She held out her hand, while propping the baby on her hip.

He only cast her a dismissive look as he pawed through the bag and dug out a well-chewed toy.

"Is there any teething gel in there? If not, I think I have some in the nursery." While Dean searched the bag again, she asked, "How do you know about teething babies?"

"Men can't know about babies?" His eyes narrowed. "Or just men who should have been in prison the last eleven years?"

Her mouth tightened. "Look, I made a presumption based on the last information I knew about you. I'm sorry. I was wrong to assume the worst."

Pulling out a tube of ointment, he uncapped it and passed it to her. "I spent a lot of time in Iraq with a family that had a baby. You pick things up."

She took the teething gel, but had her hands full with the baby. Mothers must have to practice juggling to manage a baby while doing all the tasks involved in child care.

Dean noticed her conundrum and stepped forward, taking back the gel and squeezing a dab on his finger.

"I—" she began, then said, "Thank you."

As he rubbed the medicine on the baby's gums, Eve focused her baby blues on the man with the unshaven jaw and intense brown eyes, and her fretful expression lightened. The baby made a gurgling sound that Lila would have sworn was a flirtatious coo. And why wouldn't Eve be dazzled by Dean's handsome face and tender touch? Lila had been intrigued by him since she was fourteen and first received one of his rakish grins.

He gave the baby's cheek a quick stroke with a crooked finger and recapped the teething gel. After tossing the tube on the counter, he wiped his fingers on a kitchen towel. "Now…the key to the shed? This storm isn't easing up, and I'd like to get back to my cabin before the path gets too icy."

She swallowed her retort about his impatience and ingratitude and took Eve into the living room, where her baby seat was. She settled Eve in the infant carrier and almost had her settled with a teething toy when her phone rang.

The harsh ring of the landline her parents had put in the cabin thirty years earlier startled Eve, and she gave a piercing shriek of displeasure.

Lila gritted her teeth, wanting to howl her own frustration as she strode over to the kitchen counter to answer the call. She held a finger up to Dean, asking for one more minute. "Hello?"

"Lila, it's Miriam Webber." Even over Eve's plaintive whining, Lila could hear the tension in Miriam's voice.

"Yes, hi. Did I forget something?"

"Oh, no. It's…is Eve all right?"

Lila grimaced. Having her charge crying in the background didn't make a good impression on the foster program caseworker. "She's fine. Just fussy and fighting sleep."

"Right. Well, that's not why I called." Again Miriam's tone vibrated with anxiety as clearly as Eve's cries did. "Lila, I have FBI Special Agent Dunn with me. There's bad news, and…well, I'll let him explain."

Lila's gut rolled. *Bad news? What could have—?*

"Ms. Greene? This is Special Agent Dunn." The man's deep voice was dark and grave. "I wanted to give you the heads-up that I've asked the local police to station an officer at your place. They should be there shortly."

Lila's pulse quickened. "At my cabin? Why?"

Dunn cleared his throat. "The van transporting several of The Sword cult leaders hit black ice and rolled over. The van driver was killed, and both Kent Pitts and his brother, Wayne, escaped custody."

Lila gasped. "Oh, my God! How? Weren't they hand-cuffed? Weren't there extra guards with them?"

A grunt of frustration rumbled through the line. "The US marshal riding in the back with the prisoners was injured and knocked unconscious, but whether before or after the accident is unclear at this point." Another growl. Clearly Dunn was disgusted with the situation, and Lila held her breath, knowing on a gut level that the worst news was yet to come. "The Pitts not only used the incapacitated marshal's keys to free themselves from their restraints, they stole both his and the driver's sidearms. And…the marshal's phone. Ms. Greene, the phone had text messages regarding the placement of Eve and your contact information…including your address."

Lila sat heavily on a bar stool near her kitchen counter. Her blood whooshed past her ears, making it hard to hear the special agent.

"Ms. Greene, I'm sorry. It is unconscionable that these men escaped from custody, and a full investigation will be conducted as to what happened."

She huffed a humorless laugh, her mind reeling. "An investigation? H-how does that help me now?"

He sighed. "It doesn't." Another heavy pause. "Ideally, we would move you from your location. But with this storm coming, I'm afraid it won't be safe to relocate you once the officer arrives. Ma'am, you need to lock your doors. The other cult members being transported with the Pitts tell us the brothers intended to go after Eve and Caleb, the other infant rescued from the scene this morning. We believe their intention is to kill the babies."

Chapter 3

Dean's body hummed with the tension he sensed from Lila's end of the phone call. Her expression was already bereft when she dropped onto a bar stool and the color drained from her cheeks.

"K-kill them? Why? They're just babies!"

Dean jerked his back erect and balled his fists. *What the hell?* Handcuffs? Killing babies? What was she talking about?

He'd thought he'd left the violence and ugliness behind in Iraq.

He stepped closer, his gaze intent on Lila as he tried to decipher—

A loud crack, followed by a crash, sounded outside as the lights flickered off. Dean flinched, his pulse slamming into high gear, a gut-level reaction left over from one-too-many roadside bombs while deployed.

Lila gave a startled yelp, and the baby, who'd been settling down, cranked up her whine again.

"Agent Dunn?" Lila said, the panic in her voice rising. "Agent Dunn?" She pulled the phone away from her ear and stared at the receiver with wide, anguished eyes.

Dean drew a slow breath, shoving down the nightmares that now crept into his daytime hours. Moving to the front window, he fingered back the sheer curtain and searched the yard. He spotted the large branch that had snapped off under the weight of the ice and brought down Lila's power line as it fell. "Do you have a generator?"

She didn't answer, and when he turned toward her, she was staring at near space, clearly not seeing anything. Her whole body trembled like the vibrations from the street as a Bradley tank rolled past. His protective instincts roared to life. The same loyalty and determination to defend his fellow soldiers, his country and the vulnerable citizens in the foreign lands where he was deployed now spiked in his veins for Lila. Whatever had upset her would not have a chance to hurt her as long as he had a breath in his body. He gritted his teeth in resolve as he watched her.

"Lila?" No response. *"Lila?"*

She gasped as she woke from her daze and met his eyes. She almost seemed surprised to see him standing there. "I, uh—"

Without finishing her sentence, she hurried to her front door and threw the dead bolt. Pushing aside the checkered curtains on the door window, she searched her property.

"It was a branch," he said. "Brought down your power line."

She cast a confused look toward him. "What?"

"The cracking noise. Ice brought down a branch." Then without waiting for an answer, he added, "But that's not what you're looking for, is it?"

She moistened her lips, still staring at him with a look of terror shadowing her face.

"Who was on the phone?"

"Y-you should go. I'll get the sh-shed key." She turned back toward the kitchen and took two wobbly steps before he caught her arm, steadying her.

"Forget the damn key. Who was on the phone? What did they say?"

Her throat worked as she swallowed. "The FBI. Sp-special Agent Dunn."

His grip tightened on her arm. "Why is the FBI calling you? What's going on, Lila?"

"They got away. They escaped, and…th-they want to kill the baby." She shook her head, her gaze still distant, troubled. He felt the tremor that shook her, and he put an arm around her as she started to sink to the floor. Leading her by the arm to the sofa, he pushed her down on the cushions before she fell over from shock.

He tried again. "Start from the beginning, Lila. What did the guy on the phone say?"

Her attention went to the baby, whose cries were growing louder.

She tried to get past him, batting at his restraining hands. "I have to get Eve. I h-have to protect her."

The conversation was going nowhere fast. He pushed her back onto the cushions and aimed a finger at her nose. "Stay. You're too shaken to even stand upright."

When he was sure she'd comply, he crouched by the baby carrier and lifted Eve into his arms. After a few pats on the back, the baby calmed a little, and he carried the infant back to the sofa with him.

Lila held out her arms, her expression reflecting eagerness and concern. As she drew the infant close, Lila began rocking from side to side to soothe Eve. Or maybe herself. She seemed as in need of comfort and calming as the infant.

Dean settled beside her, sitting at an angle so he could see her face. In the thin light from the window, she seemed especially wan. "Talk to me, Greene. What did the FBI want? Who got away?" He waited for her to say something, but when she met his eyes, she seemed unable to verbalize the horror gripping her. "Are you in some kind of danger?"

The answer to the last question was obvious, but he needed to get her to open up.

Lila bobbed her head, and tears bloomed in her eyes. "Did you…s-see the news this morning?"

Dean frowned. Her response struck him as odd, but he said, "No. I don't have a TV or internet at my cabin." And that was how he liked it. Unplugged from the world.

She closed her eyes and rested her cheek against the baby's head. The tender, loving gesture hit him like a punch to the gut and jacked up his protectiveness a thousand degrees.

"There was a raid this morning…on a cult compound outside of town." Her voice was as thin as mist and filled him with the same sense of foreboding. "The cult leader k-killed two young girls." She paused for a shaky breath and cut a quick glance at him. "One of them was Eve's mother."

He muttered an earthy obscenity. "And this cult leader, this *killer*, got away from the FBI?"

She nodded stiffly. "He and his brother. They s-stole weapons from the injured guards." Her gaze went to the empty gun rack over the fireplace, where he'd bet she'd gotten the shotgun she'd aimed at him a little while ago.

The feisty woman who'd tried to chase him off her property minutes ago bore little resemblance to the terrified woman sitting next to him now. His memories of Lila were more in line with the earlier version. Whatever the FBI agent had told her had been dire enough to elicit this drastic of a response from her.

"And you think these escapees might come here? To… kill the baby?" he asked, filling in the gaps from the snippets he'd heard. He knew his tone sounded skeptical. After everything he'd seen in Iraq and Afghanistan—the disregard for human life, young or old, male or female— maybe he shouldn't doubt her theory. But going to extreme measures to kill a particular baby? It didn't add up.

She angled her head and furrowed her brow. "I'm not making this up."

He raised his hands, palms out. "I didn't say you were."

"Your tone did." A bit of the fire he'd seen in her earlier returned to her eyes. "And yes, the FBI believe, based on what they learned from other cult members, that the Pitts brothers want to kill the babies." She drew and released a fast, shallow breath. "The news report I watched online earlier said the cult leader, this guy named Kent Pitts, stabbed the two teenage girls in cold blood during the raid." She closed her eyes and was silent for a moment. He waited, watched her. Disgust soured her expression. "According to the other cult members, the guy thought he was saving the girls from a worse fate."

"What worse fate?"

"Being subjected to the evils of our government and modern society."

Dean grunted. He knew there were a lot of extremist groups out there that resented any kind of authority, especially the American government and law enforcement.

Lila shifted Eve to her other shoulder, still patting the girl's back and swaying, then met his gaze. "When Miriam, the woman with foster services, brought Eve up here, she said the cult believed they had created a Utopia of some sort at their compound and only they were truly enlightened. They knew the truth about…a perfect society or some such. Swords were the weapon of choice and a symbol they all but worshipped."

"And this Pitts dude wants to kill Eve because…?"

"To save her from the big, bad world, same as the girls he stabbed." She hesitated, then added, "Oh, did I mention he called the teenagers his wives? He had several."

Dean tensed and a muscle in his jaw spasmed. "Are you saying this sicko is Eve's father?"

She appeared as nauseated by the idea as he felt. "That's my understanding. The girls were kidnapped from their families and raped. It's all so…black."

"Black?" he scoffed. "Is that the worst you have?"

She scowled her irritation with his response. "What? I'm an artist. I associate things—my feelings, people, events—with color, shapes."

He lifted an eyebrow. "As in blue for sadness and yellow for happiness?"

"No…blue is happiness. Like the sky in spring. Yellow is—" She blinked, and her frown deepened. "Are you mocking me?"

He half snorted, half sighed. "No. Never mind. The whole artsy thing is just—"

"Yes?"

He didn't want to have this discussion, didn't want to offend Lila or explain himself...

"What do you see in this ink blot?"

"Ink. In a blot."

"Anything else?"

Death. Blood spatter. War...

Icy fingers clamped on his lungs, and Dean shoved aside the flash of memory. "It's not me. I tend to see things in more straightforward terms. More cut-and-dried. Black-and-white."

"Black and white aren't colors?" Feisty woman was back, now a bit defensive as well. But defensive was better than totally freaked out zombie woman.

Dean scowled and looked away. "You know what I mean."

At least the baby had settled down some now, soothed by sticking her own hand in her mouth. Dean began processing what he knew about the threat to Eve and Lila. Something had to be done, but the ice storm threw a huge monkey wrench into the situation.

"Actually, black is the result of the absence of light, and white is a combination of all the colors in the spectrum."

He cut her a puzzled side-glance. "Huh?"

"Sorry, I prattle when I get nervous or worried." She scooted to the edge of the sofa and angled her head to check on Eve. "She seems to be settling down, so I should try to put her to bed. Look, the shed key is in a kitchen drawer somewhere. It has a green tag on it. Can you find it for yourself?"

He gave his head a dumbfounded shake. "Forget the flippin' key," he said more harshly than he intended.

Lila's eyes rounded, and she shrank back from him. The move was subtle, just a slight shift in her body angle, but he'd become highly tuned to body language in the military. A community leader who says he knows nothing about hidden weapons but can't meet your gaze. A translator who walks a bit too stiffly and checks the sky when he thinks you're not looking. The faint tremor in a voice over the comm that changes orders.

He raised a palm. "Sorry. Didn't mean to bark at you. But you can't tell me there's a killer headed this way and think I still care anything about borrowing your saw."

Lila flicked a hand toward him as she rose from the couch, Eve cradled against her chest. She tucked her dark blond hair behind her ear and gave her head a quick shake. "Whatever. Get the key or don't. But it's time you left. Obviously, I have a lot going on here today, and I don't need you in the way."

Following her from the living room, he sputtered and said simply, "No."

Lila stopped short and whirled to face him with a look of dismay. "What?"

"I said, *no.* I'm not going anywhere."

Chapter 4

Lila gaped at Dean. Not leaving? Didn't she have enough to deal with between the cranky foster baby and a murderer on the loose and looking for her cabin? A chill slithered through her at the reminder. The last thing she needed was her teenage crush hanging around. A man who was a confusing mix of scruffy and sexy, bad boy and military hero, tough and gentle. He made her head spin and her heart race at a time when she needed more than ever to keep her wits about her.

A murderer wanted to come after Eve!

"Dean..." she began, trying to sound reasonable, which was not easy with his brawn towering over her and his intense dark eyes boring into her. "You can't—"

"I don't know *can't*."

His reply confused her further. "Wha—?"

"*Can't* isn't in my vocabulary." He squared his shoulders. "I don't do *can't*. *Can't* is for quitters."

She sighed and dodged Eve's head as the baby wiggled and almost smacked into her chin. "Look, as much as I appreciate the whole Zig Ziglar act, my world has kinda imploded in the last few hours, and I need—"

"A bodyguard," he said, at the same time she said, "—you to leave."

His pronouncement rattled her, and she blinked at him.

"You need a bodyguard," he repeated and stepped toward her. "If there is a nut-job cult guy headed up here, you need more than a shotgun you're unwilling to fire to protect you."

She wanted to protest, to convince him she could shoot a man if needed, but…could she?

"Until you have the assurance of the FBI that all danger from this Pitts character has passed," he said, "I'm not leaving this cabin. Not without you, anyway. The truth is, we should all clear out until this cult guy is captured."

His offer to protect her silenced her. For several seconds, she fumbled mentally to process his offer—no, his *dictate*. He hadn't asked if she wanted his help; he'd declared he was staying, her wishes be damned.

Finally she cleared her throat and managed to stutter, "Special Agent D-Dunn said…um, a police officer is coming."

"Good." He jerked a nod. "That's the least they can do."

"With this ice storm and bad road conditions, Special Agent Dunn said that moving anywhere is dangerous. Besides, since they've sent someone to watch my place, there's no need to move me anywhere. Anyway, you don't have to—"

"But the cop's not here yet. And while having a cop, probably a rookie, sitting in his patrol car in your driveway is helpful, it's not enough. I'm staying."

She should be affronted by his high-handedness, but she was…relieved. Because in truth, the idea of the Pitts brothers hunting down the babies, the prospect of protecting little Eve should one of these dangerous men show up at her cabin, scared her spitless. She didn't want to be alone—even if his company made her nervous and uneasy on a different level.

The fact that Dean was strong and skilled with a weapon didn't hurt. She might have questions about his integrity, based on his youthful crimes of vandalism, petty theft and trespassing, but she'd never heard anything about him being violent or vicious.

When she made no reply, Dean strode to the front door, unlocked it and yanked it open. "So—" He took the shotgun from the porch, where he'd set it and came inside. "Is this thing loaded?"

It wasn't. "Well…"

He groaned and rolled his eyes. "Geez, Lila! You threatened a trespasser, a potential thief with an unloaded weapon? Are you insane?"

She frowned. "We are still talking about you, right? I'd have thought you'd be glad to know I couldn't have really hurt you."

"What if it hadn't been me?" He stalked into her kitchen, lit only by the watery daylight from one small window thanks to the power outage, and started opening drawers. "Do you understand how vulnerable you are up here by yourself?"

"What are you doing?" She carried Eve into the kitchen, closing drawers in his wake.

"Cell reception is spotty at best. The nearest neighbor is on the other side of the ridge," he continued as he searched her kitchen, "and emergency help is at least thirty minutes away. Probably more, given the ice storm."

"What's your point?" She slammed shut a cabinet he'd opened.

He lifted the shotgun by the barrel. "Where's your ammunition for this thing? Since we're stuck here, we need to be ready if one of the Pittses gets here before the cops do."

She shuddered and nodded toward the back of the house. He was right, of course. And it rattled her to think he'd been quicker to think through the ramifications and needed preparations. She had a duty to protect Eve, and she'd let Dean distract her, even if briefly. "I, um…in the laundry room."

He headed down the dark hall, still lecturing her, his tone just short of angry. "The locks on your front door wouldn't keep a hungry bear out, much less a seasoned burglar. You still haven't answered me about whether you have a generator. And I'm guessing your windows can be jimmied open from outside with a screwdriver if they're like the ones at my parents' cabin."

"If you're trying to frighten me—" She swallowed hard. She'd never considered all the weaknesses in the cabin's security. "It's working."

Lila pushed past him to reach into a cabinet over her washing machine. Taking the box of shotgun cartridges down, she shoved the ammunition into his hand.

He sighed, and in the semidark room, the sound seemed amplified. "I'm not trying to scare you. But if you're going live up here alone, you have to think about these things. Take better precautions."

"We've never had a problem in all the years my parents vacationed here or rented the place in the off-season. Even when *you* went on your crime spree as a teenager." She hated her cattiness as soon as she spoke it, but *his* preaching to her about staying safe from thieves was sublime irony, and her own edginess was sharpening her tone. She took a breath to calm down. He was, in his own way, trying to help.

A grunt rumbled from Dean's chest. "If I didn't break in here, it was because I didn't want to, not because I couldn't," he growled. "And a track record is simply history, not a predictor of the future."

Eve was getting especially squirmy, and her whimpers were tuning back up to full cries of distress. Lila could imagine the tension in their voices was a factor in the baby's fussiness. She lowered the volume and hostility in her voice when she replied, "I agree this cabin is far from Fort Knox, but it is quiet and inspiring and restful. That's all I was concerned with when I moved here a few months ago. I didn't realize I'd need to keep a murderer at bay or—" she waved a hand toward him "—neighbors from stealing from my ax."

"Give it a rest. I would have brought the ax back." He brushed by her and disappeared down the hall, leaving behind a hint of his scent—wood smoke and crisp soap. She stared into the blackness of the laundry room, quaking at her core. But whether her tremors were from the fear that still hovered like an apparition, from their heated discussion, or from the casual contact of his body as he scooted past, she couldn't say. Probably all of the above.

Eve rubbed a damp fist in her eye, a clear indication

of how tired the baby was. "Okay. To bed with you, little one."

She stopped at the nursery and found Chloe sleeping in the crib. "Hey, you. That's not your bed. Scat, cat." She nudged the sleepy feline, but Chloe didn't budge. "Vamoose, fuzzy girl. That's the baby's bed."

Chloe tucked her head down and got comfortable again.

"Come on, Chloe. Please, move." Lila gave the cat's butt a push.

Still Chloe ignored her until Eve let out a loud wail of discomfort.

Putting her ears back, the cat gaped wide-eyed at the baby then jumped out of the crib and scurried out the nursery door. Probably to hide under Lila's bed, if she knew her cat.

"Sorry, Chloe!" Lila changed Eve's diaper before putting her in the crib. The little girl fought sleep for a minute or two while Lila patted Eve's back and stroked her head before Eve's eyelids drooped closed for good. With a flip of a switch, Lila turned on the nursery monitor and picked up the receiver. When she tiptoed out of the bedroom, she found Dean on the couch, the shotgun across his lap as he loaded it.

She watched his deft movements in silence for a moment, and without looking up from his task he said, "You have a cat."

"Yes. Why?"

"I almost shot it."

Lila tensed. "What!"

"It came tearing out of the nursery and startled me."

Her jaw dropped. "So you shoot first and ask questions later?"

"Did you hear me shoot anything?"

She tucked her hair behind her ear. "No."

He glanced at her and lifted one eyebrow in a manner that said, *So there.* "Any other animals around here that might burst out of the shadows?"

"Are you always this jumpy?"

"Only since my last tour. I guess it was the proverbial straw that broke me."

Lila pulled her shoulders back and regarded him with a frown furrowing her brow. And how was she supposed to take that announcement? Sympathy and a new edginess toward him tangled in her chest. If a cat could startle him, how did he expect to protect her and Eve?

While she studied him, he said, "I apologize for yelling earlier. I didn't mean to scare you."

"You didn't."

He cut a brief, dubious glance in her direction. "So pale and shaking are your norm?"

"I—" Lila puffed out a breath through pursed lips. "Okay, so you rattled me. But I was already upset because of the call, and the baby crying and…" She raked her hair back from her face with her fingers and cast a glance toward her front door, double-checking that Dean had relocked it when he came back inside with the shotgun. "Besides, you're one to talk if Chloe running into the hall frightened you."

"I said startled, not frightened. I'm good."

She hummed her skepticism, then continued to watch him silently.

Another few quiet seconds passed, marked by the loud ticking of her mantel clock. "I do have a generator. Out back. It's old, but I think it still works."

He nodded. "I'll take a look when I finish here."

Lila rubbed her arms. The cabin was drafty on a good day, but without the electric heater and with the wind beginning to pick up outside, the temperature in the cabin was rapidly dropping. "I should build a fire," she said, mostly thinking aloud.

Dean looked up from the shotgun. "I can do that."

"No. I can handle it." She hurried over to the hearth and kneeled. As she started stacking kindling and split wood on the grate, she added, "Thanks."

"Hmm?"

"I said thank you. For your help. I know I've acted anything but grateful so far, but…" She sat back on her heels and dusted her hands. "I am glad you're here. I appreciate your precautions. This whole horrifying situation—ice storms and escaped murderers wanting to kill innocent children—I don't know why I'm lucky enough to be caught in the middle of this insanity, but…it would be even more terrifying if I was facing it alone. We may have gotten off on the wrong foot this morning, but thank you for overlooking my judgmental assumptions about you and volunteering to stick around until—"

Dean grunted loudly and shook his head. "You're right."

She blinked. "What?"

"You do prattle when you're nervous."

She huffed a sigh. "Oh. Sorry."

He stood from the couch and propped the shotgun against the side table. "Whatever. Just an observation. I'll take a look at the generator now."

With a nod, she turned back to the fire she was building, struck a match and held it to the shreds of paper she'd stuffed under the wood. Once the fire caught the logs, she followed Dean outside, taking the shotgun with her.

He crouched by the generator and tinkered with the motor. Before she even reached him and without turning, he said, "It didn't crank on my first try, but I think it just needs a little maintenance."

"How did you—"

"You have a light step, but I still heard you coming."

"I could have been the killer. The cop, an animal."

He sent a you're-not-funny look over his shoulder.

"I smelled your perfume, too."

"I don't wear perfume."

"Shampoo, then. Or body lotion. Whatever." He rose to his feet and faced her. Arching one eyebrow, he let his gaze dart to the shotgun and back to her face. "You smell like flowers, and I've been trained to be fully aware of my surroundings at all times."

"I see." Knowing he was so keenly alert to her scent and the sound of her approach sent an odd tickle to her belly. Such an intimate awareness was usually reserved for close family…or lovers. She pushed the sensation away and said, "And yet Chloe almost got shot."

"Give it a rest. I wouldn't have really shot at your cat." He sighed and added, "I was surprised by the cat, yes, but I'm okay. Really. Don't look at me like that."

"Like what?"

"Like I'm a time bomb. I'm fine. Just…don't sneak up on me again. Okay?"

She raised a hand. "Fine."

"This should only take a minute. You can wait inside if you want to get out of the cold."

She glanced toward the front door and considered going in. It was cold out. A damp, bone-chilling cold. But somehow, as strange as it seemed, she felt safer outside. With Dean. She gave a wry chuckle with that realization, and her exhaled breath made a white cloud.

As Dean continued tinkering, she alternated between studying him—his chiseled profile, which had only improved as he aged—and glancing nervously to the frosted woods, where the icy branches shimmered as they swayed in the chilly breeze. She tried to appreciate the sparkle of the ice with an artist's eye, but the notion of a killer lurking in her woods tainted even the fairylike beauty of the wintry scene. The ping of ice pellets created an added tension, like the ticking of a clock.

While her attention was focused on the wind picking up and the clatter of frozen branches swaying in the increasing gusts, Dean cranked the generator. The engine roared to life.

For the second time that day, she yelped her surprise. Clapping a hand over her thundering heart, she spun back toward him. "Geez, Dean. A little warning next time?"

He arched an eyebrow. "Now who's jumpy?"

She rolled her shoulders to loosen the tense muscles. "Can you blame me? With a murderer headed up to my cabin?"

He dusted off his hands and twisted his mouth in a noncommittal moue. "You need to distract yourself somehow. Stop thinking about it."

"Really?" She sent him a skeptical eye roll. "How do you propose I do that?"

He shrugged as he rose from his crouch. "Paint."

She shook her head. "No. Too many distractions."

"Then you could make us lunch."

"How can you even think of food? My stomach is in knots."

"So I get nothing in exchange for fixing your generator and providing you with power?" For the first time, she heard a teasing note in his tone that did as much to calm her as any distraction she could think of.

She tried for a similar lightness, even though her voice remained strained. "I guess you've earned some soup. Maybe a sandwich, too, if it means you'll stop growling at me like a hungry bear."

"Grrr!" he replied with a droll smirk, but the low rumble from his throat was far more sexy than it was intimidating. "I'll stop growling at you if you promise to stop aiming shotguns at me and bringing up my less-than-noble past."

She twitched a grin. "Deal."

He placed a hand at her back to steer her inside, and while the gesture was minor in the big picture, a warm sense of reassurance flowed through her. Dean was here. He was competent, confident and in control of the situation.

Wow, I've sure done a one-eighty with regard to him in the last hour, she acknowledged as she headed inside with him.

She led him into her kitchen, where she took out a container of homemade vegetable soup, some cold cuts and condiments. "The bread is over there." She pointed toward her counter.

"In the bread box?" he asked, opening the wooden storage. "Imagine that."

She chuckled at herself. "Hmm. Yeah." Then with a playful grin, she tipped her head. "I'm ingenious that way. Guess where I keep my cookies?"

He faced her with an expression of exaggerated intrigue. Raising one dark eyebrow, he opened the drawer in front of him. "Cookies? You have cookies?" He moved to the oven and the dishwasher, opening each in turn, then moving closer to her. "Am I getting warmer?"

She chuckled at his playfulness. She remembered his sense of humor from their earlier acquaintance. His ability to make her laugh had been one of the things that first drew her to him. Along with his dark good looks. And his bad-boy image.

"Colder."

Despite her direction, he moved closer to her, checking more drawers. When he reached her, he grabbed the hem of her sweater and flipped it up to bare her midriff. "Are they in here?"

With a startled gasp, she swatted his hand away, smoothing the sweater back into place. "Dean!"

"I don't know about you, but I think I'm getting warmer." He edged closer, crowding her personal space. He tucked her hair behind her ear, allowing his crooked finger to brush her cheek. "What do you think, Lila? Am I warmer? Are you?"

"Dean, I—" The rest of her sentence snagged in her throat when he leaned in to steal a soft kiss. Her head spun dizzily, and a flash of heat raced through her blood. Desire coiled in her belly, and her most intimate places throbbed with longing. Warmer? Oh, yes. In an instant, he'd managed to set her on fire.

He placed another breath-stealing kiss on her lips, then stepped back, snapping his fingers as if inspired. "The cookie jar!"

With a puckish smile, he crossed the floor to the opposite counter where her whimsical Kermit the Frog cookie jar sat. When he lifted the lid and spied the peanut butter cookies she'd made yesterday, he crowed, "Score!"

He gobbled a cookie down in two bites, wearing a smug look. "The cookie jar. You can't fool me, you minx."

Lila pressed a hand to her belly, where a host of butterflies flapped furiously. "Gee, I thought that one would stump you."

Outside, another loud snap echoed through the woods, and a stiff wind whistled through her eaves. The haunting noises were enough to spoil the brief moment of levity. Reminded of her situation and the looming threat to Eve, Lila's muscles tightened again. Moving stiffly, she took a pot from her lower cabinet and set it on the stove. "So...soup? It's vegetable beef."

The soft shuffle of his feet across her hardwood floor was her only warning before he stepped close behind her and set his hands on her shoulders. Her flinch spoke for itself. She was all wound up and ready to shatter.

"Soup is fine, but I can heat it myself." His low murmur and warm breath near her ear didn't help calm her. If anything, it stirred her pulse to a fevered pitch.

She bit her bottom lip, still damp from his kiss, and tried to center herself. "What happened to me needing a distraction?"

His fingers dug into her shoulder muscles, kneading... tantalizing. "Yeah, a distraction would be good. You're as tight as a drum."

Her hands shook as she pulled the lid off the soup and dumped it in the pan to heat. She closed her eyes as he continued massaging her shoulders. The deep strokes felt divine, and she had to brace her knees to keep from melting into a puddle of goo. The hypnotizing massage was muddling her thoughts. Fueling the lust in her core. *I should stop him...*

Instead, she prayed he'd never quit. If she died now, she'd die happy. A small moan of bliss slipped from her throat as she let her head loll forward, giving him better access to the stiffness in her neck and upper back. *Hussy!* her conscience hissed.

He chuckled softly, and his hands moved up her nape into her hair. "If you keep making sexy noises like that, I'm gonna have to kiss you again. This time, for real."

Finding the air in her lungs to speak was difficult, but she managed to rasp, "Dean, I can't… I don't want…"

His hands stilled, dropped from her arms, and she almost wept for the lost contact. She turned to face him, ready to defend her choice, while at the same time regretting her hesitance. Damn Carl and the pain he'd caused her! This reluctance was his fault, his legacy.

"What don't you want? Me?" Dean ran a finger along her cheek, and she shivered. "'Cause I don't believe that. That's not what your body is saying."

He stood close enough for her chest to brush his, for her to have to tip back her head to meet his gaze, for her to note that his bister eyes grew even darker when he was aroused. What was darker brown than bister? Zinnwaldite? She gave her head a shake. Who cared? Wasn't it enough that they were intently focused on her, that she could read his desire for her in those dark, brooding depths?

"Okay, I'd be lying if I denied feeling something for you, but…" She wiggled loose of his grasp with a defeated sigh and stalked to the living room, stewing. "I followed my heart in the past and got burned. This time, I have to listen to my head."

She heard the clomp of Dean's boots as he crossed the floor, sensed him moving up behind her.

"Are you telling me," he asked, "that there is a *this time*?"

Chapter 5

The road was slick. Really slick. Wayne already knew that, thanks to the transport van crash, but keeping the piece-of-crap SUV he'd hot-wired on the road was harder than he'd imagined. He'd picked the SUV thinking it would have four-wheel drive, that it would handle the icy roads better, but whoever once owned this rattletrap had done as lousy of a job maintaining it mechanically as he had with the exterior. The gears stuck and wouldn't shift into four-wheel drive and the steering was so loose, he could jerk the wheel a good six inches left or right before the damn SUV responded. He'd lose the SUV and steal something else if there was another car around. But he'd already reached the outskirts of Collins Ridge and was headed up into the foothills. Nothing out here but forests, wild animals and the sleet-crusted highway.

Wayne set his jaw and tightened his grip on the steering wheel as the tires slipped again. Kent had trusted him to take care of Eve. To humanely end his niece's life. To save her from the indignity of foster care, the blind dictates of bureaucracy and a life under the tyranny of misguided government drones.

The idea of killing a baby, his own niece, didn't sit well with him, but he saw Kent's reasoning. And his first duty was to his brother. He had his orders, and he'd carry them out. What's more, he'd take down anyone who tried to stop him, too. For instance, this Lila Greene woman who'd taken Eve. Was she just in the foster system for the check, like his foster mothers had been? Would she stand aside when threatened and let him take Eve with him or would she put up a fight? If she tried to stop him, he'd shoot her.

He had no problem with that. Funny, though, that any show of actually caring about her charge was exactly what would get the lady killed. Wayne didn't dwell on the irony long. He needed to focus on his driving. The sooner he did his job, the sooner he could meet up with Kent and they could disappear. They'd set up a compound in another state with new names and build a new family. The Pitts brothers would not be shoved in a box or ruled by any government. They would remain free, follow The Truth and The Sword would rise again.

"I gotta tell you, Lila," he said as she turned to face him, "listening to your head is fine most of the time, but I've done tours with too many young guys who died with regrets." He moved closer, and she would have backed away from his touch but her legs bumped the edge of her coffee table. Without pushing past him or climbing backward over the furniture, she was trapped.

"The girl they should have married before being deployed, the apology they never gave their dad, the risk they should have taken in business. Heads are good for some things, but don't let it talk you into missing something you'll always regret losing."

Lila closed her eyes. It was so hard to think straight when she looked into Dean's dark eyes.

"I swear to you, Lila. I will do everything in my power to keep you and Eve safe."

She drew a lungful of oxygen to fight the dizzying effects of his nearness. "Even be honest with me? Can you do that?" She opened her eyes again to read his reaction to her boldness.

He hesitated, his gaze narrowing slightly. "Honesty, huh?"

"Is that a difficult concept for you?" She tried to keep a stern tone, letting him know she wouldn't be trifled with, but her voice cracked when she met the mesmerizing heat in his eyes.

"Okay, how's this for honesty? I've had a thing for you since I was fifteen. I've always thought you were beautiful. Sexy. Intriguing." His hand skimmed her cheek, and he leaned in for a kiss. "I wanted you back then, but I knew you were a good girl. I figured you wouldn't want someone with my reputation, so I never asked you out. That's my regret, and I don't want to repeat it."

She turned her cheek to him, struggling for a steady breath and her reasoning powers. "As I recall—" she had to pause and clear her throat "—you did try to kiss me at the Fourth of July fireworks…" She cut a quick glance up at him, catching his dark gaze. "The summer before our senior year of high school."

"As *I* recall—" Dean pitched his voice to a low, sultry whisper and slid an arm around her waist "—I didn't just try to kiss you. I succeeded. And you kissed me back. More than once." He leaned in, catching her lips again, then moved his mouth down the line of her jaw and nibbled his way toward her earlobe.

As much as her teenaged self had wanted to drape her arms around his neck and savor the caress of his kisses, her adult self reminded her wavering heart of his reputation. The pain of Carl's betrayal was too fresh, her resolve not to repeat her past mistakes too firm to throw caution aside. Even if she knew a few moments of passion with Dean would be bliss. Her traitorous body buzzed with anticipation and pleasure. Fortunately, her head still worked. Planting her hands on his chest—dear heavens, he was solid and taut with muscle!—she rallied enough composure to push him away. "Don't."

Dean lowered his hands and gave his head a quick shake. "Okay. I'll respect your wishes, for now, but… I had to give it a shot. I didn't want to live with the regret of letting a second chance with you slip past untried."

Lila finger-combed her hair away from her eyes as she walked slowly over to her palette, her head spinning. Eve, a gunman, Dean, an ice storm. Any one of those was enough to process in a day, but all of them at once?

Chloe sat by the sliding glass door to her screened porch, pleading with sad eyes and a soft meow to be let out. Spring through autumn, the porch was a favorite hangout for her cat, but Chloe couldn't get it through her head that it was too cold to go out in winter. Being in no mood to play the in-and-out and in-and-out-again game with her cat, Lila did her best to ignore Chloe's beseeching expression.

"It's not that I'm unwilling to try, Dean—" she cast him a glance for understanding, not unlike the one Chloe was giving her "—but I need to be sure about you before I take a leap that could get me hurt. You've only been back in my life a few hours. And while the physical chemistry may have been reignited on sight, we have eleven years of getting reacquainted to consider."

"I get that." He slipped his hands in his jeans pockets and rocked back on his heels. "I can give you time. My plan is to be at my parents' cabin for the next couple of months. I have a seasonal job lined up with a friend starting in April. But until then…we have time to get to know each other again."

"Once this killer is caught. And Eve goes to her biological family…"

He inhaled deeply and nodded. "Right. The Pittses will be caught, Lila. There's a huge manhunt for them. It's just a matter of time."

The question was—would the Pitts brothers be caught before or after they reached her cabin, and she had to fight for Eve's life? Biting her bottom lip, she paced a bit more. She stopped at her easel and lifted the paintbrush she'd been using when she'd received the call about Eve. She'd been so crazily distracted since then, she'd allowed the paint to dry on the brush. She'd have to throw that brush away. And she'd wasted a good amount of expensive paint, which was now caked on her palette as well.

Whatever. She had bigger problems to deal with…

No sooner had the thought entered her mind than a plaintive wail came from the nursery, loud enough that the baby monitor was overkill.

"That nap didn't last long," Dean said as he followed her into the nursery.

"No, it didn't. Poor thing. I know she's hurting…and scared without her mother." When Lila stroked Eve's head to soothe her, she found the baby's skin unusually warm. "Oh, no."

"What?" Dean stepped closer to peer over her shoulder.

"I think she's running a fever."

Pulling to a stop along the isolated mountain road, Wayne consulted the GPS unit mounted on the dash of the SUV he'd stolen. According to the device, he was almost to the house where the police had taken Eve. A secluded mountain cabin. He grunted smugly. Nice try, Enemy, but he'd found the place. He wondered briefly how Kent was doing locating Caleb.

Guess I'll find out soon enough.

Rather than give away his approach, give the foster family time to hide Eve or arm themselves, he cut the engine of the old SUV and climbed out to walk the last quarter mile or so to the driveway. The wind and pelting ice were as cold as a witch's soul, but Kent wouldn't take any excuses for not doing the job right. Precaution, planning…he wouldn't let his big brother down.

As he neared the driveway, the rumble of tires on the slick mountain highway warned him of a car's approach. He left the road, sneaking into the line of trees in time to see a local police squad car ease past. The cop craned his neck, eyeing the woods where Wayne stood behind a tree, then stopped and opened his driver's side door. "Hey, you there! Come out with your hands up then lie face down on the ground!"

Wayne's heartbeat increased three-fold. He would not—could not—be caught now and sent away. The cop could shoot him in the back for all he cared—he'd rather rot in a grave than in a cell—but not before he finished the mission Kent had sent him on.

He put a hand on the gun tucked in the waist of his pants, the Glock .40 he'd lifted from the injured US marshal. Then, stepping from the trees as directed, he raised the gun and fired.

The cop quickly ducked back into the protection of his squad car and drew his sidearm. Wayne hurried forward, trying to get off the fatal shot before the cop could return fire. But a powerful blow and a sharp, burning sting in his thigh knocked him down before he could make it ten steps.

With The Sword I will fight for my right to live free, seek The Truth and defend myself from The Enemy. The mantra Kent had drilled into him over the past thirteen years gave him the courage and the energy to block out the pain and fight on. The cop was an obstacle to completing his mission, and he knew how to deal with an obstacle. Eliminate it.

Dean reached around Lila, his body pressing against her back, and he laid his hand on the infant's forehead. "Yeah, she is warm. You have a thermometer?"

Lila nodded. "I'll be right back." She hurried to the bathroom and pulled out of the cabinet a basket of supplies she kept on hand for her foster babies. She checked the expiration date on the bottle of liquid acetaminophen and dug out the baby thermometer. Returning to the nursery, she handed the medicine to Dean and uncapped the protective cover on the thermometer.

"What the hell is that?" Dean asked.

"What do you think?" She bumped him out of the

way with her hip and gently placed the tip in Eve's ear. A second later, the device beeped and she checked the reading. "One hundred point one."

Dean took the thermometer from her and gave it a once-over. "What happened to the old-fashioned glass stick put under your tongue?"

She chuckled. "Yeah, you try to get a baby to hold a glass stick under her tongue." She took the acetaminophen back from him and uncapped the dropper. "You don't want to know where they put thermometers in babies before this doohickey came along."

He sent her a wry look. "I'm well aware of where parents used to take a baby's temperature."

"Hmm." She eased the medicine dropper between Eve's lips and squirted the sugary medicine onto the baby's tongue. "The family in Iraq did things the old-fashioned way, I take it."

He gave her a quick one-shoulder shrug. "Something like that."

She flashed Eve a lopsided smile as the baby smacked her lips and swallowed her medicine. "I love this age. Teething crankiness aside."

He grunted an acknowledgment. "Why is that?"

"Pardon?"

"Why is this age—six months, you said—so special?"

"Oh. Well…because they start interacting more with you. Babies begin babbling and trying to talk, and they will laugh at silly things like funny noises or games. They can sit up, and they start eating solid foods, which is always an adventure."

"Always a mess, you mean."

She bumped him with her shoulder. "Grump. I think

a baby face smeared with strained fruit is the cutest thing on earth."

He sent her a dubious side-glance. "To each his own."

Outside, a loud crack reverberated through the woods. Dean jerked up his head, his attention darting to the window. His body seemed tense, his muscles rigid as he stared out into her yard.

His reaction puzzled Lila. "Another branch breaking from the ice?"

He flicked a quick glance at her, and a muscle in his jaw flexed. "Maybe."

"Maybe?" She recapped the bottle of medicine and set it on the dresser next to the crib.

His expression modulated as if weighing his words. "Probably."

She tipped her head, studying him. "Dean?"

He fingered aside the curtain and stared out at the icy lawn with a dark scowl.

"What time did they say that cop was supposed to arrive?" He let the curtain drop and fisted his hands at his sides as he crossed the room to her.

Lila flipped her wrist to check her watch. Well over two hours had passed since she'd received the phone call from Special Agent Dunn. "I was under the impression they were sending someone out right away." She furrowed her brow, and a nervous flutter gathered in her stomach. "They should be here by now."

Chapter 6

Dean didn't answer right away, and Lila watched him with a puzzled expression. "Don't you think the cop should be here by now?"

"Maybe." His tone hinted she was being unreasonable. "It *is* icy out there."

"Really?" she said, the word dripping with sarcasm. "Hadn't noticed."

"I just mean, the roads are bad."

Eve made a soft snuffling sound and poked her thumb in her mouth. Dean took Lila's arm and steered her out to the living room.

"You can't tell me you aren't wondering what's taking so long for the policeman to get here," she whispered.

"Don't freak yet. The ice means it's gonna take longer to get up here."

"Yeah, well…let's hope it takes the Pitts brothers longer to get up here, too."

He motioned toward the corner of the room, where her canvas was set up. "Why don't you paint or something to take your mind off of the wait? I'll go bring in some more firewood and…maybe take a look around the property to see where that last branch fell."

"Why does that matter? Power's already out," Lila said.

He took a moment too long to answer before turning up one palm. "It could…have blocked the driveway."

She eyed him skeptically. He was hiding something, she was certain. But if he wanted to check the driveway or bring in wood, who was she to stop him? She hadn't asked him to stay and guard her. She had the shotgun, loaded and ready now, thanks to Dean. And ice or not, the promised police protection had to arrive soon. Didn't it?

"Fine. Check the driveway. Just…be sure you lock the door behind you." She shuffled over to her landscape and sat down. She wasn't in a mood to paint, but he was right that she needed to stay busy. Since all the paint on her palette had dried out, she squeezed another dab of green and one of black and began mixing the two to get the right shade for the evergreen trees she was working on.

He shoved his arms in his coat and headed out, pausing to turn the thumb latch on the door. "I won't be long. Stay inside. Got it?"

The severity of his tone sent a chill through her. She hadn't planned to go anywhere, but why had he felt it necessary to warn her? "Dean?"

He stopped, turned back to her. "Yeah?"

"Where are you really going? Did you see something outside from the nursery?" Even as she asked she brushed back the curtain of the window by her easel.

"No. I didn't see anything."

She glanced back at him, gauging his truthfulness.

"Really. I'm just…restless. Curious," he said, still not convincing her. He aimed a finger at her. "Stay put. I'll be right back."

She angled her body and craned her neck to see out the front window as he headed off. He was carrying her ax. Maybe he did think there was a branch blocking the drive. Maybe she was being too suspicious because of Carl. She hated the idea that her ex had eroded her ability to trust. She really didn't want Carl to still have that much power over her. With a huff of frustration, she turned back to her painting.

Intentionally clearing her mind, she decided she needed to give Dean the benefit of the doubt. Unless, or until, he gave her reason to distrust him, she'd take him at face value. Though he seemed a bit gruff at times, he'd proven himself helpful and considerate of her needs today. That had to count for something. Right?

Dean clenched his teeth as he marched through the increasingly hard-driving ice and flurries of snow. He'd hated lying to Lila, but he didn't need to upset her without proof of his suspicions. The crack they'd heard from the nursery was no branch falling. It was a sound he'd heard enough times to last him a lifetime. A noise that echoed in his nightmares. A gunshot.

And not a hunting rifle or shotgun, either. A handgun. Probably in the .38-to-.40 caliber range, he'd wager.

He took small, careful steps as he crossed into the woods surrounding Lila's cabin, both to avoid slipping on the ice and to make as little noise as possible as he made his way toward the road. He hoped the clacking of icy limbs, nudged by the wind, and the pinging of sleet would cover the sound of his footsteps crunching through the frozen ground cover.

He stayed behind large trees as much as possible, zigzagging his way toward the small state highway that crossed the mountain. A movement to his right caught his attention, and he ducked behind a wide trunk as he scanned the scenery. A small doe trotted past, flicking her ears as the ice pelted her.

Two more loud cracks reverberated through the woods, followed shortly after by a third pop of equal volume, if different pitch. The doe bolted away, startled by the noise, and Dean's heartbeat sprinted as well.

He squeezed the handle of the ax, his only weapon, and thought longingly of his personal sidearm back at his cabin. He'd intentionally left the shotgun with Lila, not wanting her left alone and defenseless while he conducted his reconnaissance. Knowing whoever was out there was armed, he steeled himself. He couldn't allow himself to think about the images that danced at the periphery of his mind, the memories of firefights gone sideways or home-to-home searches where his team had been betrayed, ambushed.

He forged on, being all the more careful to move stealthily, stay out of sight. When he neared the road, he slowed his pace even further, crouching low to stay hidden by the thick underbrush. Through the leafless winter branches of the forest, he spotted the black-and-white. The driver's side door was open, the engine was running. Someone was behind the wheel, but the cop seemed to be looking down at the floorboard. Dean checked the woods around him carefully. He scanned high and low, searching for any sign of life. The woods were eerily still, quiet. Even the birds were silent.

But the longer he watched the officer in the squad car, the more his lungs tightened, his dread building. The guy hadn't moved, and common sense, gut instinct and experience told Dean the officer would never move again. With a final careful look around him, Dean made his way to the idling squad car. He eased up to the back bumper, keeping low, and scuttled to the open door. He could smell the burned gunpowder, indicating a recently fired weapon. The cop was slumped forward against the steering wheel. The ominous certainty in him grew, a black cloud roiling in the sky ahead of a vicious storm.

"Hey," he whispered. "You okay?"

He didn't expect an answer, but on the off chance the cop was alive and Dean startled him, he didn't want to get shot, either. He drew up even with the open door. The cop's arm hung limply at his side. Dean slid two fingers to the man's carotid artery to check for a pulse and encountered a warm sticky residue. When he pulled his hand back, his fingers were coated with blood.

Mouthing a foul word that didn't express even half of his dark roil of emotion, Dean wiped his hand on the snow at his feet. The red smear left behind mocked him.

He tugged the dead man's shoulder to lean him back against the seat. No matter how many times he saw the physical evidence of violence on a body, it never got easier for Dean. He tried not to look at the gaping wound in the man's neck. Instead, he reached across the cop's body to take the gun from his right hand. The person who'd shot the cop was out there, armed and likely headed to find Eve. He wouldn't go back to Lila's without a better weapon than an ax. The barrel was warm, so the officer *had* gotten off at least one shot.

Dean turned his back to the gruesome scene, his guard up, all of his senses tuned to the woods around him. The killer had to have left a trail. Footprints, broken branches, tire tracks...*or blood.*

Dean's breath stilled when he spotted the dark drips about twenty feet in front of the police cruiser. Staying low behind the car, he checked the canopy of branches around him again carefully. He saw no evidence of anyone hanging around. That made sense. Killers didn't generally stick around after shooting a cop. But the blood droplets said the guy was wounded. How badly? How fast could the guy move?

Despite all his questions and uncertainty, Dean knew two things for certain. One, he needed to report the cop's death and get backup sent immediately. But a check of the cruiser's radio found the cord to the hand mic had been cut. Dean mumbled another curse word under his breath. *A smart killer.*

Truth two—the cop killer's ultimate destination was Lila's cabin. Eve. Somehow, despite the ice storm, one or both of the Pitts brothers had found Lila's address and made it onto the mountain. He had to get back to Lila's...like ten minutes ago.

Wayne Pitts hobbled back toward his stolen SUV, gritting his teeth against the pain. The cop's bullet had struck the muscled part of his thigh, which meant his leg hurt like hell every step he made. But at least it hadn't broken a bone. Or hit a major artery. He'd seen guys with seemingly survivable leg injuries bleed out before an ambulance could reach them. Just the same, he knew he needed to disinfect the wound, stop the bleeding and wrap his leg. Kent would insist that Wayne's mission came first, his own needs second. But Kent wasn't here, and as much as the guilt of letting his big brother down twisted in his gut, Wayne knew he had a better chance of finding Eve and making it off that mountain alive, ahead of the US Marshals, if he tended his leg first.

He'd figured The Enemy would send the police after him and Kent. They were fugitives, after all. The Enemy wouldn't take their escape lightly. He just hadn't expected to have a cop intercept him at the remote driveway to Lila Greene's house. They'd been fast to deploy that cop, had been one step ahead of him, and that rankled. How had the cops known where he was headed? The Enemy was trickier, quicker to react than Wayne had given them credit for. A mistake he wouldn't make twice.

As he plowed through the trees, headed back to the spot down the road where he'd hidden the SUV, he felt a sharp sting on his ear, a tug on his knit hat. A thorny branch had caught the side of his face and scraped his ear. He growled his frustration and fury with the disruptions to his mission and for the agonizing pain in his leg. His bullet wound might not be life-threatening, but he was beginning to feel light-headed and slightly nauseated. Kent would have no patience with such complaints, so Wayne pushed on. The SUV was in sight, and he staggered toward it. He could bind the leg with strips from his undershirt, but how would he clean the wound?

Spots appeared at the edges of his vision, and he tripped over a root he hadn't seen and landed on the ground with a bone-jarring jolt. Pain shot like lightning through his leg. He cried out and grabbed for his injured thigh. The spots in his vision closed in, and his world went black.

* * *

While Dean was gone, checking the driveway, Eve woke again, still feverish and cranky. Lila lifted the baby from the crib and carried her to the bathroom, where she fixed a cool damp cloth to dab the girl's forehead and cheeks. Under normal circumstances, a slight fever and teething issues would not daunt Lila, but given the ice storm, the escaped cult members and Dean's return from her past, Lila was more than a little unnerved today. She cradled Eve in her arm and strolled into the living room just as Dean burst through the front door, letting in a blast of frigid air as he stomped in.

"Well?" she asked.

His expression was more grim than usual, and she held her breath as he set aside the shotgun and stripped off his coat. "Well what?"

"What did you find?"

He shook his head, modulating his expression. He untied and pulled off his hiking boots, setting them closer to the fireplace to dry. "Nothing."

Here we go with the terse act again. "So there were no branches blocking the drive?"

"No."

"No sign of the cop?"

He squared his shoulders, his jaw tightening. "No."

She sighed her impatience. "Should I call that FBI agent and tell him his guard never showed?"

Dean jerked his chin up a notch. "No."

"But—"

"I mean... I'll do it. You have your hands full." He nodded to the wiggly, whimpering baby in her arms.

She shifted Eve to her shoulder and patted her back.

"This isn't your problem. If the FBI agent needs to be called, I—

"Really?" He shook his head and gave her a frustrated scowl. "There's independent and capable, and then there's stupidly stubborn. You're dealing with a little more than your average fostering case here. I can help with this situation. Let me."

He was right, of course, even if his curtness did sting. As much as she wanted to prove she didn't need a man to rescue her, she was dealing with extraordinary circumstances. An escaped killer, an ice storm, a vulnerable baby in her care. Lila bit her lip and scanned her countertop for the pad of paper where Miriam had written the emergency numbers. "The FBI agent's contact info is on that pad." She tipped her head toward the counter.

He stepped over to retrieve the sheet and took her cordless landline from its cradle. "I'll, uh…take it back here." He started for the nursery, the farthest room from the living room. "It's quieter."

"Or I could—" But he disappeared before she could finish her offer. A ripple of unease slid through her. She didn't know Dean well, but even to her unfamiliar eye, he seemed edgy. Even before he left to check the driveway, he'd been acting strangely. Although, she'd already seen he was more tightly wound than the average person under normal circumstances. Was his persistent tension a sign of PTSD? Who was she to say? Her uncertainties about him were one more reason not to harbor any ideas of striking up a relationship with the bad boy from her past.

She settled on the couch with Eve, still swabbing the baby's face with the cool rag and murmuring soothing coos to calm the girl. A moment later, Dean's voice sounded beside her and she startled.

"Hello? Agent Dunn? Yeah, my name is Dean Hamilton. I'm a neighbor of Lila Greene's."

She glanced to the end table, where Dean's voice was being broadcast from the baby monitor. *Oops*. She grinned as she stretched toward the receiver to turn it off. But the device was just beyond her reach. She started to scoot down the couch, closer to the receiver, when Dean's words caught her attention.

"Yes, sir. We have a situation up here, and you need to send backup. STAT."

A situation? Lila frowned.

"The cop you sent to guard Lila is dead."

Lila gasped, and an iciness sank into her marrow.

"I found him in his squad car at the end of Lila's driveway with a GSW to the neck," Dean continued, and a numbing horror spread through her.

"I found a blood trail leading into the woods around Ms. Greene's property. Looks like the perp was wounded in an exchange of fire. No eyes on the dirtbag. I hauled ass back to Lila's cabin to make sure she and the kid had protection." He paused, then said, "Yeah. One or both of the Pitts brothers sounds right to me. That was what you were expecting, right?"

Another silence, during which Lila shook herself from her daze, and her brain began ticking rapid-fire thoughts. Dean had lied to her. He'd found the cop dead and told her he'd found nothing. Or was he lying to the FBI agent? But why would he do that? Or had Dean killed the cop? No, that didn't make sense. Why report the killing, if he'd done it? Where was the shooter now?

The questions tumbled one on top of the other in the space of a few anxious heartbeats.

"Dean Hamilton," he repeated. "My family owns the cabin on the other side of the ridge. I did two tours with the Army Special Forces in Afghanistan and more recently in Iraq. I can protect her, but you need to get your men up here to find this cretin."

Lila heard a snapping branch outside her cabin and jerked her gaze to the front window. The wind was picking up, and the sleet was changing over to snow. The roads would only become more treacherous and impassable as the blizzard conditions worsened. She was stranded up here with a killer on the loose in the woods. She pulled Eve closer to her chest, both in a protective gesture and seeking comfort for herself.

"She has a shotgun, and it's loaded, but I have a .38 back at my place."

She blinked at the baby monitor. Dean. She wasn't alone. Dean was here. He'd sworn to protect her. But could she trust him? Was he who and what he claimed? He'd lied to her when he got back from his trip outside, but...

"I don't like waiting here in her place like sitting ducks. I want to move them to my place."

Lila sat taller. Move them?

"No. The roads are bad, and he might be watching the driveway. We'll hike out."

A buzzing noise started in Lila's ears. As the shock of what Dean was saying wore off, she stood, holding Eve close, and began pacing restlessly. This whole situation, the entire day, had been surreal. She really didn't know where to begin processing everything that was happening. But she knew having Dean decide her fate was unacceptable. She would not let herself be bullied into choices affecting her safety or her foster baby's. Eve was her responsibility, and she would decide how to protect her.

As if she sensed the importance of the call they were listening to, Eve tucked her head against Lila's chest with a snuffling exhale and quieted.

"How long will that take?" Dean said. "A helo can't fly in this weather."

Irritation sank in its claws. Lila clenched her teeth and mentally began preparing her arguments for whatever plan Dean had devised. He had lied to her, just like Carl had so many times about so many things. While one part of her brain could admit she was hypersensitive when it came to dishonesty, because of Carl's duplicity, another part of her mind rejected that justification. She would not, could not, be party to any more deception and betrayal. Even as her more rational side argued that Dean must have a good reason for his lying, her wounded heart hardened, reinforcing her protective walls. That Dean had lied about something as important as her safety, withheld information she *needed* to know about the fate of the cop, showed her Dean was untrustworthy. She couldn't justify putting her life or Eve's in the hands of a man who could be so deceptive.

"Cell reception up here sucks. No, you're right. Fine. Yes. We'll wait until we hear back from you here."

Reason number two why she would not be leaving her home. It seemed crazy to her to leave the place where Special Agent Dunn could contact her and vice versa. She kissed the top of Eve's head as she patted the baby's back. The baby's skin was still warm, but maybe the Tylenol was finally kicking in.

Dean finished his phone call, and she heard his heavy sigh filter through the baby monitor. He didn't return to the living room right away, and as Eve drifted to sleep in her arms, she used the excuse of putting the infant back in her crib to check on Dean.

He stood near the window, glaring out at the snowy woods, his brow heavily creased. The thin light from the window threw his brooding countenance in stark relief, highlighting the sharp angles and square cut of his jaw. Lila's pulse did a quick, giddy two-step at the sight of him. The natural reaction of a woman to his striking looks, she assured herself. But a physical attraction to Dean, one she'd had since she was a teen, didn't mean she had to lose her head with him. *Don't make the same mistake again.*

He jerked to attention when she came into the room as if he hadn't heard her approach. "Oh, hi. I, uh… It's started snowing."

"Yeah. I know," she whispered stiffly as she eased over to the crib and slowly lay Eve on her side to nap.

"Is she feeling better?" he whispered back, clearly taking his cue from her.

"Or else she's plumb worn out."

Every muscle in her body was drawn tight with anxiety, anger and hurt. She wanted to rail at Dean, strike out at him for the pain his deception caused her. The deep disappointment. She'd wanted Dean to be different, she realized. Maybe it was unfair to allow Carl's sins to color her perceptions about Dean, but the heart wasn't always rational. Sometimes self-preservation was the stronger instinct. Knowing she was being unyielding and forming opinions without giving Dean a chance to explain didn't ease the ache of Carl's betrayal that Dean had reawakened.

She wanted to believe he'd changed in the past eleven years, as he claimed. She wanted to believe that the chemistry she felt with him could be backed up with a level of trust and respect that she could base a relationship on. Yes, she'd set a high standard for him to meet, a watermark even she didn't meet some days. But knowing how difficult she'd made it for anyone to get past her trust issues, her broken heart didn't change the stabbing ache of disappointment. She'd set high hopes along with her high standard, and at his first opportunity to prove his merit, Dean had let her down.

She wanted to kick him out, send him on his way back to his own cabin. But…

The cop you sent to guard Lila is dead.

She had to fight to keep the tide of panic from overtaking her. As angry as she was at Dean, clearly there were bigger issues to deal with. Pushing aside the aching disillusionment and nagging rationalizations that sliced through her, Lila lingered by the crib, tucking a blanket around the baby and stroking Eve's head with a trembling hand as the baby dozed off. Deceptive or not, Dean had told the FBI agent he would protect her, protect Eve. She needed him here as long as the cop killer was in the area. Acid puddled in her gut, and she gripped the side of the crib to stay upright.

This can't be happening to me!

Dean moved up beside her and stared at Eve as well. Even just his presence standing next to her eased the anxious knot tangled inside her. As hurt as she was, she couldn't deny having a brawny protector here until the Pitts brothers were caught was a definite boon. She needed to ask him about the call, but she hesitated. If he didn't tell her the grisly story of what he'd found, she could pretend for a few more minutes that all was right with her world.

Denial is why things got so bad with Carl. She'd ignored the missing money, blaming her own bookkeeping skills and questioning her memory. She'd allowed Carl to take secret phone calls and lamely believed the explanations of his absence that didn't quite add up. She'd been a fool and hated how she'd allowed Carl to dupe her for so long. Deep down she knew this was at the root of why she expected so much from Dean. She drew harsher lines in her personal relationships because she knew she had allowed things to go from bad to worse with Carl. She was determined not to give an inch ever again.

And now Dean expected her to believe his lies? No! She would keep her guard up, shove down the attraction she felt toward him and keep him at arms' length—which was difficult when he was so sweet to Eve.

Even now, the worried look that had been etched in Dean's expression when he'd stood by the window softened as he studied the little girl. "She's cute."

"Very." Lila tore her gaze from Dean's tender expression. She didn't want to acknowledge that he was kind and patient with the fussy baby, even if most bachelors wouldn't be as understanding. Knowing he had a soft spot for Eve would make it harder to fight her growing attraction to him. She waited a moment to see if Dean said anything about his phone call.

But he didn't. Why would he? He'd gone to lengths to hide the truth from her, made his call in private—or so he'd thought.

"So," she began, trying to keep the quaver of stress

and frustration from her voice, "did the FBI guy know what the holdup was with the cop? Are they still sending someone?"

"No. He didn't know what had happened to the cop." He paused then added, "But he's looking into it and sending backup."

A nibble of truth, but still no mention of his ghastly discovery. She gritted her teeth. She wondered how long he planned to continue his deception, keep his silence.

She reined in her irritation and her fear as best she could. She'd play along with his farce, give him the rope to hang himself, but would keep her guard up. While she believed Dean meant to keep her and Eve safe, she didn't intend to depend solely on him. She exhaled a cleansing breath and tried to come to terms with what she faced. She couldn't be stupid like she'd been with Carl. She couldn't turn a blind eye to the danger she was in. She'd take her own precautions. But what exactly did that mean?

Arming herself with kitchen knives and piling the furniture in front of all the doors?

"What else did he say?" *Come on, Dean, just 'fess up!*

"He wanted to know who I was."

"Of course." Lila's hurt and frustration grew with every stilted response. Moments earlier she'd been kissing this man, hoping that he'd changed, believing maybe they could build on their attraction. *Please, just give me the truth! I need to know where I stand. Where* we *stand.*

When Eve stuck her thumb in her mouth and sucked loudly, Lila's heart squeezed. One day she hoped to be watching her own baby sleep. She wanted a house full of children. And, of course, the husband who would give her those babies. She wanted the whole American dream. Family, security, a white picket fence. She sighed mentally. Someday. She just had to be patient. Her Mr. Right was out there.

Dean rubbed a hand on his unshaven chin and the soft scratching sound sent an odd tingle through her. Her head might know he wasn't her Mr. Right, but her libido hadn't gotten the memo. He hitched his head toward the door, signaling for her to follow him out, and after a final pat on Eve's back, Lila tiptoed out to the hall.

"Something you wanted to talk about?" she asked quietly, offering him yet another opportunity to come clean.

He shook his head. "Naw. I just thought we should let her sleep. She's been so fussy and all."

She crossed her arms over her chest and raised her chin. "You're sure? Nothing to tell me?"

He hesitated, his gaze narrowing suspiciously. But again he said, "Nothing."

Disappointment slashed through her. Even when she'd given him ample openings to be honest, he'd chosen to hide the truth from her. To her, the sin of omission was as bad as a flat-out falsehood.

She followed Dean when he walked into the living room and squatted in front of her fireplace. With the iron poker from her fireplace tool set, he began jabbing the logs, breaking them apart and shifting them in a way that would smother the flames.

Arms still crossed angrily over her chest, she frowned at him. "What are you doing? Don't you know that will kill the fire? I'm kinda enjoying being warm today."

He shot a glance over his shoulder. "Yeah, I, uh… figured since the generator was going you'd want to conserve firewood."

She arched an eyebrow and cocked her head skeptically.

He faced the grate again, still banking the fire and hedging. "I mean, who knows how long this weather will last and if the generator quits…"

"I want a fire. Build it back up, please." Her words were polite, but her tone meant business.

He stood and dusted his hands. "Not a good idea."

"Why not?"

"Just…trust me. Okay?"

She scoffed. Trust was the one thing she was short on today. "Why should I?"

His hands stilled, and his face scrunched in disbelief. "Pardon?"

"Why should I trust you?" Lila moved her hands to her hips in clear challenge.

"What's your problem?" Dean straightened his back and looked her up and down.

"Well, let's see… I have a violent and probably deranged cult leader gunning for the baby I'm fostering, an ice storm raging outside…" She ticked off the items on her fingers.

He pulled a face. "You know what I mean. Why are you acting mad at me?" He stepped closer to her, and she stiffened. "Have I not been trying to help you today? I fixed your generator, helped with the cranky baby, went out looking for the missing cop—"

She raised her chin. "And that's reason to just blindly trust you?"

He spread his hands. "What do you want me to say? I know I was a delinquent as a kid, but I've changed. If you'd give me a chance, I'd like to prove that to you."

His hurt and puzzled frown would have broken her

heart if she hadn't just heard him lie about what he'd found during his exploration down her driveway. *Just confront him*, a nagging voice said. *Clear the air so you can move forward. Maybe you can still build something with him if...*

She shook her head, squashing the thought before it fully formed. "No."

He released her, but his dark look of confusion and frustration remained. "Why *no*? Can you tell me you aren't glad I'm here, that we have a second chance to get to know each other? Honestly, you can't deny that you feel the heat between us."

"Honestly?" She chuckled wryly at his repeated use of the word. "Yes. I feel it. I did then, and I do now. But—"

"And isn't that something worth pursuing?"

She fumbled with the gold chain she wore, nervously sliding the coin charm back and forth. He wanted to pursue something with her? The notion both galled her and made her giddy. A steamy affair with Dean sounded tempting, and she was flattered he wanted more than a few stolen kisses with her. But how could he propose a relationship with her moments after deceiving her? She couldn't possibly get involved with someone with such a dim respect for the truth.

"Lila?"

She pivoted and paced a few steps away from the tantalizing scent of him, the virile energy that seemed to surround him and draw her in. Forcing moisture to her mouth, she said, "You need more than basic biology—a physical attraction—to make a relationship work."

"Agreed. That's why people date. To get to know each other."

"I know, but you're not..." She paused, sensing his

mood change. He tensed his shoulders, and his expression grew defensive.

"I'm not the same person I was eleven years ago. If you'd give me a chance to prove that, I—" He cut himself off, clamping lips in a tight line. "Never mind. I won't ask again."

The evidence of his wounded pride clawed at her. "Dean…"

"No, forget it." He raised a palm and stalked away. After retrieving his boots from the hearth, he dropped on the couch, his jaw taut and his movements jerky as he jammed his feet in his boots and tugged on the laces.

Guilt gnawed at her, but upon reviewing the exchange, she kicked herself for assuming the blame for his mood. She'd pushed him away, yes, but she had every right to. No matter how much chemistry they shared, she wouldn't put herself in a position to be hurt by another man who couldn't be completely aboveboard with her. She needed a man she could depend on and believe in.

Then, as it became clear that he intended to leave, her heart thumped an anxious cadence. She wouldn't beg him to stay if he was determined to go back to his cabin, but the idea of being alone with Eve frightened her. In a couple short hours, she'd come to count on Dean's presence through this crisis. "So that's it? You're leaving?"

He didn't answer her, but his surly silence was loud and clear. She pressed a hand over the rapid-fire beat of her heart. *Don't panic. He promised to protect you and Eve.*

But how much weight could she give his word? Could she trust his promises? Rather than stay in the living room, where the emotions were as thick as a West Virginia fog, Lila ducked into the nursery and checked on Eve.

The baby slept soundly, her lips parted and her breath soughing softly. Tears burned Lila's eyes as she gripped the crib's side rail. Had she pushed too hard? Had she blown it because of her doubt and distrust? Her caution and suspicion may have cost her the protection she needed. And the chance of a fresh start with a man she'd been drawn to since she'd been a teenager. Had she driven Dean away? Had she driven Carl into the arms of another woman? Her stomach swooped at the inkling that she was as much to blame for her breakup as Carl. A nagging insecurity that had plagued her for months returned.

She wouldn't take the blame for Carl's unfaithfulness or unscrupulous behavior. Nor would she excuse Dean's deception. She was tired of making excuses for the men in her life. And yet...

Damn it! Was it possible Dean had her best interests at heart? She replayed Dean's words, his blank expression. His deceit had been intentional, she was sure, but she hadn't called him on it yet, hadn't allowed him a chance to explain. The phone conversation replayed in her head next, this time coupled with a chilling realization of what she'd overheard Dean tell the FBI agent. The cop had been *shot*. How could she have let Dean's deception overshadow that horrible truth? A man had been killed today just yards from her cabin, and the murderer was lurking in her woods.

A cold, wet slap to the face jarred Wayne from the groggy darkness that sucked at him. His eyelids fluttered open, and he blinked at the web of winter-bare hardwoods and snow-laden evergreens above him. Snow and sleet spit in his face, and when the wind kicked up, the branches over him swayed and dropped globs of crusty snow and ice. Swiping at his face, he realized it was one of these clumps from overhead that had pelted his face and roused him. His leg ached, and when he sat up, his head spun. A shiver rolled through him as he glanced around. How long had he been passed out? His clothes were damp, and he was chilled to the bone after lying in the snow and sleet for God knew how long.

He groaned, seeing the SUV he'd stolen sitting twenty feet away. Why couldn't he have made it to the damn truck before he collapsed? He brushed more ice and snow off his coat and out of his hair and struggled to his feet. Tooth-grinding pain slithered up his leg when he put weight on it, and he bit back a shout of agony. Until he could assess his situation, he needed to lie low. Still, he let a silent string of invectives roll through his mind.

He had to pound his fist on the door handle, breaking a thin layer of ice off, before he could wrench the driver's side door open and slide inside. Once there, he leaned his head back and gulped a few deep breaths. He steeled himself before peeling back the fabric around the new hole in his pants to inspect his wound. The scent of his blood made Wayne's gut roll, and the raw appearance of the bullet wound didn't help.

Grow a pair, Wayne! You have a mission to complete. Kent's voice in his head seemed so real, he looked around him, expecting his older brother to be sitting next to him, castigating him with a disapproving glare.

His mission. Wayne closed his eyes, inhaled deeply and trained his thoughts on what he had to do. He couldn't fail Kent. His big brother had always been there for him, and he would always be in Kent's debt for saving him from that horrid foster home.

Reaching in his pocket, he pulled out the blood-splattered paper he'd taken from the front seat next to the cop, a printout from one of those GPS mapping and directions websites. According to the small map, he was a stone's throw from Lila Greene's place. He'd have to backtrack to the cop's car, then hike up the unpaved road, where the police cruiser had been parked.

But first…

He turned on the seat and searched for the tools he'd need to patch up his leg and finish his task. In the glove compartment, he found a bottle of hand sanitizer, which would sting like hell but would disinfect his wound. With more looking, he discovered a gym bag under the backseat. The T-shirt inside was small and pink—he'd stolen a woman's vehicle apparently—and he easily ripped it along the side seam to make a bandage to wrap around his thigh. He found an energy bar and half-frozen bottle of water in the gym bag as well, and he quickly opened and gobbled up the sustenance.

When he heard a rattle in the bottom of the bag, he dug deeper and found a bottle of Pamprin. Definitely a woman's SUV. He was about to toss the bottle aside when the words *pain relief* caught his attention. He read the label. Aspirin, acetaminophen and caffeine. That all sounded good to him. Nothing girly about those ingredients. He frowned, debating. He could imagine Kent laughing at him, mocking him. *Got menstrual cramps, little brother?*

But Kent wasn't here, and his leg was throbbing. *Screw it. What would it hurt?* He swallowed two tablets and pocketed two more for later.

Wayne then laid his other supplies out and tore a bigger hole in his pants over his gunshot wound. He'd tend his injury, hydrate and head out again. Within the hour, sooner if possible, he needed to be off this mountain. He was less than a mile from Lila Greene's cabin. Even with his bum leg slowing him down, he could finish the job he'd come for in that time frame. His brother's child would not suffer a life in The Enemy's corrupt foster system. Very soon, Eve would join her mother in the afterlife.

Chapter 7

Dean watched Lila stalk into the nursery, and guilt sat like a pit in his gut. After telling her he'd changed and that she could trust him, he'd lied to her. Forget his reasons. A lie was a lie when it came to trust. Worse, it was obvious she could tell he'd lied, and she was furious with him. Not the best way to build the foundation of a relationship with a woman he cared about. But keeping the dark truth from her had been a conscious choice. She was already frightened enough knowing the Pitts brothers had escaped, that her life and the baby's were at risk. If he'd told her he believed at least one of the killers was already on the mountain, that the policeman sent to protect her had been murdered less than a mile from her home, Lila would freak.

Hell, he was a little freaked himself. He'd thought he'd left this kind of violence and danger back in Iraq.

Restless, he crossed the room to the baby's diaper bag. Preparing the bag with supplies for himself and Lila as well as Eve would at least give him something to do until he worked some other things out, until Special Agent Dunn called back with his update and approval to move the baby to a safer location.

If he could buy a little time, find a way to break the news to Lila gently—was there such a thing when it came to a murder on your property?—maybe he could soften the blow by showing her he had a plan. Step one, the idea he mentioned to Special Agent Dunn, was to get Lila out of this cabin. The Pittses were coming here. He had no idea what had delayed them—other than some degree of injury based on the blood trail he'd found at the cop's squad car—but Lila's best defense would be to not be here when they arrived. So he would move her and the baby. Pronto. That meant packing up baby supplies, weapons, warm clothes and—

He paused, his heart stilling when a soft sobbing whispered from the baby monitor. But it wasn't Eve crying. It was Lila.

Dean's chest tightened with a fresh twist of compunction. Based on the way Lila had been acting a few minutes earlier, he'd wager he was at least partly to blame for her tears. And if they were going to get out of her cabin anytime soon, he needed to put things right with her.

Hell. He dragged a hand down his cheek and groaned. He'd rather face a firefight than a crying woman.

Steeling himself, he quietly entered the nursery. The sight of Lila sitting in the rocking chair, her face in her hands, her shoulders hunched forward, her back shaking as she sobbed, landed another sucker punch to his gut. She was the image of dejection and pain.

If she weren't in such imminent danger, he'd turn around and walk away from her right now. Not because he was scared to deal with her tears, but because he wanted no part of causing her any grief. He'd been all wrong for her when he was seventeen, and though he'd turned his life around years ago, he now had new issues to grapple with. Lila didn't need someone who woke from nightmares in a cold sweat and who jumped at sudden loud noises. The military doctor said he just needed time and counseling, but how could he think of starting a relationship when his head was still a mess?

The second he placed a hand on her back, she gasped and jerked her head up. "Geez, Dean. You scared the crud outta me," she whispered harshly, swiping her eyes with the back of her hand.

He crouched in front of her, blocking her escape. "You're crying."

She averted her face, keeping her eyes cast down and to the side. "Wow. You're observant. Give that man a prize."

"Why?" He put one hand on her knee and grasped her balled fist with his other, stroking her wrist with his thumb.

"Forget it." She wrested her hand from his, but when she put it back on her lap, he took it again and squeezed.

"Why?" When her face crumpled, clearly fighting fresh tears, he slid a hand along her cheek and cupped her jaw. In a low tone he asked, "What did I do?"

Her lips compressed in a line of frustration, and with a heavy sigh, she whipped a hard, brown-eyed glare at him. "You lied to me."

His guilt rolled over again. "Um, technically I—"

"Don't even think of denying it," she scoffed quietly,

her eyes flashing with her pique. "Omission is just as bad as a lie. Especially when you assured me you hadn't seen anything suspicious on your walk. I didn't ask you to come in here and take over. Don't you think I need all the facts if I'm going to protect Eve and myself?"

He twisted his mouth and slowly nodded, feeling a little like a scolded schoolboy. "How did you—?"

"You came in here to make your call to the FBI agent. I overheard the whole call thanks to the baby monitor."

Dean blinked his surprise and cut a glance to the device sitting on the dresser by the crib. *Hell. Of course.*

"Which is—" she dropped her chin and stared at her hands "—how you heard me crying, I'm guessing."

He blew out a slow breath through his lips. "Yeah."

A strained silence fell between them for long seconds before he said, "Lila, I'm sorry. I—"

"Didn't you think I had a right to know my police protection wasn't coming? That my guard had been *murdered*?" Her volume and pitch were growing with her hysteria. "That the killer was somewhere out there—" She flung a hand toward the nursery window, her eyes growing wide, as if the truth of what she was saying was sinking in. She sucked in a shallow raspy breath. "Dean—"

"Shh." He put a finger to her lips, then stood, tugging on her hand as he did so. "You'll wake Eve. We'll talk in the other room."

Lila bit her bottom lip, moisture filling her eyes, and she cut a glance to the crib. With a tremulous nod, she stood and followed him out to the living room.

Before he could sit on the couch, she launched into him again. "Isn't it enough that I have this killer after

Eve without having to sort out whether I can trust you or not?"

"You can."

"I was counting on you to keep us safe. I thought, gee, he's a trained soldier. Who better to guard us? But that doesn't mean I've surrendered all control of my life and my choices to you. I needed the truth, Dean. I needed to know I could trust you."

"Lila, I understand why you're upset, but—"

"Do you? Do you *really*?" The way in which she emphasized the question told him he'd be smart not to answer.

He scrubbed his two-day beard and sighed. "Lila, I didn't tell you because I didn't want scare you."

She scoffed. "Well, it didn't work. 'Cause right now, I'm terrified!"

He raised both hands, palms out in conciliation. "I was hoping to find a solution, come up with a plan of action, before I broke the news to you. I thought if we had a plan, I could buffer you from some of the shock."

She paced away, sucked in a shaky breath and walked back toward him. "And? Do you have a plan? You told Agent Dunn we were moving."

Dean nodded. "That's the plan at this point. If the Pitts brothers know where you live and are coming here, I'd rather not be here waiting for them."

"But… Eve. All the things I need to care for her are here. The crib, the food and diapers, the toys and—"

"We'll take baby supplies with us, of course. And we can improvise what we can't take with us. With luck, the US Marshals and FBI will have the Pitts brothers back in custody by nightfall, and you can come back here. But right now, my family's cabin is safer. Not knowing the status of the phone service at my place, Special

Agent Dunn asked that we wait here until he contacted the US Marshals about what I found and called back on your phone. But I want to be ready to move the minute he calls."

She cast her glance around her home, lingering on the view out each window. "All right then… Her car seat is over there. Do you know how to install one or should I do it?"

He hesitated. "There's a catch."

Her face fell, and her shoulders dropped. "Of course there is."

"We can't take your car. Not only would the sound of the engine alert the killer to our move, negating the effort, but the roads are nearly impassable. The highway to my place is steep and narrow and…too dangerous."

Lila's complexion had drained of color. "Then what?"

"We hike. It's uphill most of the way, and it will be slick, but if you have good winter boots—"

"And Eve?"

"I'll carry her. And her diaper bag."

When Lila looked to the baby carrier that sat in the middle of the floor, Dean shook his head. "Not in that. If you don't have a backpack sort of carrier, I'll rig something up with blankets or scarves."

"You're serious? You want us to hike to your cabin… with a baby…in a blizzard?" She aimed a thumb to the nearest window.

Outside, the wind whistled in her eaves, and a blur of snow whipped through the air.

"You'd rather wait here for the Pittses?"

Lila wrapped her arms around her middle, while a wild, frantic look danced in her eyes. "No. I just…"

"All right then. Time's wasting. Let's pack up."

Chapter 8

Digging to the back of her closet, Lila found a backpack her family had used for hikes and transferred most of Eve's baby supplies from the diaper bag to the backpack. She took enough diapers, formula and changes of clothes to last through the night. Just in case.

She tried not to dwell on the idea of spending the night at Dean's cabin. This was business, not personal. Not the intimate arrangement implied.

With a further raid of her closet contents, Lila helped Dean prepare a slinglike getup to carry Eve securely nestled against his chest. Not only would the sling, made from two of her pashmina scarves, make it easier for Dean to carry the baby, but being wrapped up against Dean's brawn, under his coat, Eve would also be snuggled in a pocket of warmth. Lila was almost jealous of her tiny charge. The thought of burrowing close to Dean,

wrapped in his arms and thick soft blankets for the du-
ration of this ice-storm-turned-blizzard, sounded heav-
enly to Lila. Even though he'd lied to her. But his heart
had been in the right place…

No! He had no right to keep such important information from her. She wasn't a child that needed to be
shielded from harsh realities. Scared or not, it was better she knew the truth. The truth…

A twinge in her gut called her a hypocrite. Didn't he
deserve to know the whole truth about her situation, the
reason why she'd been so angry?

She sat down on her couch to put on her hiking boots
and glanced toward the door, where Dean was fastening
his coat around Eve. Taking a deep breath for courage,
she blurted, "My fiancé cheated on me."

He stopped fiddling with the buttons on his coat and
raised a curious look. "Come again?"

"I was engaged until last summer. I called it off, because I found out Carl was cheating on me and lying
about it."

Dean's face darkened in sympathy and disgust. "The
creep." He clenched his jaw then added, "Sorry."

She grunted an acknowledgment. Or maybe a dismissal. Because his cheating had only been the final
straw. "Thing is, I wasn't surprised. I was…almost relieved. Hurt, of course, but also relieved." She jerked
harder than necessary on the laces as she tied her first
boot. "I'd come up here to the cabin to take a break
from him and do some thinking. See… I'd figured out
he was stealing from me. Taking money from my wal-
let, using my ATM card to make withdrawals without
my permission."

Lila glanced up at Dean and found his dark eyes

latched on her. The intensity of his gaze sent a shiver through her. Dropping her gaze to her feet again, she started lacing the second boot. "And I caught him in a couple of white lies. He'd say he was working late, when he'd really be getting drinks with the guys. He'd say he had to cancel dates with me because he was sick, only to find out he'd gone to a ball game with his roommate." She gritted her teeth and sent Dean a scowl. "And friends of mine told me Carl used to bad-mouth and belittle my art when I wasn't around. He'd say things like, 'When we marry, she'll have to get a real job. No more kindergarten projects and doodling.'"

Lila gnawed her bottom lip as the complex whirlwind of emotions linked to Carl battered her anew. Not just hurt and anger, but embarrassment for having been fooled as long as she was. Grief for the lost future she'd planned. Frustration that she'd been such an easy target for his manipulation. "I got mad at him when I learned about the ATM withdrawals and said I needed a week away to think. But I got back early and caught him with another woman and…"

Bowing her head, she pinched the bridge of her nose, trying to stem the flood of tears. She'd wasted enough tears on Carl. She was free of him and his dishonesty and lack of ethics. She should be rejoicing, not crying over the breakup.

The sofa cushion beside her dipped, and she whipped up her chin, meeting Dean's concerned frown.

"Lila, this cretin—"

"Isn't worth my breath or tears. I know." She forced a stiff smile to her lips and shook her head. "I just wanted you to know why I'm so sensitive about lies. About honesty and trust. Why I got so mad at you."

"Damn," he muttered under his breath. "Lila, I'm—"

She moved a hand to his knee to cut him off. "You didn't know. I understand that. But I still need—" To her horror, her voice cracked, and the tears she'd been holding at bay rushed to her eyes.

Dean had his arm around her shoulders, pulling her head under his chin in seconds. "Lila, honey, I'm sorry. I thought I was sparing you unneeded worry. I—"

"I know. I'm not saying…" She tried to pull back, but his fingers splayed at the base of her skull and held her close. He cradled her close with one arm and held Eve against his chest with his other. Rather than fight him, she indulged in the contact that did more to settle her nerves than anything else had today. She savored his embrace, putting her arms around him, around Eve, in a hug that centered her.

"For what it's worth," he said, his lips pressed to the top of her head, "honesty and integrity are important to me as well. Not that my decision today reflects that, but… When I said I turned my life around at the boot camp I went to when I was seventeen, I meant it. I had drill captains and a counselor there that made me see the destructive path I was on."

Lila flattened her hand over Dean's heart and drew comfort from the slow, steady beat against her palm. She stilled as she listened to his deep drawl. Even Eve seemed lulled by the melodic baritone of his voice and suckled her fist quietly.

"I got a dose of reality at boot camp that has stayed with me. I committed myself to making a positive impact in the world, being a man the world could respect rather than someone they pitied or resented."

Lila curled her fingers into his shirt. "Dean…"

"Those values were driven home in the military. I never want to be the kind of person I was as a kid again. I won't accept less from myself."

"Dean." She lifted her head and met his gaze. "I accept your apology."

He twisted his mouth in a reluctant grin. "Thanks."

She could still see the shadows of his regret and doubt lining his face, and before they set out on their trek to his cabin, she wanted the matter settled. Framing his face between her hands, she caught his mouth in a kiss that had the heat and fervor behind it that she'd been longing for since the first gentle brush of his lips earlier.

His fingers tangled in her hair, and his warm lips opened to hers, responding with a sweet seduction that made her head spin. He shaped her mouth with his, then swept his tongue in to tease hers in a heady dance.

Sliding her arm around his neck, she clung to him, allowing the kiss to continue, lost to anything but the way Dean made her feel. Safe. Alive. Vibrant.

In a matter of hours, Dean had uncovered the deepest part of her soul, the fragile hope for her future that she'd carefully bubble-wrapped and buried to protect it from the kind of hurt she'd known with Carl. Even her artwork had reflected the lack of passion in her life and suppressed pain, the loneliness and frustration with the direction her life had been going. Her colors had been drab, her brushstrokes uncertain and amateurish. But the spark of desire that flickered inside her made her wonder...

Did she dare to put her faith in Dean? Not just for protection today, but to keep her heart safe if she opened herself to a possible relationship with him? What if—

A particularly stiff wind buffeted her windows and

made the trees around her cabin sway and creak. A now-familiar crack sounded near her front door, followed by a loud thump on her roof.

Dean jerked, his body tensing. His reaction sent a frisson of alarm through her. She pulled back, gauging his thoughts by his eyes. He recovered quickly, but for a heartbeat, she'd seen his distress.

"Dean? What is it? That was just a branch breaking." She glanced to the window nervously. "Wasn't it?"

He drew a deep breath and, pulling away from her grasp, rose to his feet. "Yeah. It was."

"You're sure? You seem upset."

He flashed her a strained half smile. "You have my word. But it's a reminder that the storm's not getting any easier for hiking. We need to get moving."

"I thought you said Special Agent Dunn wanted us to wait until we heard back from him."

"He did but…damn it, what's taking so long? I know he's trying to coordinate with the local police and the US Marshals, but I've been on special ops with the army that took less time to plan."

As Dean stalked to the window and stared out at the snowfall, Lila thought back to earlier events today. Other times when the crash of icy branches—or what she now knew were gunshots—had echoed through the woods. He'd tensed then, too. Twitched. She rubbed her sweaty hands on her jeans and studied him. He'd served several tours in violent parts of the world. His reaction made sense…

"It's PTSD, isn't it?" she asked in a hushed tone.

He whipped his head around to give her a startled look. "What?"

"The reason you jump at sudden loud noises. Do you have post-traumatic stress?"

His brow furrowed and his mouth firmed to a taut line. "Most of us coming home from battle have at least a few nightmares."

"How bad is yours? Do you see a counselor?"

"Can we not talk about me? We have more important things to deal with right now." He stomped away from the window, his hand gently cradling Eve's bottom despite the stiff movement of his steps. "Get her hat. I'm tired of waiting for Dunn to call back."

"Dean…" Lila pushed off the sofa and found Eve's tiny knit hat, but she kept a concerned eye on Dean. "Please, don't brush me off. I know things are crazy right now, but you're important, too. I want to know what you're going through, what help you're getting."

He spun to face her. "Why? Why do you care?"

She straightened her back, blinking. "Why do you care about Eve and me? I just…care. And because I think I should know what you're dealing with if we—"

The shrill ring of the house phone interrupted her.

Dean snatched up the receiver. "Dunn?"

He nodded as he listened. "Yeah, we're walking out now. How long will your men be? Roger that." He hung up and jerked his head toward the door. "Okay, let's move."

Wayne stopped to lean against the trunk of a pine tree and rest. The cold wind stole his breath and made walking more difficult. His leg had grown stiff and numb, but he could drag it, put weight on it without too much pain. He just had to keep his mind on something else.

Focus on taking the next step, doing the job he'd been given. *Don't fail.*

He had Lila Greene's cabin in his sight through the swirling snow, and he wanted to survey the property, decide his best approach. He put a hand on the gun he'd lifted from the US marshal at the van wreck. He'd only used a couple rounds on the cop, so he should have plenty of ammunition to finish the mission. He checked it again anyway, just to be certain. He didn't want any screwups. Kent would expect no less than perfect execution of his mission.

He chortled. *Execution.* Yep, that's what it would be for Lila Greene if she got in his way.

His gut flipped a little at the thought. Would he really kill a woman for his brother? And yet…how could he not? Kent had rescued him from the Hambridges, his last foster home, where he'd been abused, neglected, used as a paycheck by a drunk and her bastard husband, who didn't care about any of the children in their care. Not even their biological kids. It had been hell. And Kent had saved him from that cesspool, from the beatings and hunger and fear. Yes, he would kill for Kent. He'd die for Kent if needed.

With The Sword I will fight for my right to live free, seek The Truth and defend myself from The Enemy. The mantra Kent had drilled into Wayne's head replayed like a chant. If he repeated the line, said it in his head over and over again, maybe he could block out the ache in his leg and the bone-chilling wind and snow.

A movement at the front door of the cabin yanked him from his deliberations, his maudlin remembrances. A man walked out on the front porch, a pack strapped on his back and a lump under his coat. Wayne slipped behind the tree, out of view and watched.

Next out of the cabin was a woman with long, dark blond hair past her shoulders and a red knit hat pulled low over her ears. She turned and locked the front door then followed the man down the steps, holding his arm as they negotiated the icy steps to her driveway. Were they really going out somewhere in this blizzard? Was that even Lila Greene? Could it be someone from Child Services moving Eve out of Lila's care? Who was the man? A cop? And where was Eve?

Wayne shoved down the panic that bubbled in his chest. Nothing had changed. His mission was the same. He'd follow these people…after he checked the cabin for the baby.

He'd wait until they drove away and—

But they didn't get in the sedan parked out front. The man dressed in dark winter garb led the blonde woman toward the trees, into the woods. They were hiking out. Away from the cabin. But going where?

Wayne dug in his pocket and pulled out the folded printout with the area map. There was little on this mountain road other than Lila's cabin and an abandoned coal mine. But they weren't headed toward the road. They were headed up the hill, into the forest and over the ridge. Gritting his teeth, Wayne squinted at the map. Another road branched off the highway and wound around to the far side of the mountain. The map showed what could be other cabins in a cluster on the far side of the ridge. Hamilton-Gamble Camp Road, the tiny print read. A family camp? More houses?

As the man and woman disappeared into the swirl of white and dense trees, he heard a faint wail. A baby's cry.

Eve! They were moving Eve to the homes on Hamilton-Gamble Camp Road. He'd stake his life on it.

Examining the map again, he frowned. The most direct route to those homes was to hike straight north, over the ridge. But the man in black was leading the woman off to the east. Wayne's gut told him that despite the direction they were headed, the man was taking Eve and Lila Greene to one of the houses to the north. Rubbing his aching leg, he contemplated the steep hill to the north. He could climb it. He had to. He wasn't fast enough or stealthy enough with his bum leg to catch up to the man and woman and mount an effective attack. But he could hike the steeper more direct route to Hamilton-Gamble Camp Road and cut them off. Then cut them down.

"Dean, where are you going?" Lila panted slightly as she hurried up beside him and tugged on the sleeve of his coat. "Your parents' cabin is that way." She pointed her thumb to the north.

"I'm aware of that."

"Then why—"

"Look at you." He dipped his head toward her, indicating her labored breathing. "You're already out of breath. The climb over the ridge, the direct route, will be steep and slick. The rocks have a sheet of ice under the snow. This way is longer—"

"I'll say!"

"But considering we're hiking with a baby and—" he gave her a once-over "—I'm guessing an inexperienced hiker, this way has an easier slope, better terrain for traction."

Her expression modulated, and she nodded. "Okay. And a better term would be out of practice."

"Huh?"

"I'm experienced with hiking, but I'm out of shape."

Dean arched an eyebrow and sent her a sly grin. "I kinda like your shape."

Lila blinked at him as she processed his flirting, and he continued through the web of branches, clearing a path for her as best he could. The trees provided some buffer from the howling wind, but occasionally a glob of snow would be blown down from the upper branches as they swayed in the stormy blasts. Lowering his head and squinting against the sting of flying snow and sleet, Dean trudged on.

"What about our tracks?" Lila asked as she caught up to him again.

Even though he was carrying the baby, the shotgun and the pack, Lila had to take two steps to match every one of his long strides. He made a mental note to slow his pace for her, even though his instinct was to rush, to get back to his cabin as quickly as possible and get them out of the elements.

Lila hustled a step in front of him and blocked his path. She waved a hand to the trail they'd left. "Won't the killer see our tracks and be able to follow us?"

Dean turned and considered her point. Maybe it would be prudent for him to do something to try to cover the prints. But the snow wasn't that deep yet, and the swirling wind and steady accumulation would soon blot out their footprints.

"It's a coin toss." He met her eyes as she hunched her shoulders in the blustery chill. "If we spend the time erasing our path, something Mother Nature is working on already, we risk having the guy catch up to us because of our delay."

"And we have the baby out in this nasty weather that much longer," she added, worrying her already-chapped lip. She held his gaze, and the faith he saw in her expression filled his chest with a surprising warmth. "Your call."

Her trust in his leadership, his judgment, spread a balm over the dings to his soul left by her earlier presumptions about him. Cupping the back of her head, he leaned in to steal a kiss. Her cold lips parted, and he found the heated recesses of her mouth with his tongue before backing away. "Thank you."

The pink in her cheeks from the cold deepened to a rosy hue, and her pupils dilated, a telltale sign of her desire.

As he withdrew his hand, he swiped the knit hat from her head. "If you're worried about being spotted, a red hat is less than subtle in the snowy woods." Setting the shotgun aside, he stuffed her hat in his coat pocket and took his knit cap off. "Use mine."

"But—"

He tugged the knit cap into place and drilled her with a silencing look. "I'll be fine."

Lila frowned but didn't argue the point. As she turned to fall in step with him again, her feet slipped. At the same time that she grabbed for his sleeve, he caught her arm to steady her. Without questioning the move, he pulled her close and wrapped her in a hug that sandwiched Eve between them.

She curled her fingers into his coat and clung to him. "Geez, if the ground is this slick here, you're probably right about climbing the cut-through trail to your house."

For several seconds, she made no move to leave his embrace, and he savored holding her. Being close to Lila felt natural, felt right. In all the years that had passed since he'd crushed on Lila as a teenager, he'd never forgotten her, or the opportunity squandered to be with her because of his rebellious and wild mischief. He didn't regret going to boot camp—the place had saved his life, turned him around—but he regretted like hell that he'd blown the chance to have something real with Lila. And now fate had put them together again, given him a do over. He wouldn't blow it a second time.

When Eve squirmed and whimpered a protest, Lila backed away, parted the edges of his coat enough to press a kiss to the baby's cheek and checked that the small striped knit hat covered Eve's ears.

With an awkward grin, Lila carefully stepped away and continued up the slope toward his cabin. He retrieved the shotgun and scanned the woods, keeping a vigilant eye out for anything that seemed off. Not knowing what had happened to the cop killer rankled. Was the shooter dead, lying in the woods just beyond Lila's driveway? Or was he even now stalking them like prey? An itch at the base of his neck told Dean the latter was most likely. That the killer had yet to show himself made him all the more wary.

He trudged on through the snowy detritus of the forest, sticking close to Lila should she slip again and keeping half his gaze on the scene around them.

Eve wiggled in her sling, her strong baby legs kicking his stomach. Having her nestled under his coat, strapped against him this way, felt odd. Her movements and her baby powder scent were a constant reminder of the young life that was in his hands. Being responsible for Eve, holding her against him, stirred a combination of fierce protectiveness and mellow warmth he'd never experienced before. Was this what it felt like to be a parent? The primal urge to protect coupled with an unconditional affection?

Dean didn't know about the parenting thing, but he knew for sure Lila and Eve were his entire focus at that moment. He was honor bound to protect them, and he would fulfill that duty at all costs.

At all costs, he had to reach the crest of the hill and cut off Lila Greene and the man with her before they could lock themselves inside at their destination. Wayne told himself to ignore the pain in his leg and forge on as quickly as possible. Law enforcement backup would be here soon. If Lila was moving her location, they had to know he was in the area. Someone had probably found the dead cop. Time was of the essence, and he couldn't stop to indulge his need for rest. The incline to the summit of the ridge was even steeper than it appeared. Wayne had to climb, using his hands to grab at rocks or roots to help pull him up the hill. His injured leg was stiff, and his thigh throbbed. The effort of climbing the sharp incline took more energy and muscle power than walking, and he had to concentrate on his goal, his mission to keep from vomiting. The pain was that bad.

With The Sword I will fight for my right to live free, seek The Truth and defend myself from The Enemy. With The Sword I will fight... He repeated the mantra over and over to stay focused. To stay conscious. He could not fail Kent.

When the terrain leveled out a bit, he found a hefty

stick under the crust of ice and snow and used it as a crutch to help him move through the stormy woods. One more step. One more… Must…not…fail…

Chapter 9

"So," Lila said as she trudged behind Dean, "what exactly did Special Agent Dunn tell you? Are they meeting us at your cabin? Sending a SWAT team? Have they located either of the Pittses yet?"

He slowed to a stop, giving her time to catch up, and turned full circle, studying the woods and hillside around them. "Yes. He didn't say. And I don't think so."

She stopped as well and used the break to stretch her torso and roll her shoulders. Walking hunched forward to avoid the stinging sleet and to balance on the slope was killing her lower back. "Huh?"

"The answers to your last questions, in order. He said they were getting four-wheel drive vehicles ready to head up here. They were going to post men at your cabin and meet us at mine. The storm is too fierce to fly a helo, but they'd mount an air search as soon as the winds died down. I took that to mean they hadn't found either of the Pittses yet."

The blizzard was not as intense here among the trees and shielded by the mountain, but the wind still howled and the wintery mix pelted her cheeks.

"Oh. Well, how far out are they? How long will it take them to get up here?"

"I don't know. They were leaving from the command center in town. The important thing is help is on the way. Lots of it, from local police to FBI and US Marshals. Everyone wants these killers caught." He flashed an encouraging smile before heading off again.

Help was coming. That should make her feel better, but she'd been promised help in the form of a local cop to guard her house and the policeman had been murdered. That truth balled in her gut and left her nauseated. A man had *died* trying to protect her and Eve. The way Dean was protecting her. If anything happened to Dean…

With a shiver, she shook off that thought. Dean knew what he was doing. Backup was coming. Law enforcement and lots of it. She had lots of help to protect Eve from the evil men gunning for her.

"So…speaking of help, why not let me carry something?" Ducking her head against the sting of sleet and snow, she hurried her steps to keep up with him. "I won't let it slow me down, and it only seems fair…"

"I'm good. Besides, my cabin's not that much farther."

"I should be the one carrying Eve." Lila tried not to sound winded as she argued her point. Having Dean carrying everything might be expedient, but she hated the feeling of being coddled. She'd been taking care of herself, financially and logistically independent from her parents, from any man for years. She might need Dean's military skills and brawn to protect her, but she could carry a backpack or her foster baby, for crying out loud. "Besides, what happens if we do run into trouble?"

He cut a glance over his shoulder. "Then I'll protect her with every resource I have."

"I mean..." She grabbed the sleeve of his coat to slow him down and gain his full attention. "I don't like the idea of you firing the shotgun while you're holding the baby. It's not safe."

He opened his mouth as if to counter her point, but snapped it closed again. He furrowed his brow and huffed his exasperation. "She gets heavy after a while, and I was trying to make it easier for you. We still have about half of a mile to go."

"I can handle her." She paused. "Unless you want me to take the gun. You shouldn't have both. I could probably be fired from fostering if they found out I let you carry her and a weapon."

Dean sent another searching look around the area. Because of the ice storm and blowing snow, the wildlife—chipmunks, birds, squirrels and rabbits—that normally scurried about the forest was noticeably absent. They were hunkered down weathering the storm like she should be.

"Fine." He handed her the shotgun—not the choice she wanted—and her gut swooped. Could she shoot someone, kill someone, in order to defend them from a killer. "Dean..."

When she glanced back at him, he was peeling off his coat and unwrapping the homemade sling around the baby. Eve, who'd been dozing and snug, woke with an angry cry when the cold air hit her. "Take off your jacket. The sling will go under it."

She exhaled a silent breath of relief and quickly shucked her coat. Setting aside the shotgun and propping it against a tree, she took the baby from him. Next, Dean pulled the drape of scarves from his chest and moved closer to Lila.

"Shh," she cooed to the baby, holding her snugly and rocking her by swaying. "You'll be warm again in a minute."

"Stand still, and I'll tie her on you."

Lila followed his directions, turning this way and that, lifting an arm when told to as he recreated the crisscross sling to securely support Eve. She propped a hand under the baby's bottom and fumbled to rebutton her coat. Swatting her hands away, he refastened her buttons, his gaze intent on her face rather than his work.

Lila shivered, more from his steady gaze than the cold. "What?"

"Nothing. I just like looking at you. Always have. You're beautiful, Lila."

His compliment warmed her better than a hot toddy by a roaring fire. Or rather the sentiment behind the kind words. He liked looking at her. He liked...*her*. He had romantic feelings for her. Feelings that had been in place for a long time.

And how did she feel about that? *Happy. Hopeful. Scared.*

She wanted a relationship with a good man. She was ready to settle down and start a family. Dean seemed like a good choice, but was she seeing what she wanted to see in him despite her history with him, his track record? It had been eleven years. He said he'd changed, and so far today his actions had proven that. Mostly. They'd need to date, of course, take the time to get to know each other, fill in the gaps of those eleven eventful years.

Her heart thudded against her ribs as she perused his face, as if the chiseled lines and rugged angles held all her answers. He was, without a doubt, handsome. Sexy as hell, really. She wanted to paint him, the brooding expressions and intense light from his eyes. Heck, she wanted to paint him with chocolate sauce and raspberry jelly then lick him clean!

A tiny noise escaped her throat when the erotic image flitted through her mind and kicked up her pulse.

His eyes lifted from her buttons to her gaze. "Hmm?"

"Nothing," she rasped, then gathered a fortifying breath.

When he finished with her coat, he took the gun from where she'd set it, brushed the snow off the stock and tipped his head toward the hill. "You lead. I'll cover your six."

"My six?" She wrinkled her nose, puzzled, as she started trudging through the windblown drifts.

"Protect your back. It's just military lingo for guarding the rear, as in the six o'clock position."

"Oh." She thought about the life Dean had led since she last knew him. Several tours in war zones. Special Forces. No wonder his instinct seemed to be to protect, to defend. It was his training. Yet he'd seen enough horror to damage his psyche, leave him with nightmares and a hair-trigger response to loud noises.

A strange lump balled in her gut, thinking of Dean in the line of fire, near explosives, at risk as he served his country. She was at the same time proud of him and terrified by the thought. But that was then. He was home now. The danger was behind him.

Or was it? She'd unwittingly thrown him into a horrible situation. She remembered his knee-jerk reaction to loud noises as she stepped carefully over a fallen tree trunk, pushing aside the frozen branches that impeded her path. "So, Dean…you never answered my question earlier."

"What question is that?"

"About your PTSD. You mentioned nightmares, and I saw your reaction to the cracking ice, the loud pops. Are you seeing a counselor?"

He muttered a curse word. "I don't want to talk about it."

"Dean, you can't sweep it under the rug and think—"

"I'll be fine."

"Dean…" She stopped and turned. This was a conversation she needed to have face-to-face. But as she pivoted toward him, her balance off a bit thanks to Eve's weight at her chest, her feet slipped again. She didn't fall, but Dean was quick to catch her arm.

"Thanks." She found her equilibrium and raised her chin. "You need to talk about your experience overseas. If not to me, then to a professional."

"Please, Lila. Can we not have this discussion here and now? I just want to get you and Eve to safety, and the longer we dawdle out here…" He scrubbed a hand over his face and scowled.

She puffed her cheeks and blew out a sigh of resignation. "If I give you a pass on this discussion now, will you promise to talk about it when this mess is over?"

With a hand gripping her elbow for support, he turned her back toward the trail. "Why is this so important to you?"

"Because…it is." Frowning her discontent with his

avoidance, she resumed hiking. With one hand cradling Eve and her other reaching for trees or shrub branches to steady herself, she picked her way over the icy and uneven ground. "If we're going to have any kind of relationship, I think you—"

"Are we? Going to have a relationship?"

She grunted. "An important question, but you changed the subject. Answer my question first, Mr. Hamilton."

"Exploring a relationship with you has appeal."

"Appeal?" She chuckled wryly and ducked a low limb. "Wow. Such faint praise."

"Last time I checked, appeal was a good thing. I'd be lying if I said I hadn't thought of it. And I know how you feel about lies so…yes, I've considered it. Often. And for many years. I've made no secret of how I feel about you, Lila. I want you. I care about you. I'd like to see where things might go between us. Is that what you want to hear?"

She smiled, even though she knew he couldn't see her face. "It's a start. Women like to be wooed, Hamilton. Just remember that."

"Wooed? What year is this, 1850?"

"I'm just saying, if—"

"Give me the baby, and you don't have to die." A man appeared in front of her as if from thin air. He had a leg bound in a homemade bandage and a large stick he used as a crutch. He glared at her with deadly intent in his bloodshot eyes as he aimed a gun at them. "Come on, sister. Give me Eve."

Chapter 10

Dean grabbed the back of Lila's coat and had yanked her behind him before she could fully process the threat. He ditched the backpack with a quick shrug of his shoulders and flick of his arms. A staggering heartbeat later, he'd raised the shotgun and aimed it at the man. "On the ground, hands out, or I'll blast a hole in you."

The man countered by shifting his handgun toward Dean. "I'm in charge here. And I only want the baby. Hand her over and that can be the end of it. But if you have a problem with that, I'd be happy to kill you, too."

Lila gasped, terrified that Dean would play the hero and get himself killed.

Sure enough, he squared his shoulders and placed himself between her and the gun. "I know who you are, Wayne Pitts."

Lila blinked. How did Dean know that? How much more had he kept from her?

"The wise move for you is to surrender without incident." Dean kept his tone cool and even, but the chill behind his words brooked no argument. "There are more than a dozen FBI agents and US Marshals descending on this mountain as we speak. They know where you are, where we are headed, and will not hesitate to take you down like the murdering scumbag you are if you give them any reason."

Wayne Pitts snarled, his nostrils flaring in hatred and disgust. "I'm sure there are cops comin'. I'm prepared to die. But my brother gave me a mission, and I will complete that mission, if it means killing you to do it."

"Dean..." Lila whispered, her voice thick with fear and doubts. "Please."

But please what? Don't get yourself killed? Certainly. Don't rile the man with the gun? Also good. Don't let the man get Eve? Definitely.

Wayne Pitts motioned with the gun as, hobbling on his stick-crutch, he edged to the right. "Step aside, man. I've already killed a couple of men today when they got in my way, and I will do it again."

Dean shifted his position to match his opponent's movement. "Buddy, I killed more than thirty men in the line of duty with my Special Forces team. And I will do it again to protect Lila and that little baby from you."

Lila struggled to draw a breath as the standoff intensified. Damn it, where were the FBI agents Dean mentioned? Was there really help coming? Maybe he'd lied to her again to keep her from panicking. *Please, God, send help!*

Dean cocked the shotgun and aimed it. "Last chance, Pitts. *On the ground.*"

Lila saw the slight narrowing of Wayne's eyes, guessed what it meant just before—

"Dean, look out!"

Swinging his stick in a wide arc, Wayne lunged. The stick caught Dean broadside and sent him sprawling on the frozen ground. Dean groaned and clutched at his head, where a trickle of blood ran down his temple.

"Dean!" Lila moved toward him, wanting to help him, but Eve's weight at her chest and the baby girl's whimper of distress reminded her of her first duty—*save Eve*.

Wayne stumbled then braced himself on the stick again as he jerked his attention back to Lila. He pointed the gun at her again. "Come on, Ms. Greene. Hand over the baby."

He knew her name? A shiver raced through her before she remembered how the Pitts brothers even knew where she lived. The injured US marshal's stolen phone had had her contact information, Agent Dunn had said.

"No. Never." She crept backward away from Wayne, knowing she couldn't outpace a bullet and hating the growing distance between her and Dean. But she couldn't let Eve's uncle get his hands on her. It galled her that Eve's own family was trying to kill her.

Wayne hobbled closer to her, his eyes wild. Her attention locked on the unstable man and the weapon he waved at her. "Don't make me shoot you, Lila. 'Cause I will. Kent wants me to free Eve. I gotta do th—"

With a sweep of his leg, Dean knocked Wayne to the ground and rolled to his knees to hover over his opponent. With a hand at each end of the barrel, he jammed the shotgun against Wayne's throat.

Lila's mouth dried as she backpedaled, inching away from the fracas and cradling Eve's head against her chest.

She followed the struggle between the men, waiting for an opening when she could do something to help Dean without putting Eve at risk.

Wayne thrashed his arms, his hips, gasping for air and trying to free himself, and Dean swung a leg over his opponent so that he pinned him to the ground. But Wayne still held the handgun and bashed it against Dean's head. Dean grunted in pain and blinked hard as if fighting to stay conscious.

Capitalizing on Dean's brief vulnerability, Wayne bucked hard and shoved at the shotgun crushing his throat. He sucked in a deep breath and seemed energized by the influx of oxygen. Growling his fury, Wayne aimed the handgun at Dean's face.

"No!" Lila screamed.

Dean slapped Wayne's weapon askew just a fraction of a second before the chest-rattling concussion of the gun firing.

Lila flinched, but her breath stuck in her lungs. Eve loosed a shriek of fear that voiced what Lila couldn't. A bone-chilling terror. *Dean!*

Above them the crackling of ice preceded a brief rain of snow clumps and ice bits shaken from the tree, whether by the gunshot or the errant bullet.

The struggling bodies continued to writhe, grunting and grappling for possession of the handgun and the shotgun. For dominance. For their lives.

Because, Lila acknowledged with a churning nausea, the likelihood was this fight between Dean and Wayne Pitts would only end when one was dead. Whether she or Eve was dead as well was undetermined.

Go! Get out of there! A voice of self-protection

screamed in her head. And she considered it. If only because she had to keep Eve safe.

But she couldn't—wouldn't—abandon Dean like some selfish coward. He was risking everything for her. How dare she consider running away like a yellow-bellied wimp?

Dean had pinned Wayne's gun hand to the ground, but in order to keep Wayne from twisting loose, Dean had discarded the shotgun, tossing it a few feet away, and straddled his opponent's legs to keep him immobile. "Lila!"

She jerked herself from her shock and met the quick glance he aimed over his shoulder.

"Get the gun!" Dean said, his voice rough and winded.

Forcing her numb and trembling legs to work, she edged toward the heap of tangled men and weapons. The butt of the shotgun was just beside Wayne's foot. Keeping a protective arm around Eve, she reached for her father's hunting gun.

Dean cut a side-glance and shook his head. "No, the other—"

Wayne read the situation as well, and with a grunt, he wrenched his body, unseating Dean, then thrashed his good leg toward Lila. Flinching away from his kick, she fell on her bottom with a tooth-jarring thump. Eve continued her piercing, frightened wail, which only rattled Lila further.

The grabbing and fist-throwing fight resumed between Dean and Wayne. Lila's gut roiled with guilt. She'd misunderstood Dean's intent and now...

Again the handgun fired, and bark-laced snow sprayed from the trunk of a nearby tree. She had to do something! She had to end this. She had to save Eve, save herself...

save *Dean*. Any misgivings about Dean's past evaporated in an instant when she considered a future without him, without the second chance she'd been given with him. She wanted Dean. Wanted the promise of a future with him. Wanted—

Another blast of the handgun. And a sharp cry of pain.

Dean's face twisted in agony, and his body, his shoulders, curled inward.

No! Oh, no no no no! "Dean?" she rasped. "Dean!"

Though clearly injured, Dean managed to take another swipe at Wayne, a stiff-handed jab that caught his opponent in the Adam's apple.

Wayne coughed and stepped back to suck in a wheezing breath.

Tears burned Lila's eyes and froze on her eyelashes as she scuttled back from the fight. With one arm around Eve, she clambered to her knees and searched the snow for the shotgun. Her own panicked gasps joined Eve's cries as she hefted the gun and staggered to her feet. Dean was hurt, and she needed to find an opportunity to run interference for him, needed to help shift the advantage to him.

But she had Eve, had to put the baby's safety first. She had the shotgun, but even if she wanted to shoot Wayne, Dean was still tangled up with the cult escapee, and she didn't have a clear shot. As she ran rapid-fire possibilities through her head, Dean's knees seemed to buckle, and she noticed the blood blooming at his waist. He *had* been shot!

A sob caught in Lila's throat. Her hand shook as she flexed and tightened them around the shotgun. She just needed a small opening, one clear shot. *Never pick up a weapon you don't have the skill and will to use.* Thanks to her father she had the skill, and to save Dean, she'd find the will…

Wayne swung an uppercut that sent Dean to the ground. Dean didn't get up, only rolled on his side groaning. Seizing his advantage, Wayne fumbled to his feet and swung a kick at Dean's temple.

Fury raged in her blood, pounding in her ears for Wayne's cheap shot, and she squawked her disgust with the low blow.

Wayne turned toward her, licking blood from his split lip, his breathing labored. "Give me…the kid."

"Dean!" She longed to race to him, help him, but Wayne blocked her path.

The Pitts brother swayed on his injured leg and leaned against a tree trunk for support. With a glance around him, he found his homemade crutch, now cracked, and flung it aside with a snarl of disgust. "With The Sword I will fight for my right to live free, seek The Truth and defend myself from The Enemy."

Shoot him! the voice of self-protection shouted. Shaking to her core, Lila raised the shotgun and aimed it, holding the weapon as far away from Eve as she could. "Stay back. I'll shoot. I will!"

But could she? Really? Oh, God! Was Dean right? When cornered, did she have the courage, the chops to kill a man in order to protect Eve? Taking a man's life was no small thing.

Wayne only narrowed his eyes, and he limped closer. "The work of The Sword will not be denied. The Truth will prevail, and The Enemy will be cut down."

"Cut down? You would really kill a baby?" Lila rasped, her heart breaking. Dean had yet to move, and she could barely see for the blur of her tears. She swiped at her face with the back of one hand as she inched backward. "How can you be so heartless?"

"I have a mission. Kent gave me orders. I have to free the child."

For a brief moment, she though she saw a flicker of remorse, of reluctance, cross Wayne's face. Was it a trick of the light? Wishful thinking? If she could play to the possibility he had second thoughts...

"Free her?" Lila asked. "How is killing an innocent child freeing her?"

"Death frees her from this life. From the domination of The Enemy. The Sword teaches The Truth." He almost seemed to be chanting, droning mantras by rote. The words he muttered methodically seemed to center and calm him. Could she keep him talking? Buy time until the authorities arrived?

"I will save my brother's daughter from the evils of government control and a corrupt foster system."

Lila stiffened her back. "I'm not corrupt! I care about the children I take in."

Wayne only shook his head. "That's what they all say. But I saw firsthand the ones who took in child after child merely to get the government check. Foster children to fund their drug habit, to use as personal maids and free labor. To slap around when they stood up for themselves."

Lila's jaw dropped. "Do you mean you—? Why didn't anyone report these parents? That's...that's horrible!"

Wayne lifted a corner of his mouth in a wry, sad smile. "Exactly."

"But that's not what the foster system is about! You

can't judge me based on that. I would never treat my foster children that way."

"Just give me my niece," he said through gritted teeth, clearly losing patience.

Lila cast another look toward Dean. He had yet to move, and her heart squeezed painfully. *Please let him be all right!*

"Look, what if I gave you my word, my personal vow that I will not let anything happen to Eve? This baby deserves a chance at life, and I intend to see that she gets that chance."

"Life among The Enemy is no life at all."

Lila swallowed hard. "I am not your enemy and certainly not Eve's. I will protect her and see that she has good care. Please! Just put the gun down!"

"You first. Hand the child to me, and you may live." He inched closer, one limping step at a time. Though his steps wobbled, the gun remained steadily trained on her. "My mission is only to free Eve."

Lila raised her chin. "And mine is to see that you don't hurt her!"

Through the whistling wind, the crackle of ice in the trees, Lila thought maybe, just maybe she heard an engine. A car? An ATV? Was help *finally* arriving?

"Help me! We're here!" she shouted.

Wayne stiffened, his face growing darker, sterner. "You shouldn't have done that."

His finger tightened on the trigger, and she heard a click. Wayne's face reflected confusion, and he tried again to shoot. Nothing happened.

Lila was not an expert in firearms, but she knew enough from listening to her father over the years. His weapon had either jammed or was out of ammunition.

Relief swept over her hard and fast, weakening her knees. Yet her danger hadn't passed. Dean was still on the ground, and the weapon malfunction seemed to enrage Wayne. He charged toward her, his hobbling steps brisker, more determined. His mouth was set in a grim, bitter line as he closed the distance between them.

Gasping, Lila clutched the shotgun with both hands, a finger on the trigger, prepared to shoot if she had to. She stumbled backward, taking bigger, quicker steps. "Stay back. I swear I'll—"

Her heel hit a root, and suddenly her feet lost traction on the ice. She went down hard, without so much as a free hand to brace her fall. The butt of the shotgun hit the ground as well. The jarring bump meant her finger squeezed the trigger, and a blast of buckshot fired into the air. The kickback of the gun smacked the barrel against her cheekbone and vibrated through her arms to the bone. The cacophony of the blast rang painfully in her ears, and she blinked, stunned. She had no time to process what happened. The blast had only spooked Wayne, slowed him a fraction of a second. She still had to get away from—

A pattering sound like rain preceded a stinging thump on her neck. A loud, now familiar, cracking echoed through the woods as well. Ice. A branch. Around her, the buckshot pellets fell back to the ground, accompanied by frozen shards and clumps of snow dislodged from the branches above. Curling her body around Eve, a hand pillowing the baby's head, she rolled, turning her back up to the falling debris.

"What the—" Wayne began, but didn't finish.

Wrapped around Eve, face in the snow as she was,

Lila didn't see what happened next. But she heard a dull thwack. A pained grunt. Gurgling. Then silence.

When all was silent again, the rain of ice and buckshot over, she raised her head, shaking snow from her hair. She checked Eve first, saw no indication of injury, though the little girl bawled angrily for having been sandwiched between Lila and the snow. Taking a tremulous breath for courage, Lila pushed to her knees... and turned.

Wayne lay on his back, crumpled in the snowy underbrush, his eyes staring sightlessly toward the sky. An icicle pierced the soft tissue at the hollow of his throat.

Her stomach rolled and she averted her eyes. Then clutching Eve close to her, she scrambled to her feet.

"Dean!" With small penguin-like steps, she hurried over to her fallen protector. Sinking beside the man who'd come to mean so much to her in such a short time, she patted Dean's cheek, checked for a pulse. She nearly sobbed when she found the strong steady throb in his throat. "Oh, thank God!"

A large red mark on his temple was quickly darkening to a bruise. She probed at the spot, searching for a goose egg. She'd learned in her first-aid training before becoming a foster mother that an external lump was far preferable to internal swelling that would crowd his brain. His lack of response bothered her as well. Remembering the bloom of red she'd seen earlier, she jerked up his shirt and found the wound on his torso. The seeping wound in his side seemed small for all the blood on his shirt. But she had no idea what sort of internal injuries he might have.

Staunch the bleeding. Jerking the knit cap from her head, she pressed the hat against his wound while she fumbled mentally for a better way to stop his bleeding. She pictured the diapers and burp rags in the knapsack, and cast her gaze around her to find the discarded backpack. Digging out a couple of burp cloths, she balled them up and pressed them into Dean's bleeding side. She pulled the scarf from her neck, and after poking it behind Dean's back, she tied the wad of burp cloths tightly against his side. "Come on, honey. Open your eyes. Say something!"

Eve had cried so long and hard she'd given herself the hiccups. Lila rocked back on her heels, putting an arm around Eve as she crooned, "It's all right, sweetie. It's going to be okay."

But was it? Would Dean make it until help arrived? What was she supposed to do with an unconscious, bleeding and possibly concussed man, a baby and a dead body in the midst of a snowstorm? She closed her eyes and made an intentional effort to calm her breathing. *Don't panic. Dean said help is coming.* Had she imagined the sound of an engine she thought she'd heard? The woods were eerily quiet now but for the soft moan of the wind in the upper branches and the pinging of sleet and snow.

She cradled Eve close and swayed slowly side to side, hoping to soothe the baby, but she found she needed the calming motion herself. Dear Lord, she'd killed a man! By accident. But Wayne Pitts was just as dead, accident or not.

She shivered—from the cold and from guilt. She could better understand Dean's lingering trauma from his days in combat. Cutting a quick glance back toward Wayne, she whispered a quick prayer for the man's soul and asked forgiveness for her part in his demise.

Turning back to Dean, she cupped his chin, tried spritzing his face with snow. She needed him to wake up. *Please, please, Dean, wake up!*

"Lila Greene!" a male voice called from down the hill toward her cabin.

She gasped and jerked her head up, scanning the snowy woods. "Here! I'm here!"

Dean jolted then, his arms coming up defensively in front of him before he grimaced in pain.

She laid a hand on his cheek. "Easy, honey! It's me. Lila. It's over."

Dean scrunched his eyes shut and groaned, sliding a hand to the side of his head where Wayne had kicked him.

"Dean, be careful! You're injured." She tried to examine his gunshot wound, but he batted her hands away.

"Pitts…" Dean groaned, still trying to sit up and look past her.

"Is dead." She shuddered and nodded in the general direction of the body, the deadly icicle still protruding from Wayne's throat. She shifted her attention to the snowy woods, searching for the cavalry.

"Hello? Please hurry!" she yelled in the direction the voice had come before, "Dean is hurt!"

Finally, the crunch of feet in snow and panting of out-of-breath government agents filtered through the trees as a group of four men approached, weapons drawn. "Show us your hands!"

"It's okay," she called back. "This is Dean Hamilton. He's with me. Wayne Pitts is there." She aimed a finger at the still man. "I'm pretty sure he's dead."

"And the baby?" The agent leading the group wore a jacket that read US Marshal.

Lila stroked the crying infant's head. "Safe. Scared but safe." *Like me. I'm safe thanks to Dean.* The realization of all Dean had sacrificed, all he'd been willing to put on the line to protect her and a baby he had no connection to, was a demonstration of how the bad-boy teenager had changed. He'd come out of boot camp, his tours in the Special Forces and eleven years of maturity a different man. A man she could trust. A man she could *love*.

Lila met Dean's gaze as the lawmen surrounded them and her heart filled will a confidence and promise that made her chest ache. A good ache. A healing, hopeful ache.

"My name's Marshal Talley. I'll take the little girl, ma'am," the lead marshal said. When Lila hesitated, he added, "Just to check her for injury, so I can report back to headquarters. Standard procedure."

Giving Eve a kiss on the top of her head, Lila slipped the baby out of the homemade sling.

"Hi there, princess," Marshal Talley said in a soft, kind tone and, surprisingly, Eve quieted and looked at the man with blinking curiosity. "You're going to be okay, little darling."

A man wearing a coat that read FBI knelt by Dean and checked his pupils, examined his head injury and surveyed the bloody gash just under his ribs. Another one of the arriving marshals stood over Wayne's body and grunted. "I'll be damned. Ice stabbed him like a dagger." He glanced to the men around him. "Or a sword. Poetic justice, huh?"

While Lila watched the law enforcement officers move carefully about the scene, Dean took her hand and laced his fingers with hers. "Are you…okay?"

His thready voice concerned her. "I'm fine now that this is over." She gave him a weary smile. "You've lost a good bit of blood. Are you in much pain?"

"I'm okay," he muttered. "I'm o—" His eyelids fluttered, and his eyes rolled back as he fell silent.

"Dean?" She squeezed his hand. "Dean!" She raised a stricken, questioning look to the man assisting Dean. "What happened? Will he be all right?"

Rather than answering her, the man pulled a hand radio out of his pocket and raised it to his mouth. "Dispatch, this is Special Agent Bolinger. We need medical transport off Mount Collins at Hamilton-Gamble Camp Road. STAT!"

The sounds of a busy hospital wing seeped through the cobwebs of sleep as Dean woke for the second time the next morning. His first waking had been at some ungodly hour before dawn, when the nurse came in to draw blood and check his vitals. Now a soft light filtered through the window blinds, telling him the sun had risen. The familiar scent of flowers told him before he opened his eyes that Lila was there. The quiet murmur of a news report told him she was watching television.

Lila was there. Knowing that was better than any painkiller they could give him. She was safe. Eve was safe. Wayne Pitts was no longer a threat. He didn't know all the details of what had happened on the mountain after he'd blacked out, but he'd learned that much during brief snatches of lucidity as he was transported by litter to his house after he was shot. He'd been in and out of consciousness for the slow ride down the icy mountain by ambulance to the ER.

Lila hadn't accompanied him. She'd been checked by

the EMTs and declined further medical care at the hospital in order to stay with Eve. Or so he'd been told. He had yet to confirm anything with Lila himself, in large part due to the heavy-duty painkillers they gave him that meant he slept hard through the night.

"I dreamed about you last night," he said now without even opening his eyes.

"How did you—" The sound of the TV commercial disappeared.

"You smell like flowers. Remember?" He blinked her into focus then and felt his heart catch at the sight of her. She really was the prettiest woman he'd ever known. And she was smiling at him. For him.

"How are you feeling? The doctors wouldn't tell me anything. That whole patient-privacy thing, ya know."

"Mmm," he murmured in acknowledgment. He stretched carefully, still quite sore from his injuries, and tried to shove aside his drowsiness. The TV was still on, just muted. "Slight concussion. The GSW was a glancing hit. Damaged muscle and cracked a rib, but no organ damage. So I'll live to fight another day."

She lowered her eyebrows as she frowned. "Oh, no, you don't. Your fighting days are over, bucko."

"Bucko?" He chuckled at the term, and a sharp ache spun through his torso. "Oh, ow! Don't make me laugh. The rib…"

She held up her hands defensively and grinned. "You're the one who thought my grandfather's moniker was funny."

He lifted a corner of his mouth. "I thought it sounded old-school." He reached for her hand, and she laced her fingers with his. "Where's Eve?"

"With her maternal grandparents. They were located

last night and picked her up early this morning at the Collins Ridge PD station." She bit her bottom lip. "It was so bittersweet. Seeing them meet the grandchild they didn't know they had while grieving the loss of their daughter." She shook her head. "But you could tell they fell instantly in love with her. Eve's grandmother couldn't stop kissing her and crying. But smiling, too. Like I said, happy and heartbroken at the same time."

She stared down at their joined hands, her expression pensive.

"And you?" He pushed the incline button on his bed with his free hand, propping up for the discussion ahead. "How are you holding up?"

"I'm tired. It was a long, sleepless night, worrying about you, dealing with Eve, replaying—"

He tightened his grip on her hand. "Don't replay. It serves no purpose."

"Says one who knows?"

He drew a slow, careful breath. "Yeah. One who knows."

"So can we talk about that now?"

At the edge of his vision, an image on the television caught his attention. And a name—Pitts.

"I don't mean to push, but if we—"

"Hang on," he said, stopping her with a raised hand. He pointed to the television screen and said, "Turn that up."

She cast a look to the TV and sucked in a sharp breath as she used the remote to unmute the news story.

"—confirm that Wayne Pitts, younger brother to escaped cult leader Kent Pitts, died yesterday. Authorities are withholding details surrounding Wayne Pitts's death until an investigation can be conducted."

Again he squeezed Lila's hand. "You did nothing wrong. The investigation is a formality."

She nodded. "Special Agent Dunn has already gone over it all with me. I'm all right."

"Kent Pitts," the news report continued, "who escaped custody while being transported to federal lockup, is still at large and is considered armed and dangerous. Citizens are warned not to confront Pitts should they see him, but notify police immediately."

Dean scowled. "If Kent is still at large, Eve—"

"Is still at risk, yes." Lila pressed her other hand on top of their joined hands. "She and her grandparents were taken to an FBI safe house."

He compressed his lips, not yet satisfied. "And you?"

"I was never the real target, just a roadblock to be dealt with. Agent Dunn has a man stationed at my place, just in case, but they don't think I'm at risk anymore. They've let the media know Eve has been moved to a new, secret location. If Kent has an ear to the news, he'll know I don't have her."

Dean shifted his legs, restless to be out of the hospital. "I should be the one protecting you. I feel like I failed you yesterday. I—"

"Failed? Don't be ridiculous! You went above and beyond for me and Eve!" She reached for his cheek with her free hand. "Who knows how this would have come out if you hadn't been there. Dean, I..." She gazed into his eyes and nibbled her bottom lip. "Thank you."

She leaned in for a kiss, and he caught the back of her head to hold her close for a second kiss. And a third and...

"About my PTSD..." He rested his bandaged forehead gently against hers. "I'm seeing a military shrink and am taking things one day at a time. No quick fixes, but in time…" He sighed. "I have every reason to believe I'll be all right."

"Good." She kissed him again, threading her fingers through the hair around his ear.

He traced the line of her jaw with a fingertip. "So that brings us back to…us."

"And a second chance to see if this attraction might lead to something more?" She tipped her head, and the corner of her lips twitched in amusement.

He nodded, then winced when his head throbbed.

She moved to sit on the edge of his hospital bed, laying a hand on his chest. "Easy, bucko. I'm not going anywhere." Lila snuggled closer, adding, "I'm all-in. I believe we were given this second chance for a reason."

He smiled at her, ignoring the ache in his scalp when he wiggled his eyebrows. "See, we're already on the same page."

"But you have to promise me—" Her expression had grown serious, and he knew where she was headed.

"Complete honesty. You got it. I am not Carl. I'm not the Dean you knew eleven years ago. I hope you know, yesterday I was only trying to protect you, make an untenable situation easier…"

She nodded. "I get that."

"Lila?" he said, his heart so full of hope and happiness it ached, right along with his head and cracked rib. "The truth is…I think I'm falling in love with you."

She stilled, and her startled gaze latched on to his. "Dean?"

"Yeah."

"In the interest of full disclosure," she said formally,

though a smile played at her mouth, "I need to correct something I told you yesterday."

Dean angled his chin and raised his eyebrows, intrigued. "And what's that?"

"I said I considered happiness to be blue."

"Like the sky in spring. Right."

"Right. Well, I do think blue is a happy color but… my own happiness is bister."

He drew back and gave her a puzzled look. "It's what?"

"Bister. A shade of dark brown."

He let his skepticism show on his face, and she hurried to explain.

"It's the exact color of your eyes when you look at me and smile. You make me happy."

Her answer knocked the breath from him.

She snuggled closer and stroked the side of his face. "I love your smile. I love the way your face lights up when you're happy. I love that you have a reason to smile again. But most of all, I'm falling in love with you, too."

He let her words soak in. Were they sappy? Sure. But he didn't care. Lila Greene was making him feel all sorts of mushy things. He might not have the same flowery way of expressing himself, but he had the same marrow-deep joy and affection filling him up. So he answered her the best way he knew how. "Hoo-ah!"

* * * * *

Dear Reader,

Writing gets me through hard times and extreme weather. Writing *Claiming Caleb* was especially fun for me because I got to write snow and ice when the outside temperatures here were pushing one hundred! Throw in the West Virginia mountains, a hunky FBI agent and a woman who'd wanted a baby more than anything, except not at the price of her sister's life, and you've got true distraction. Plus a crazed cult leader and his brother, an ice storm and a rekindled romance from the past, and I had exactly what I needed.

I hope you enjoy reading Garrett and Michelle's story—oh, and baby Caleb's, too. While you read, I wish for you a warm, crackling fire and a gentle snowfall. And love, of course. Because love is what matters most of all.

Enjoy,

Karen Whiddon

CLAIMING CALEB

Karen Whiddon

To Animal Rescuers everywhere.
Your purity of heart and dedication make me
glad to be a part of you.

Chapter 1

Michelle Morgan held the sleeping infant, gazing down at his innocent, precious face and tried to summon joy. Though she'd dreamed of a baby for years, she'd never imagined such a blessed gift could come with so much sorrow.

He had Lydia's eyes, the same light green as Michelle's own. Her younger sister had been way too young at eighteen to have a child, and far too young to die at the hands of a man she'd trusted.

Murder. As she gently rocked the baby she'd been told Lydia had named Caleb, Michelle tried to wrap her mind around the circumstances that led to Child Protective Services bringing the baby here.

Like everyone else, Michelle had been riveted by the continuing news coverage of the standoff between law enforcement and Kent Pitts, the charismatic leader of the cult called simply The Sword—a group of maybe fifty people with a compound in the hills near Collins Ridge, West Virginia.

Unlike everyone else, she'd been a wreck of nerves and emotion because her younger sister, Lydia, was inside. And now Lydia was dead, at Pitts's own hand. Michelle still reeled from the shock of learning the cult leader had considered her eighteen-year-old sister one of his wives.

When Lydia had run off and joined the cult right after graduating high school, Michelle had begged and pleaded for her to reconsider, to no avail. Now Lydia was dead, leaving Michelle with a huge hole in her heart and a tiny baby who would never know his mother.

Lost in her thoughts, the knock on her door—a sharp rapping, really—made her jump.

After one quick glance at the baby, still sleeping, she placed him in the makeshift crib she'd created using a dresser drawer and blankets. Taking a deep breath, she opened the door a crack and gasped. *He* stood there, the man who'd haunted her dreams for the past five years, the man she'd once loved to distraction and whom she'd never forgotten.

Garrett Ware.

Keeping her door cracked, she peered out at him, heart pounding, her breath making puffs in the cold air. Snow had started to fall, coating his blond hair with white flecks. She noted he wore an FBI vest over his winter jacket and also the new hardness to the line of his jaw.

"What are you doing here?" she asked, feeling foolish, when clearly he'd come for a work-related purpose. "I've already been contacted by your people and told of the loss of my sister."

Tilting his head, his bright blue gaze never left her face. "May I come in?"

His formal tone, as if they were strangers, put yet another pain in her heart.

Silent, she stepped aside and pulled the door open wide enough for him to pass.

"I'm sorry about Lydia," he told her, his tall and solid bulk making the room seem even smaller. "I was there, disguised so she didn't know who I was, but I knew she was there. I tried to save her, I swear to you I did, but I was too far away and didn't have a gun. By the time I got to her, she was already gone."

Stone-faced, she nodded. "The agent who called told me all the details. Even about the sword with the curved blade. How Kent Pitts used it for some religious rituals and in the end to stab my sister." She took a deep breath, momentarily feeling as if she was under water. "I wasn't aware you were there."

She tried not to accuse him, but if she knew Garrett Ware at all, she knew he already suffered enough guilt for the two of them. The sorrow in his bright blue eyes attested to that.

"I went in undercover. MM, I promise you I tried to stop him."

MM. The nickname he'd always called her, and which she no longer used. "I believe you," she said. "And if that's why you came by, thank you. It helps a little knowing someone was trying to take care of her in the end."

Still he didn't move. "I couldn't get her out of there. There were two of them—Lydia and the other girl he'd made his newest wives. He didn't trust me—it was almost like he sensed something. I had to be careful, being undercover and knowing the operation was going down."

He swallowed, inhaled deeply and looked away. "None of us dreamed he'd do such a thing. He killed them, MM. Stabbed them both, right in front of me."

Once, seeing the agony in the too-taut lines of his neck, she would have gone to him and tried to soothe him, to offer comfort. Now, with her own pain plus five years of separate lives in between them, she didn't move. "Thank you," she said, her quiet voice shaky. "Now if you don't mind, I'd really like to be left alone."

His gaze slid past her to little Caleb, still asleep. "I heard there was a baby or two." He moved closer. "They were able to get the children out after Pitts had been arrested. I never got to see them."

"At least he didn't kill them." The trace of bitterness in her voice made her weary. "Little Caleb here is all I have left of Lydia."

He nodded, and it suddenly dawned on her she still had no idea why he continued to hang around.

"If you're here to apologize for something you couldn't help, there's no need." Part of her wanted him to go, to take his handsome self out of her space, so her breathing could return to normal.

The other part...well, she wanted him to stay. Once, he'd asked her to marry him and she'd accepted. When everything had fallen apart, they'd gone their separate ways, lived their separate lives. Not once had he made any attempt to contact her, which meant he'd never wondered about the woman he'd professed to love forever. Until he hadn't.

She could live with this—she *had* lived with this. Until now. Until he'd shown up at the door of the one-room cabin she'd rented to be close to the compound and her sister. Now, one look at him and every emotion came rushing back.

The long look he gave her set off alarm bells. "You truly don't know why I'm here?"

"No. Should I be worried?"

"Yes."

His one-word answer made her blink and cross her arms. "Garrett, what's going on?"

"I take it you haven't been watching the news."

"I turned it off after Pitts was captured. The last I saw, he was going to be arraigned and then they were transporting him to the prison up in Preston County. Why? What did I miss?"

His grimace told her to brace herself. "The storm is worse northwest of here. It's moving this way, but the roads out that way, especially in Preston County, are sheets of ice."

"And?"

A muscle clenched along his strong jaw. "The transport van crashed. Kent Pitts and his brother, Wayne, escaped."

She swore softly.

"That's not all," he continued. "Kent has sworn to find and kill both of his children."

For one second, stark terror turned her blood to ice.

"Why?" The word burst from her. "I don't understand. What kind of man would want to take innocent lives?"

"I think you already know the answer to that. Kent Pitts is crazy. His brother, Wayne, does whatever he says. They appear to believe killing the babies is better than letting them live among unbelievers. That's why I'm here."

Still not understanding, she blinked.

"To protect you," he said. "You and little Caleb there. The bureau has assigned me to watch over both of you until the Pitts brothers are caught."

Garrett had told himself he could handle seeing Michelle again. After all, five years had passed since she'd called off their wedding. And while he'd understood her reasoning completely, it had taken a while for the hurt to fade. Longer than it should have, actually. At least now, he was completely over her.

Until she'd opened her door, her curly red hair just as wild, her long-lashed green eyes still as bright and beautiful and he'd realized he wasn't. Not by a long shot.

He could smell something delicious simmering on the stove. Stew, maybe? His mouth watered. Michelle had always been a talented cook, and he hadn't had time to eat dinner.

Glancing at the innocent sleeping baby, he reminded himself he had a job to do. He'd already failed to save Michelle's younger sister. Damned if he'd let either of the Pitts hurt anyone else.

"I'm here to do a job, nothing more," he said out loud, wondering if he reminded himself or her. "You won't hardly even realize I'm here."

"I doubt that's possible. In case you hadn't noticed, this is a one-room cabin."

Her dry tone made him narrow his eyes. He glanced at the window, noting how the storm had intensified so that all he could see was swirling white. "Well, we'll just have to make do. We're stuck here, at least until the weather lets up."

Though she nodded, her tense expression never relaxed. He found himself itching to run his fingers through her hair the way he used to, to tug her close and claim a kiss.

Stunned, he moved away, making a show of thoroughly checking outside. "It's really coming down now. On the drive up here, the sleet and freezing rain had just turned to snow. The roads are bad and getting worse."

"And they're saying the snow is going to be mixed with more ice," she told him. "At least, the last weather report I watched predicted that. It sounds like this storm has the potential to do a lot of damage. Downed trees, power lines and impassable roads." She shuddered. "I'm glad I was able to stock up down in town before all this mess hit."

Turning from the window, he made a quick decision. "I'd planned to get you out of here, take you and the baby someplace safe. With the roads the way they are, I'm thinking it might be better to wait out the storm."

"I agree."

"On the positive side, the storm will make it equally difficult for the Pitts brothers to find you. If we can't get out, they won't be able to travel far."

Frowning, she tilted her head. "If they're on foot, I don't think they'll last long in the weather."

"We think there might be an accomplice or two. Pitts grabbed an injured US marshal's phone. Not only does he have the location of both the babies, but he has a way to connect to any of his people on the outside for help."

"Then I'm glad we're having such a monster storm," she immediately said. "Looks like I picked a good time to cook stew."

At her words, his stomach growled. Loudly. He

grinned at her; he couldn't help it. "I thought that's what I smelled."

Briefly, she smiled back. "Would you like some? I haven't eaten yet and since it appears you'll be here awhile, I might as well feed you."

Which meant she might be secretly pleased. The MM he remembered loved nothing more than cooking for people. Especially for him.

Swallowing hard, he reminded himself again that all of that had been in the past. Still, she'd offered him food, and no way was he going to pass up a chance to eat her delicious home cooking. Since it now appeared they'd be bunking together for a couple days, he figured he'd offer to cook some, too. Michelle knew he was a horrible cook.

"Garrett?" she prompted. "Are you hungry?"

"I could eat."

When she dished up the stew, he noticed she only made one bowl, placing it on the small kitchen table. "What about you?" he asked.

"I've lost my appetite." Her dry tone left no doubt as to the reason why. "I'll have some later."

With a shrug, he took a seat, inhaling deeply the fragrant steam. "This smells delicious," he told her, his mouth watering as he reached for his spoon.

"I almost forgot, I made bread, too." She placed a good-sized chunk on his plate. "Enjoy."

He dug in.

"I always did love your stew," he told her after swallowing the last spoonful and pushing away his empty bowl. "That was delicious. Thank you."

"No problem." She inhaled, her gaze sharp. "But do

me a favor. For as long as you're here guarding Caleb, don't bring up the past."

Surprised, he considered her words. "I'm not sure if I can do that," he finally answered. "I can't just pretend nothing ever happened between us. Yes, it's been five years, but we'll never be strangers."

"Then I'm afraid I'm going to have to ask you to not speak to me at all." She crossed her arms again, her defensive expression telling him she meant it. "I just lost my sister. I'm grieving. I can't deal with you dredging up old hurts. It's just too much."

He wondered about that. Did she mean she still mourned his loss, the same way he did hers? "None of that matters," he said. "I'm here to do a job, to keep you and that baby safe. We'll have to figure out how to work around that, but I won't pretend not to know you."

"You don't." Her flat tone matched her pursed lips. "A lot can happen in half a decade. I've changed. I'm sure you have, too. I'd venture to say you don't know me at all."

Outside, the wind drove something into the side of the cabin. The loud clang made Michelle jump and woke the baby. The instant Caleb began to cry, Michelle rushed to comfort him. Garrett grabbed his parka and put it on before he headed outside to check out the sound.

The instant he stepped into the storm, ice pellets stinging his face, snow swirling in the howling wind, he realized that unless the Pitts brothers had gotten help, they were dead men. If they were on foot, they'd have to break into a house and lie low until the storm had passed.

Which meant he'd have a little time before they reached Michelle and her charge. He'd been around Pitts long enough while undercover in the compound to understand when the cult leader obsessed over something, he'd move hell or high water to get where he needed to be.

And Pitts had sworn to kill his children rather than see them raised by nonbelievers. Though Garrett had no idea which one they'd go for first—Caleb or the baby girl.

Tramping around all four sides of the cabin took longer than it should have, battling the force of the wind. He kept his head down, watching for footprints, even though he knew they would have already been obliterated.

When he reached the front door again, every unprotected part of his skin stinging from cold, he stamped the snow off his boots and went back inside. Once he'd closed and locked the door securely behind him, he divested himself of the heavy parka and gloves and went directly for the woodstove to warm his frozen hands.

When he looked up, he met Michelle's gaze. She'd taken a seat in a rocking chair and held a bundled-up baby. Caleb had fallen back asleep.

The instant their eyes met, Michelle gazed back at the infant, her face so full of love and tenderness, it took his breath away.

He felt like he'd been punched in the gut. She looked like she'd been made for this moment, cradling the infant protectively, her head bent, long hair falling in a curtain around her shoulders. The dim light gave everything a surreal feeling. Homey too, despite the danger lurking just out of sight.

Damn. Turning away, he shook it off. He needed to be on his guard. Such a distraction could endanger them both.

"I did a complete perimeter check," he told her, his

tone brisk and businesslike. "Nothing there. Must have been the wind."

She nodded, most of her attention still focused on the sleeping child. "I thought as much."

He searched his mind for something else to say. Something banal, a bit of empty conversation, the way two strangers might talk.

"The stove does a good job of helping to keep it warm in here," he said. "We need to make sure the fire doesn't die out, especially tonight while we sleep."

Again she nodded. "I've got plenty of wood. I was thinking about dragging the mattress off the bed and moving it closer to the stove. It'd be a lot warmer that way."

Which brought up another interesting question. Where did she intend him to sleep?

"About our sleeping arrangements," he began.

"Shhh." Moving carefully, she rose and placed the sleeping baby back in his makeshift crib, which appeared to be a dresser drawer lined with blankets.

He waited until she'd finished, trying not to eye her shapely backside. With a hot flash of desire, he remembered the feel of her in his hands.

Angry at himself, he shoved the thought away. "I can sleep on the couch," he said, his tone leaving no room for discussion. Not that he expected any. She wasn't about to tell him she wanted him to share her bed.

Shake it off, Ware, he told himself.

"That's fine," she answered, exactly as he'd expected.

As he was about to reply, the power went out.

Chapter 2

Though on some level she'd been expecting this due to the ferocity of the storm, the sudden darkness startled Michelle. She froze. For a second, all she could hear were the ice pellets pelting the metal roof of the cabin, the crackling fire in her woodstove and the even sound of Garrett's breathing. Close. Too close for comfort.

Then, as her eyes adjusted, she hurried over to Caleb, reassuring herself he was all right and still sleeping.

"He's fine," she said, more to reassure herself than anything else. "It's a good thing I brought in a lot of wood. If the power doesn't come back on, that woodstove will keep us warm."

"Good." He strode to the window, moving close as if he could actually see past the whiteout snow. Silhouetted against the outside light, she could see his shoulders were still as broad, his waist just as narrow. She'd always considered his the perfect male body. No wonder no other man could ever measure up.

Damn. Swallowing hard, she had to tear her gaze away from Garrett. Needing an anchor, she focused on the still-sleeping baby.

From this moment on, she told herself, nothing would matter to her but her precious charge, Caleb. So what if she couldn't stop thinking of how Garrett made her feel? All of that paled in comparison to her need to keep the baby safe.

Just then, Caleb stirred and began to cry. Michelle hurried over and picked him up, checking his diaper. He needed a change, which she managed to do. She fumbled a bit, feeling awkward under Garrett's watchful gaze.

The infant's cries became wails. Though it wasn't yet time to feed him, she judged it close enough. "I need your help warming a bottle," she told Garrett. "I can't use the microwave, so we'll need to use a pan of water on the stove."

More nervous than she should have been, she grabbed one of the bottles she'd made earlier out of the fridge and handed it to Garrett. Then, still bouncing the wailing baby, she located a saucepan. "Fill that about half full with water and—"

"I know what to do,' he said, cutting her off. "Remember, I used to help take care of Georgia's kids for extra money after school."

Preoccupied with trying to calm the now almost hysterical baby, she nodded. She remembered very well, since she'd often kept him company when he'd been stuck at home watching his little niece and nephew, Kayla and Chris. He'd always been great with kids, which was why she'd been so shocked when he'd said he didn't want any of his own.

The past, she reminded herself sternly as she bounced baby Caleb, walking from one end of the room to the other.

"It's ready," Garrett announced, squirting a bit of the bottle on his wrist to test the temperature before handing it to her.

As soon as the baby felt the nipple against his rosebud mouth, he began to suckle. "Blessed silence," she said, unable to tear her gaze from his precious little face as she watched him drink.

Garrett made a sound, something unintelligible and strangled. When she raised her head to look at him, she was surprised to see an expression of such tenderness that it stole her breath.

Suddenly, the entire scene—ice pellets pelting the tin roof, the crackling fire, storm swirling outside and the now content baby—felt way too cozy.

And wrong. But then, nothing about her life ever since Lydia had decided to join a cult right after graduating from high school had been right.

Hopefully, that would soon change. At least, once Pitts was recaptured and the storm ended. Then she'd go back to Ohio and her tidy little house and get busy starting the paperwork to formally adopt Caleb.

Once the baby finished his bottle, she put him to her shoulder to burp.

"Here." Garrett held a dish towel. "Put this on your shoulder in case he spits up."

"Thank you." She did exactly that. Once Caleb had made a good belch, she placed him back in his warm, makeshift crib, where he promptly fell back asleep.

"He's a good baby," Garrett remarked. "Looks a lot like your sister, too."

Suddenly exhausted, Michelle nodded. "I'd forgotten how much work they are."

"You never had one full-time, like I did." His sister had been an alcoholic and later a drug addict. Garrett had cared for her two children through his entire teenage years and as much as he could while he attended West Virginia University.

Michelle wondered what had happened to them, how they were doing these days. She was on the verge of asking, then she shook her head. Best to let the past remain the past.

"Do you usually use the woodstove for heat?" Garrett asked.

"Partly." She pointed to a window unit near the bed. "That thing there helps, too. It can be set for heat or to cool. But since it relies on electricity, the woodstove will have to do until the power comes back on."

He nodded. "It might get a bit chilly in here if the outage continues longer than a few hours."

"I'm thinking about dragging the mattress over closer to the stove," she said, and then immediately blushed.

Apparently, he correctly read her expression. "No worries, I've got a thermal sleeping bag out in my truck. I'll be on the couch."

He eyed her. "As a matter of fact, you and the baby can use it. I'll be fine with blankets."

"I'm afraid Caleb might suffocate," she told him. "He'll be fine right here bundled up next to the stove."

"As long as you don't let that fire die out."

"I won't."

He shrugged. "Be right back," he said, putting on his parka and heading outside once more to retrieve his gear.

Though he moved fast, the instant he opened the door, icy air blasted inside. Darkness had fallen, and with no outside light due to the lack of electricity she wondered how he'd find his way to his truck in the wind swirl of the blizzard.

Waiting, she found herself holding her breath until the door opened again, bringing another blast of frozen air and Garrett.

Snow coated his hair and shoulders as he removed his heavy coat. "Even though I wouldn't have thought it possible, the storm is getting worse." He dropped his bag on the floor and went over to check out her stack of firewood.

"It's enough for another day," she told him, starting to feel uneasy. "Maybe a day and a half."

The worry lines creasing his forehead did little to reassure her. "Hopefully, the worse part will be over before then."

"I have more wood stacked outside," she told him.

"Is it covered?"

She shook her head. "No. When I heard it might storm, I should have put a tarp over it."

"It'll be wet, but if I bring some more in now, maybe it will have time to dry."

Without waiting for her to agree, he put his coat back on and stomped off out into the storm.

She stood in between the baby and the door, not wanting even a hint of the freezing air from outside to hit him.

A soft pounding made her jump. She hurried over and pulled the door open to let Garrett, his arms full of wood, inside.

After placing the first stack on the floor near the stove, he took one more trip. "There," he said, sounding satisfied. "That should hold us over."

Eyeing the mountain of wet wood, she shook her head. "Exactly how long are you thinking this storm will last?"

The clear blue of his eyes cut right through her as he met her gaze. "There's no way of knowing. Better safe than sorry."

Somehow she managed a nod, aware she couldn't let him know how much even the thought of being trapped in a twenty-by-thirty room with him for several days made her feel uncomfortable.

With only the woodstove for lighting, the darkness gave the room an air of intimacy. She tried to shake it off, reminding herself he was there to protect her and Caleb, nothing more, but even knowing that didn't help much.

"It's been a long day," she finally told him, stifling a yawn. "If you don't mind, I think I'm going to turn in. Caleb probably doesn't sleep through the night yet."

He helped her move the mattress, quietly nodding when she asked him if he had everything he needed to sleep on the sofa.

"I'm good." He actually sounded cheerful. "I can use one of those pillows. Along with my sleeping bag, I'll be fine."

Now what? Should she change into her pajamas? Even though they were flannel, she'd still feel strange. More uncomfortable. It'd be warmer to sleep in her jeans, but not as comfortable.

In the end, she decided to go with the flannel. Luckily, the tiny little bathroom provided a modicum of privacy.

When she emerged in her sensible and warm pj's, she went hot all over as Garrett's gaze swept over her.

"You haven't changed at all, have you?" he asked with a slow grin.

Her heart skipped a beat at the beauty of that grin. Recovering, she shrugged and turned away. "I have no idea what you mean," she said, even though she knew exactly what he meant. Every winter since she'd been a kid, she got out her flannel pajamas. Always plaid, though the colors varied. She figured she had five or six pairs of them.

While she'd been changing, Garrett had added wood to the stove, so a nice little fire crackled merrily behind the grated metal door. "Thanks," she murmured, wishing she didn't feel so self-conscious.

After making sure she had Caleb in his makeshift crib where she wanted it—taking advantage of as much warmth as possible, though careful it wasn't too much—she slipped under her own sheets and covers. Since she normally slept in a chilly room with several blankets, she worried she'd be too warm, but once she got comfortable, she figured she'd be fine.

Closing her eyes, she prayed she'd fall asleep quickly. Without dwelling on the past she'd shared with Garrett.

As Michelle got settled for the night, every rustle of fabric felt like fingers tracing over the nerve endings under Garrett's skin. No matter how many times he reminded himself of his job, his duty, he couldn't stop wondering if her skin would still feel as silky smooth. Or if she still smelled like tangerines. He'd thought about getting close enough to tell, but had judged it too dangerous to his equilibrium.

So instead, he let his mind keep replaying the last moments at the compound, right as the FBI broke through. As long as he lived, he'd never forget the stark terror on Lydia's pretty young face as she'd watched her leader—and husband—plunge his sword into one of his other wives, Rachel. And then Pitts had turned on her. Lydia had barely had time to scream before he'd gutted her, letting her crumple to the floor like discarded garbage.

The other seven wives had scattered then, out of their minds with terror, thinking they'd die soon, whether at Pitts's hand or The Enemy's, as Pitts called them.

Stunned, Garrett had tried to stop the bloodbath, but two of Pitts's lieutenants had grabbed his arms and by the time he'd fought them off, Lydia was already dead.

Immediately, he'd thought of Michelle and how much her baby sister's death would hurt her.

Shaking off the horrible memory, he rose and checked on her and the baby. Michelle had burrowed under her blankets, only the top of her head poking out. He stood there, fighting the urge to kiss her, and then padded back to the couch. The window behind him needed to be resealed; a mean draft sent gusts of icy air down the back of his neck.

After placing his sleeping bag on the couch, he unzipped it and crawled inside. Eventually, his blood warmed and he allowed himself to drift off to sleep.

He awoke some time later to a much dimmer room. Despite the wood he'd added to the stove earlier, the fire had burned down to smoldering embers. Unzipping the sleeping bag and moving as quietly as he could, he grabbed a few more pieces of wood and opened the door in the front of the stove. Once he'd placed the wood inside and felt satisfied everything had caught satisfactorily, he moved over to check on the baby and Michelle.

Little Caleb still slept soundly, apparently warm and cozy from his proximity to the heat of the stove. Michelle, on the other hand, had managed to kick off her blankets and sheet and lay curled in a ball, shivering violently despite her flannel pajamas, still sound asleep.

He covered her, first with the sheet, and then with what must have been five blankets, taking care not to wake her. Then, heaven help him, he leaned in and breathed in her scent. Which was exactly the same as he remembered.

Tangerine. As he straightened, the memories came rushing back. Michelle sitting on the gate of his pickup, head thrown back as she laughed at something he'd said, the sun catching her hair just right and setting the curls ablaze with color.

His chest tightened as scenes flashed across his mind. Michelle on horseback, daring him to race to the river. He'd let her beat him, and she'd rode that horse right into the water, laughing all the way.

Their first kiss. The first time they'd… He swallowed tightly.

She'd been a handful, the younger Michelle. But she'd loved him as fiercely as he'd loved her. They'd both thought they'd be together forever. Until they were making wedding plans, and she'd thought to ask him about children.

As long as he lived, he'd never forget the pain in her eyes when he'd told her he didn't want any.

"Ever?" she'd asked, her bottom lip trembling. Right then he'd wanted to gather her in his arms and hold her, to promise her anything. But the one thing he wouldn't do was lie.

They'd sworn to each other that they never would. So he hadn't. And he'd lost her.

Pushing the painful thoughts away, he returned to the couch and tried like hell to will himself back to sleep.

He must have dozed, though he'd tossed and turned so much he didn't wake rested. Caleb had awakened once, making mewling cries revealing his hunger.

Garrett hadn't moved from his cocoon while Michelle stumbled around warming a bottle. He'd watched through half-closed eyes as she fed the tiny infant while sitting up on the edge of her bed close to the stove. She'd been made for this, he realized. Even half-asleep in the middle of the frigid night, the peaceful contentment glowed on her lovely face as she gazed down at Caleb. Despite the underlying sorrow over the loss of her sister shadowing her eyes, having an infant to take care of brought her a measure of peace.

A familiar ache—one that had been absent for several years—tightened his chest and throat. No. He closed his eyes and turned his head away, refusing to dwell on what might have been.

After the baby had gone back to sleep, Garrett listened again to the sounds Michelle made as she crawled back into her now-cold bed. He was torturing himself, yet he couldn't seem to keep from imagining her welcoming him under her heavy blankets, her silky skin smooth under his touch.

Triumph surging through him, Kent Pitts lifted his face to the sting of the ice pellets mixed with snow, and smiled. Once again, events had proven his fate would not be denied. Not by pseudo–law enforcement or weather. In fact, he could easily believe the elements were on his side.

On the side of The Sword.

"Come here," Kent ordered. "Let me get those cuffs off you." He grinned, jingling the keys he'd snagged from the downed guard's belt.

One click, and his brother's hands were free.

Now that they'd taken care of that, he directed Wayne to deal with the injured guard. Wayne would use the gun, whereas Kent preferred swords. Much more personal, as well as sacred to the order he'd founded.

Turning his back, he waited until the sound of a gunshot rang out. Squinting into the distance, which the storm made slightly difficult, Kent calculated how long they had until dark. "Grab his jacket," he ordered. "And get the one off the driver, too. Hats, gloves, whatever winter gear they have. We're going to need them. Oh, and his cell phone, too. There might be information on there we can use."

"Gotcha," Wayne replied, already sounding busy.

Again he waited, rubbing his hands together to try and warm them. Finally, he judged enough time had passed. "You ready, Wayne?"

Immediately, his younger brother rushed over, two heavy winter parkas in his arms. Both of them had US Marshal emblazoned on the back. "Yes, Master Pitts. I am. Here." He thrust one of the jackets toward his brother. When Kent slipped his hand into the pocket, he found a Swiss Army Knife tucked inside. Another sign. While not a ceremonial blade, it was a knife. However small, it could still cut through flesh. Especially the perfect, soft skin of an infant like his son, Caleb. "With The Sword I will fight for my right to live free, seek The Truth and defend myself from The Enemy," he said softly.

Wayne smiled. As always, the mantra of The Sword bolstered his spirits, Kent could tell.

Both men hurriedly dressed. Though the coat wasn't a great fit—a bit too large—it was a hell of a lot better than trying to navigate this storm in prison-issue shirts and pants. He yanked the knit hat down on his head, covering his ears, and pulled on the warm gloves with a sigh of relief. "Let's go. We don't have a lot of time before they'll figure out what happened and send someone else after us."

Excitement shone in Wayne's eyes. "Let's do it," he said, turning back toward the van.

"Where are you going?" The steel in Kent's voice stopped Wayne short.

"To free the others," Wayne answered, his brow furrowed in confusion.

"Leave them here," Kent ordered. "They're on their own. From now on, it's just us. We're the only ones who have the courage to do what must be done in the name of The Sword."

Though Wayne's mouth fell open, he immediately closed it. He wouldn't argue, Kent knew. He never did.

"This way." Kent started forward on foot. "We'll steal the first car we come across. Or cars," he added, almost as an afterthought.

"Cars?" Hurrying to catch up, Wayne zipped his coat up to his chin. "Are we splitting up?"

"You're the only one I trust. My children must be set free from this horrible world. Foster homes." He shuddered as he said the words. "Let me have the phone."

As soon as Wayne handed it over, Kent removed his

gloves and began scrolling through texts and emails. "Here we go." Triumph filled him yet again. "The addresses where they've placed my son and my daughter. As I suspected, they're in different homes."

Wayne nodded, clearly still not understanding.

"I'm going to give you a sacred mission," Kent intoned, using what he privately thought of as the royal voice. "When we find cars, I want you to go after my daughter, Eve. I don't care what you have to do to the foster home, but you need to release her."

"Release her?"

"From this world." Struggling to hold on to his patience, Kent turned and placed both hands on his brother's shoulders. "Eve cannot be raised by our enemies. She's better off dead."

For the first time that Kent could remember, Wayne balked. "But she's just a baby," he began.

"She's *mine*," Kent snarled. "I and only I, have the right to decide what happens to her. Do you understand?"

His expression miserable, Wayne slowly nodded. "I do."

Now Kent softened his voice. "Look at me, Wayne. Don't I always know the right thing to do?"

Wayne finally nodded.

"With The Sword I will fight for my right to live free, seek The Truth and defend myself from The Enemy," Kent reminded him.

At the words, Wayne's expression cleared. Resolve replaced indecision. "I will carry out your orders. Do you want me to use a ceremonial blade?"

"No." Kent fingered the small knife, finding its weight supremely satisfying. "You have a pistol. Use that. Make it clean and make sure she doesn't suffer. Do you understand?"

Wayne nodded.

They continued walking, pellets of ice ticking at them as they made their way toward the next town. The roads were slick, especially with the black ice that you didn't even see until you were sliding, so they stuck with the grassy side of the road where they could get better traction.

"This storm's supposed to get worse," Wayne commented. "I heard the guards talking. They're saying blizzard conditions later on, mixed with ice."

Serene, Kent nodded. "Then we need to move fast. Look." Pointing at a small car lot, apparently closed due to the weather, he smiled. "We've been delivered a bonanza. Choose wisely. I'm thinking four-wheel drive."

The ability to break into and hot-wire cars was one of the things both men had learned in their youth living on the streets. Neither had forgotten and they each had a new ride less than ten minutes later.

Kent found a scrap of paper and a pen inside his vehicle, an older Ford F-150 pickup. Consulting the phone, he scribbled down the address where Eve was being housed.

"Here you go." He held it out to his brother. With a quick nod, Wayne took the paper.

"Let The Sword guide your hand," Kent intoned. "Now go."

For a heartbeat, Wayne didn't move. "What about after?" he asked. "Are we gonna meet up, or what?"

Kent lifted his hands as if drawing energy from the earth or the storm. "If allowed to do so, we will. If not, I'll see you in the next world, where our castles await us."

With a nod, Wayne closed his vehicle's door and drove off.

A second later, Kent consulted his phone and did the same. Oddly enough, the address where Caleb had been placed wasn't far from the compound where the members of The Sword had lived.

More proof, as if Kent needed any, that he trod the right path. Driving carefully but with unshakable certainty, he headed back the way they'd originally come. Toward Collins Ridge, West Virginia.

Chapter 3

When Garrett opened his eyes again, light filled the room. All the white snow reflected brightness, despite the slate-gray sky. He briefly remembered how, as a kid, that particular clarity of light had often been his first clue to snowfall and a likely day off from school.

"Morning." Her soft voice glided along his skin.

"Morning," he rasped, his body suddenly, achingly, aroused. Even the fleeting thought of her small hand wrapping around him nearly made him lose it.

Taking a deep breath, he closed his eyes and desperately tried to think of something else besides how sexy she looked in the morning, her red curls tousled as if she'd just tumbled from his arms.

He failed miserably. Deciding he had to move, he unzipped his sleeping bag enough to sit up and reached for his cell phone. Checking emails and for potential texts would ground him.

But the phone showed he had no signal. Which wouldn't be good. He needed to be able to receive updates on the Pittses' location and/or possible recapture.

He swore softly under his breath. "Are you able to use your cell phone here?" he asked.

Looking up from changing the baby's diaper, she shook her head. "No. Because this cabin sits in a valley, I had to walk up that hill behind us to get a signal. That's about the only place I could."

"On top of a hill?" He didn't bother to hide his disbelief. "How am I going to keep in touch with my team?"

She shrugged as she placed little Caleb back in his crib. "I guess you'll have to go outside and climb up the hill. I have one bit of good news. Though it's still snowing, the wind appears to have let up, at least for now."

Standing, he avoided looking at her. He stretched and crossed to peer out the window. Nothing but dazzling whiteness, as far as the eye could see.

"I wonder how much of that is ice?" she said from too close behind him.

Aware his frustration was disproportionate to the situation, he swallowed and kept his back to her. "After I wake up a bit more, I'll go check it out. Do you have any coffee? Even instant will do." Or would have to, since the electricity hadn't come back on.

"I have tea," she offered, not sounding the least bit apologetic. "I can boil water on the stove. Or if you'd rather have something else, there's Diet Coke in the fridge. Though it might be warm now. As a matter of fact…" Her voice took on a worried edge. "There's going to be some spoilage. At least I have powdered formula to mix with water. But I wonder if the remaining eggs will be okay to eat this morning. I'd planned to make scrambled eggs for breakfast."

"That depends on how cold it is inside your fridge." He turned so fast she stumbled back. Instinctively, he reached to steady her, meaning to just grab her arm until she was okay. Instead, he wound up hauling her up against him, chest to chest. As she stared up at him, for a moment he simply couldn't breathe. Unable to help himself, he lowered his head to hers and kissed her.

In an instant, the years they'd been apart melted away. Her mouth opened under his and their tongues welcomed each other home.

Garrett had no idea how long they stood like that, kissing as if they couldn't get enough of each other. His hand wound up tangled in her hair, that wild mess of fiery curls he'd always loved, while he could feel her heart beating a wild tattoo against his chest.

She gasped and jerked away. Stunned, he let her go.

Keeping a few feet between them, she took in deep, ragged breaths. "What the hell was that?" she asked, her voice shaking with emotion—either fury or angst.

Furious with himself, he swallowed hard. "A mistake." His clipped speech revealed more than he liked. "I assure you it won't happen again."

She jerked her head in a nod and moved away.

While Michelle checked out the contents of the fridge, Garrett crossed over to take another look at the tiny baby.

Full and dry and warm, Caleb slept again, his rosebud mouth pursed. Eyeing him, Garrett thought of Georgia's kids, wondering how they were now and if they ever thought of him. His older sister had disappeared with them without a word while he'd been at work. He'd searched and searched, but they might as well have dropped off the face of the earth. He could only hope they hadn't gotten involved in drugs like their mother.

Blinking, he focused again on the infant in front of him here and now. "I'll keep you safe," he said, pitching his voice low. "I give you my word. I'll protect you with my life if need be."

Finished, he turned to find Michelle watching him, her face expressionless.

"The eggs are still cool enough. I think they're safe," she said. "I'll whip up some breakfast. After that, we can take showers."

Of course, the unfortunate choice of wording brought to mind carnal images of times past. The shower had been a favorite place of hers to arouse his passion, not that it had taken much beyond the sight of her perfect body naked.

Again he found it necessary to turn away so she wouldn't see the sign of his obvious arousal.

When he'd asked to take this assignment to protect Michelle and the baby, he hadn't thought much beyond the need to atone for failing to save Lydia.

He'd certainly never expected the past would be so difficult to overcome.

Once she'd set a plate of scrambled eggs in front of him and taken a seat across the table with her own, he ate with a single-minded intensity. The instant he finished, he pushed back his chair and stood up. "Thank you," he told her. "That was delicious." And then he headed into the small bathroom for his shower.

"Wait." Her quiet command stopped him in his tracks. Heart beating way too fast, he slowly turned to find her there, so close he could lift his hand and touch her.

"About that kiss," she began and then shook her head

as she reached up and pulled him to her. When she covered his mouth with hers, it felt like a dam had burst. Every nerve ending ignited, from dying embers to a blazing inferno. Explosive.

Unbelievably, the soft flannel of her pajamas felt sexier than any silk negligee.

The sleek caress of her body mingled with the scent of tangerine made his chest ache. Damn, he wanted her. Craved her, actually. It took every bit of self-control he possessed to keep from turning the kiss into more.

While he pondered if she'd even welcome an attempt to take it further, she flashed a sexy smile.

And then, with no hesitation, she yanked off her nightclothes, standing beautiful and naked with her head held high and a challenge sparking in her emerald-green eyes.

Fully aroused, holding himself in check, he drank in the sight of her. "Are you sure?" he managed. Instead of answering with words, she used her small hands to undo his belt, then the top button on his jeans before she slid the zipper down and set him free.

Her sharp intake of breath, almost a gasp at the sight of him, made his hardness even more painful. He shrugged out of his shirt, needing to put his hands on her, to explore every curve, every nook of her generous body.

They came together as if they'd never been apart, and despite the years since the last time they'd been this close, his fingers remembered how to stroke her just so, to make her pupils dilate so she arched her back and cried out for more.

When he entered her, the sensation of *home* hit him, so strong he almost wept. With a groan, he had to hold them both still to keep her from moving or he'd lose his tenuous grip on control.

She protested, both out loud and then with a wiggle. It felt so good, he relaxed his grip on her so she could do it again.

Somehow, they made it to the bed.

And then, they both began to move in that intricate dance that felt both so familiar and so wonderful.

This, he thought, as her body clenched around him, anointing him with honey as she climaxed. *This*, as he let himself go, driving his body into hers, pleasure and pain and emotion all mixed up with the certainty that he should never have let her go.

Finally, she held on as he bucked and poured himself into her, the shuddering release stronger than anything he'd experienced in years.

Five, to be exact.

He held her after, her naked body still moist from their lovemaking, her heart still fluttering like a trapped bird under his hand.

"MM," he began, when he could speak.

"Shhh." Smiling, she pressed her fingers against his lips. "Don't. No regrets, okay?"

He went still, not sure exactly what she meant, and finally nodded.

"Now about that shower…" She scrambled to her feet, totally unself-conscious of her naked splendor. "I'm going first. Keep an eye on Caleb for me, please."

And without waiting for an answer, she strolled into the bathroom, closing the door with a quiet click behind her.

Stunned, shocked and spent, he let his head fall back on the pillow, staring at the ceiling and trying to figure out what this unexpected development signified.

Once, Michelle had meant the world to him, and he'd

hurt her badly. Damned if he'd do that again. Yet the short time he'd spent with her had made him realize he'd only been half-alive. Even his precious career, despite the hours he devoted to it, didn't fulfill him. At least, not like she had.

Wincing, he rolled over and began getting dressed. He'd made a mistake—*they'd* made a mistake, and he couldn't let this assignment be compromised just because he desired the woman he was supposed to protect.

Caleb let out a loud wail, reminding Garrett he had one more to keep safe.

Crossing the room, Garett scooped the little guy up and checked his diaper. As he'd suspected, it was wet. He grabbed a fresh one from the huge box of disposables and deftly changed it. Once done, he carried Caleb over to the wooden rocking chair, took a seat and began rocking him back, exactly the way he'd done for both of Georgia's kids when they'd been small.

Eventually, Caleb's eyes drifted closed, and he fell back to sleep. Garrett studied him, entranced at what he'd swear was a satisfied baby smile.

It dawned on him that he could get used to this.

Amazed at her body's pleasurable ache, Michelle let the shower wash away any trace of regret. She was older and wiser than that love-struck girl who'd once agreed to marry Garrett. Now she knew better. They'd made love. No, she corrected herself, they'd had sex. She had zero expectations, and if she tried really hard, she thought she could look at this as two adults enjoying an interlude of each other's company.

Yep, that's what she'd do.

Drying off, she dressed in clean jeans and a sweater and went to tell Garrett that he could have the shower.

When she stepped in the main room, she stopped at the sight of Garrett, little Caleb cradled in his arms, rocking slowly and crooning a lullaby in a low voice.

Her heart did a complete flip-flop. Then she reminded herself she'd asked him to take care of Caleb while she showered. Garrett was only doing what he did best— a job.

"Hey," she said softly, moving toward him. "The shower's all yours."

He lifted his gaze from Caleb, the glaze of bright blue sending a shock through her, exactly as it used to when they'd been younger. "Thanks," he murmured. "The baby woke up and I changed him. Would you like to hold him, or should I put him back in his bed?"

Mouth dry, she held out her arms. "I'll take him. Go have your shower."

Of course, his arm brushed her breast as he passed Caleb to her. Of course, she had to suppress a shudder, which if she thought about it was nothing short of ridiculous.

Taking a seat in the rocking chair still warm from his body, she shook her head and kept her eyes on the adorable slumbering baby. She refused to watch Garrett walk away and told herself to act less like the foolish girl she'd once been and more like the woman she'd become.

Somehow, the repetitive motion of the rocking chair lulled her into a doze. She started at the sound of Garrett rummaging in his backpack.

"Sorry." He shot her a sideways glance, a hint of a smile curling his lips. "I didn't mean to wake you. I need to check in with my team. Since I have to go to the top of the hill to get cell reception, I might as well check out the conditions out there."

About to protest, she bit her lip and nodded instead. "Be careful," she said, keeping her voice neutral. "That ice can be pretty treacherous."

Busy getting suited up in his coat and boots and gloves, he nodded. "Be back as soon as I can. Lock the door after me." And without looking back, he opened the door and left.

Turning the dead bolt, Michelle wondered why she felt like crying.

Outside, the clear air was so cold it hurt his lungs at first to breathe. Garrett stopped and took a long look at the pristine purity of the white, snow-covered landscape. He took a step, the crunch of his foot as it sank helping him judge how much ice the snow hid.

All around him, tree branches drooped and groaned under the weight of the ice. He could see several had already fallen, some larger ones blocking the road up to the cabin. Turning in a slow circle, the sunlight making dazzling diamonds of the snow, he looked for the hill that Michelle had said he needed to climb. Since the little cabin sat in a valley, there were three to choose from.

He grabbed a long stick to use to check the ground ahead of him. Surprisingly, he made it to the top without any problems and turned, noting it had been much steeper than it appeared from the cabin. Speaking of which, he could see it below, little puffs of smoke coming from the pipe chimney that vented the woodstove.

For a heartbeat he stood there and drank in the scenery. His view looked like something from a Christmas card. Rustic and perfect and cozy, albeit cold. Digging his cell phone from his pocket, he peeled off one glove and punched in the number for the Special Agent in Charge, a guy they all called Dunn.

"The state has pretty much shut down due to the ice," Dunn told him, after Garrett filled him in on his own situation with no power or cell reception. "Power is out all over the region and we don't know when it might return. The state police are asking everyone to keep off the roads. I need you to stay on top of things, keep an eye out, just in case."

"Of course." Briefly, Garrett considered asking Dunn to send in reinforcements, as more agents would mean better protection. But the same issue that might be keeping them safe also would make it difficult for other agents to reach them. Not only had downed tree limbs blocked the road in, but judging from the amount of ice that had fallen, main highways would be impassable.

"Garrett, we think they might have split up," Dunn continued. "Each one going after one child. Wayne has—"

Static garbled Dunn's voice into indecipherable noise. "Dunn?" The call went dead. Breathing a curse, Garrett checked his cell signal. No bars. Garrett secured his phone and pulled on his glove. Even though his hand had been unprotected less than a few minutes, it had already gone numb. He flexed his fingers to get the circulation going and turned to head down to the cabin and his two charges.

When he returned, Michelle let him in, not bothering to hide the anxiety in her expression. He stepped inside, exchanging the cold, crisp scent of freshly fallen snow for the slightly smoky warmth of the cabin.

"The electricity is out everywhere in this area," he

told her. "My contact didn't have any idea how long until it will come back on."

She nodded, her gaze never leaving his face. "Any word on Pitts?"

"No. My call dropped, but I think it's safe to assume that he and his brother are still at large." Taking a deep breath, he removed his gloves then his coat. "Apparently, they've split up. At least the roads—especially the ones leading up into the mountains—are impassable. Which makes it difficult, if not impossible, for Pitts to reach us."

His words didn't appear to soothe her. "What about a snowmobile?"

He stared. "That's always a possibility, but it's highly unlikely—"

"Is it?" She cut him off. "I think it's better to be prepared for the worst-case scenario, don't you?"

"Okay." He had to hand it to her. "Good thinking. We'll keep that possibility under consideration. The great thing about snowmobiles is how loud they are. We'll be able to hear him coming when he's miles away."

"True." She took a seat at the little square kitchen table and motioned him to do the same. Flexing his fingers to hasten the return of his circulation, he did.

"Let's try and outline some sort of plan," she told him, lacing her fingers on top of the table. "I feel better when I have an idea of what to do."

Again, he liked her rational way of thinking. Once, Michelle had been a fly-by-the-seat-of-her-pants sort of girl.

"Here are our potential scenarios," he said. "One, Pitts and his brother walked into the storm on foot and froze to death."

"Which no one thinks is realistic."

"Exactly." Unable to help himself, he reached across the table and touched the back of her hand. "Possibility two—Pitts called someone with the phone he stole, and he and they were picked up and taken somewhere warm."

She kept her hand still as she nodded, her green gaze intent. "And then what?"

"Beyond that, it's anyone's guess. They could still be holed up, waiting for the storm to pass. They could have gotten into a four-wheel drive truck or jeep and decided to take a chance on the ice, when it'd be more difficult for law enforcement to catch them. Or—" he dipped his chin in her direction "—they might have located a couple of snowmobiles and took off in them. Apparently separately, since Wayne was spotted without Kent."

Lowering her head, she sighed. When she lifted her chin and combed her fingers through her wavy hair, he ached to follow them with his.

"What I don't like about this is the way I feel like a sitting duck," she explained. "We should be doing something, even if it's only going on the run."

"Which we can't. Not with Caleb. It wouldn't be safe to try and go anywhere with this ice, never mind with an infant in tow."

"I know." Instead of defeated, she sounded determined. "So we need to be prepared for the possibility that he's going to show up here."

"I am prepared." He showed her his holstered pistol. "I also have a shotgun, broken down in my bag."

"I have a gun, too," she said, surprising him. "And I know how to use it."

"Good. I'm glad to hear it. But the main thing you need to do is protect that baby." He jerked his head in Caleb's direction. "Because he's going to be Pitts's focus.

You and I are merely collateral damage. He wants his son dead."

"What kind of a monster..." She let the words trail off, momentarily closing her eyes. She got up, went to the cupboard and retrieved two plastic glasses. Filling them at the tap, she handed him one. "We're lucky the pipes haven't frozen."

Accepting the drink, he gave her a wry grin. "Don't jinx it."

She nodded and took a long gulp of her water. He couldn't help but watch the graceful lines of her throat as she swallowed. He still found everything about her beautiful. And sexy. How in the hell had he been stupid enough to ever let her go?

"You know," he said, his voice steady despite the increase in his heart rate. "We can't keep dancing around what happened. We made love, MM. We need to talk about what's going on with us."

Chapter 4

Kent kept a smile on his face and his hands tight on the steering wheel. Under normal circumstances, the address on the phone wouldn't have been difficult to find. But even though it seemed as though only a few minutes had passed, the weather deteriorated rapidly. Sleet and ice mixed with snow and a gale-force wind dropped visibility to next to nothing. He was forced to creep along, keeping his speed super slow, so he wouldn't slide off the road and end up in a ditch like the prison transport van.

The radio blared a warning asking all citizens to stay off the roads. Easy to see why—only a fool or a man with a mission would even attempt to drive in near-whiteout conditions.

But Kent wasn't worried—after all, he was Kent Pitts, mouthpiece and leader of The Sword. And he did have a mission.

Kent flicked off the radio. Nothing else mattered. Kent had a duty to protect what he owned. Everything—the compound, his wives and his offspring, belonged to him. And as such, were his to do with as he saw fit. He would not allow his children to suffer, to live among The Enemy and let their unenlightened nonsense poison their young hearts.

Better off they die while they were still unspoiled, still pure. He knew all too well the evil that could happen to children in foster homes.

The whoop of a siren made his heart leap in his throat. Easing the pickup as close to the shoulder as he could, he watched as a marked police car pulled around him, lights flashing. The driver had been too intent on the road and his destination to pay any mind to a lone man driving a weathered pickup truck.

Kent knew where the cop was heading. Toward his home, The Sanctuary of the Sword. Violated, now. Rage filled him, violent and so strong he clenched his teeth and made his jaw ache.

They would pay. All of them. After he'd ensured his children had been set free, he planned to locate his secret stash of dynamite and make himself into a human bomb. He'd never been one to go out quietly. At least this way, the rest of the foolish world would never forget his name.

The truck fishtailed. He corrected, realizing he'd managed to lose his tranquility and while distracted, press too hard on the accelerator. Now that he'd eased off, he crept along at a safe snail's pace, confident that he'd make it to his destination unscathed. And undetected. No doubt the authorities were still scrambling around the area where the van had gone off the road.

Despite his abysmally slow speed, unable to see more than a few feet in front of him, he felt the truck begin to slide. Turning the steering wheel, confident it would straighten out, he was shocked when the entire truck continued past the edge of the pavement, turning once, twice and finally slamming in to a huge tree.

His seat belt did its job restraining him, though the way his head and neck jerked, he knew he'd have whiplash.

Minor inconvenience, he told himself. The engine still ran, and since the rear of the truck had taken the impact, it would only be cosmetic damage.

Shifting into Reverse, he pressed his foot gently on the accelerator. The wheels spun, kicking up more snow, and while the vehicle shimmied a little from side to side, it rapidly became clear the truck wasn't going to move.

Fine. Refusing to worry, well aware he could not, would not, be thwarted, he turned the key and cut off the engine.

Outside, the wind howled, buffeting the pickup, making him wonder what it would do to him once he stepped into it. In the end, though, he knew it didn't matter. Those given great destinies were always spared death by the elements.

Glad of the woolen hat, heavy coat and gloves, he abandoned the truck and headed into the woods. The map he'd used on the phone had indicated the address was over the nearest hill, in a valley. Surely, he could make it there on foot.

Michelle froze, struggling not to show any of the tumultuous emotions that rushed through her at his words. *We made love*, he'd said.

"It was nothing." She spoke the lie in a quiet voice, proud that she kept it steady. "Just something that happened due to extenuating circumstances."

To her shock, he laughed. A deep, rich masculine laugh that made her toes curl in her warm boots. "Blame it on what you want, but when we came together again, it was a hell of a lot more than nothing."

Heaven help her, but pleasure surged through her at his words, the unexpected warmth making her face pink. It amazed her the way such a simple statement could make her feel as if her entire body had caught on fire.

"What I meant," she began, hoping for at least quiet dignity, "was that I completely get that just because the two of us gave in to desire, nothing has changed."

"Hasn't it?" He leaned across the table, the husky undertone in his voice making her mouth grow dry. "Don't you find it unusual the way we, even after not seeing each other for five years, can pick right back up as if we were still together?"

Resisting the urge to fan herself, she could feel the twin flags of color blazing on her cheeks. "We're not together, Garrett. And you know as well as I do that lack of passion was never one of our problems."

He tilted his head while he considered her words. She fought the urge to squirm in her seat, unsure why even talking about this made her so uncomfortable.

Maybe the fact that even discussing it had her craving him again. She curled her hands into fists, her nails digging into her palms, to keep from reaching for him.

In fact, she thought as she glanced at the baby, she needed some kind of distraction. A baby crying or...

"Wait. What's that?"

Outside, somewhere in the distance, the whir of some kind of motor or machine could be heard.

A snowmobile? She swallowed hard, feeling sick. The rush of adrenaline made her shaky.

Garrett jumped to his feet. "Don't move," he ordered, grabbing his coat as he rushed toward the door.

For one stunned second, she did exactly as he'd asked and froze.

Then, muttering to herself, *To hell with this*, she got up and went for her gun. If Kent Pitts thought he could just come crashing in here and destroy little Caleb, he'd have to go through her first.

Though it felt a bit melodramatic, once she had her pistol in her hand, she instantly felt calmer. More focused. She dragged the rocking chair over by the makeshift crib, positioning herself between the sleeping baby and the door and windows.

Now, if Pitts somehow managed to overcome Garrett to make his way inside, she'd be ready.

Garrett. He wouldn't make careless mistakes, she knew. Honestly, despite the awkwardness of their shared past and the attraction that clearly still simmered between them, she couldn't think of anyone else she'd want protecting her and Caleb.

No way would Pitts get past him.

The noise cut off, sounding still a good distance away. But with the hilly mountains on three sides, noises were distorted sometimes. She couldn't really judge if the whirring motor had drawn closer or not.

A slight creak on the boards of the front porch was her only warning.

Tensing, she brought her weapon up to bear on the front door.

Garrett stepped inside, brushing snow off his coat. He stopped when he saw her, his expression registering surprise. "All clear," he said, his voice clipped and precise.

Heart hammering, she lowered her weapon and clicked the safety back on. "Just taking the necessary precautions," she said, hating the breathless tinge to her voice.

He watched while she slid the pistol back in its holster. "That noise is a chain saw," he told her. "Someone on the other hill is trying to clear his driveway."

She nodded, refusing to feel foolish. "I'm glad."

Praying he wouldn't reinitiate the earlier discussion, she checked once more on the still-sleeping baby and then got busy seeing what she could save from the fridge and freezer.

"You can probably put the meat out in the snow and it'll stay frozen." He spoke from behind her—too close, close enough to see the way she started nervously.

Glad for something to do, she reached into her freezer and handed him the still frozen—though barely—pork roast, beef tips and preformed turkey patties. "Here. Would you mind taking care of that for me?"

"Not at all." From the wry quirking of one corner of his mouth, she could tell he knew what she was doing. She didn't care. She'd do whatever it took to avoid having a heart-to-heart, semiserious talk with him. Doing so would serve no purpose than to cause them both pain.

While he dealt with burying the meat in the snow, she carried the remaining package of chicken pieces over to the sink. Some running water and this would be thawed enough for her to cook for lunch.

Then she rummaged through the fridge to see what else she could salvage. She had a couple of decent-sized potatoes she could bake, plus canned spinach.

Garrett returned and after stomping his boots on the porch, he took a seat. "Awaiting further instructions," he teased.

She flashed him a deliberately short smile. "Great. If I find something else for you to do, I'll let you know."

He leaned back, muscular arms behind his head, and nodded. She found it incredibly hard not to get lost in his overwhelming masculinity.

If she kept herself busy, Michelle could handle the silence. Sort of. But with Garrett sitting on the fake leather couch making the already tiny room seem even smaller, she couldn't seem to turn off her über awareness of him.

Maybe it was the way his blue-eyed gaze seemed to follow her everywhere she went. Or perhaps it was due to the fact that she knew he still wanted to talk to her.

Luckily, preparing lunch took as long as she could drag it out. But finally, she had the chicken and cut-up potatoes simmering in cream-of-mushroom soup on top of the woodstove. When they were nearly done, she'd add the drained can of spinach. It might be pretty basic, but it should be tasty.

"Smells great," he said.

The simple comment clogged her throat with emotion. She managed to choke out a thanks, keeping her back to him while stirring the meal more than she needed to.

The unexpected intimacy of the scene affected her more than it should have. They were trapped in a small cabin during an ice storm. What had she expected? Not this. After so many years, his presence should make her feel so many tangled and conflicted emotions.

"Maybe we should talk," she heard herself say, turning just in time to see him push himself to his feet.

Throat dry, she stood while he moved across the few

feet that separated them. Part of her thrilled at the way he towered over her, making her remember how he'd always made her feel secure and protected.

"About our past," she began, half turning toward the stove. "We should leave it alone. It's where it belongs, behind us."

"I don't agree." His quiet response made her catch her breath. "Clearly there's still something between us."

Suddenly unbearably weary, she shook her head. "Why rehash this now, Garrett? Just because we're stuck together in this cabin doesn't mean forever. You know as well as I do what's going to happen as soon as the Pitts brothers are captured."

His shuttered expression revealed none of his thoughts. "No, I don't. Why don't you tell me?"

"I'll take Caleb and go back home to Ohio. And you, you'll return to your job and your life, wherever that may be."

"I work out of the Clarksburg office," he said. "Right here in West Virginia. I have for the last four years."

She waited, but he didn't elaborate. Well, damned if she was going to say anything else. She remembered how he'd used to laughingly tell her he loved the way she rambled and talked about nothing.

Of course, he'd loved her then. Or so she'd thought.

"Why'd you go, MM?" he asked, his gaze steady. "You barely even told me goodbye."

"Don't. This is exactly what I meant when I said I didn't want to rehash the past. What's the point?"

Her protest came from the heart. Even five years later, thinking about what had happened to them brought nothing but pain.

"You wouldn't even talk about it," he continued.

"There was nothing to discuss. You wanted one life and I wanted another. You also agreed that we wouldn't be a good fit." And that had hurt most of all—she'd never forget the way he'd looked at her, the bemused contempt on his handsome face.

Though he nodded, he didn't offer an apology or words that he thought might have comforted her.

"After you'd told me that, what else was there to say, to discuss?"

"I was wrong," he said.

For a heartbeat, she couldn't move, couldn't breathe. When she found her voice again, she prayed it wouldn't shake. "Maybe you were, maybe you weren't. It no longer matters."

At that, he moved closer. "Look at me," he ordered, his large fingers cupping her chin and raising her head. "Look at me and say that again. You never were able to lie to me."

She'd had enough. Jerking away, she stumbled, her hand instinctively going out to break her fall. She connected with the edge of the pan and the hot stove.

"Yow." Despite the pain, she managed to muffle her scream. As her hand throbbed, she blinked back tears. "It's burned. I've got some aloe vera gel in my medicine bag over there. Will you please bring me that and a bandage?"

While he went looking for the items, she turned on the sink tap and waited for the water to reach a mild, cool temperature. She then stuck her hand under the running water. Instantly the pain eased.

As she watched the water flow over her hand, she noted the red and pink of the burn. Disgusted at her own clumsiness, she tried to thank Garrett for finding the aloe vera and bandage, but he shook his head. "Let me see it."

He took her hand in his, inspecting the damaged skin. "Good thinking with the water." He turned off the tap.

"Thanks. Now I just need the gel. If I slather it on and then bandage it, it'll go a long way to help it heal."

"You sound like you speak from experience."

Blinking back tears, she nodded.

"Let me," he said. Gently, he put the aloe vera on her hand. The coolness of the gel soothed instantly.

"Don't rub it in," she told him, her voice more shaky than she would have liked.

"Okay."

She watched his long fingers as he unwound the bandage, bracing herself in case he wrapped too tightly. But his touch felt surprisingly tender as he wound the gauze. By the time he'd finished, her legs felt boneless and her body had gone wet.

"I just don't understand this—" she began. Before she could finish, he covered her mouth with his and kissed her again.

She let herself get lost in the feel of his lips on hers, aching for more. The smell of lunch cooking brought her back to her senses.

Glad for an excuse to turn her back to him, she moved over to the stove to check on the chicken. It was nearly finished, and she needed to put in the spinach. She kept busy, feeling his gaze on her the entire time.

"The baby's still sleeping," Garrett told her. "I just checked on him."

"Thank you." She refused to look at him.

Once the table had been set, she moved the one-pot

meal to a platter and placed it on the table. "Dig in," she said, her voice way too bright.

If he noticed, he didn't comment. "Looks great." She noticed he also sounded a bit forcibly cheerful. What did that mean? Was it possible she affected him as strongly as he did her?

Then again, she reminded herself, what did it matter? If only she could look at this a different way, like having a fun fling from the man in her past. Which she might have been able to do if her emotions weren't so deeply involved.

She loved him. She'd always love him. She realized the truth. Despite severing all ties years ago, she hadn't been able to cut the hold he held on her heart. She wondered if she ever would, or if she was destined to spend the rest of her life loving a man who'd never feel the same way about her.

Chapter 5

If Kent Pitts had shown up in the doorway right now, Garrett would have welcomed the chance to take him down. Hell, he needed to move. To punch something. In the short time he'd spent with Michelle, she already had him tied up in knots.

Outside, darkness had fallen. Night came early this time of year. With the morning light, he'd hike back up to the top of the ridge and take another look at their situation.

Meanwhile, they were stuck here together in a cabin not much bigger than a two-car garage.

He took a look around the room, seeing the place with fresh eyes. Clearly a rental, sparsely furnished, no doubt meant to be used as a hunting cabin or a place for skiers to stay. He'd been told Michelle had rented it to be close to The Sword compound and her baby sister.

According to the report on file with the bureau, she'd made several unsuccessful attempts to get her sister out. She'd even gone so far as to hire a deprogrammer, a woman who specialized in helping young people who'd been brainwashed by a cult acclimate to real life.

Michelle had truly believed she'd get her sister out. Garrett had believed it, too. He'd spent six months undercover, trying like hell to gain Kent and Wayne Pitts's trust. He'd just started to make progress when the raid had gone down.

No one—Garrett least of all—could have imagined what Kent would do with his back against a wall. He might be delusional and drunk on his own power, but Garrett hadn't pegged him for a killer. And Garrett usually had pretty damn good instincts about people.

For the first time in his entire career, he'd failed. His miscalculation had cost two young women their lives. He would never forgive himself for that.

So why did he even begin to think Michelle could?

"TV would be nice," Michelle said, a note of wistfulness in her voice. He got what she meant. They needed a distraction—something to prevent them from feeling the need to break the silence with talking.

Especially since even talking about making love brought back the ache to do it again.

He needed to keep his mind where it belonged—on protecting the woman and child. And if he got really lucky, capturing Pitts.

With his resolve strengthened, he felt much better. Until he caught a glimpse of Michelle tidying up, and all he could think about was the feel of her body under his.

"Remember when I used to come over while you

took care of Kayla and Chris?" Her soft-voiced comment brought memories rushing back.

He made his expression blank. "Yes. Why?"

"I was wondering how they were doing now. When you and I lost touch, I thought of them often. Are they well? I imagine they must be getting pretty big now…"

Catching sight of something in his eyes, the gut-wrenching sorrow he couldn't quite conceal, her voice trailed away.

"Georgia took off with them when I was at work. This was right after you and I split up. I haven't seen them since."

Heaven help him, she came closer. She knew all too well the pain of the double loss. She laid her hand on his shoulder. "I'm sorry. I know how much you loved those kids."

Though he knew better, he couldn't keep from leaning into her touch. "I've never stopped looking for them. With all the resources I have at the FBI, you'd think I'd have gotten some kind of lead, but no. Nothing. It's like they dropped off the face of the earth." He didn't say what he feared—that his sister and niece and nephew were dead.

"Maybe Georgia cleaned up her act and is living a mainstream, small-town life somewhere," she said, even though they both knew this was unlikely.

"What about you?" he asked, desperate to distract her, since her nearness and her scent were about to drive him crazy with longing.

She stared, her frown making a tiny crease in her forehead. "What do you mean?"

"Well, you pretty much know everything about me

and my life since we broke up. While I know absolutely nothing about yours."

Her smile contained absolutely no humor. "So I'm guessing you're trying to tell me that your life for the past several years has been nothing but work?"

Pretending not to notice she hadn't answered his question, he nodded. "You remember how I told you I wanted to focus on my career. Well, I did. End of story."

"Sounds kind of lonely," she said softly, watching him with that particular kind of intensity he remembered from the days when they'd been inseparable.

He managed to shrug. "I never said I was a monk. I dated here and there, as my schedule allowed. What about you?"

Her wry smile told him the casual tone he tried for apparently didn't fool her. "Are you asking me if I'm involved with someone? Because if you are, I don't see how that's any of your business."

Now it was his turn to chuckle. "Actually, you just answered me."

"No, I didn't."

The token protest sounded weak, most likely because she knew he had her.

"Seriously, though, I really am wondering what you've been up to since I saw you last. Did you ever go back and get your masters so you could become a nurse-practitioner?"

Slowly, she nodded. "After my parents died—I'm guessing you knew about that, even though it happened after we'd gone our separate ways—I tried my best to raise Lydia. She was only thirteen when they were killed—"

"In a car crash, right?"

She swallowed and nodded. "Not even a month after we split up." Which meant she'd been grieving not only him, but her parents. "Lydia took it hard. She always was a wild child, but I tried my best to help her." The stark sorrow in her beautiful green eyes made him ache to hold her.

"She graduated high school," she continued, a note of bitter pride coloring her voice. "She even got a free ride to West Virginia University. Instead of going to college, right after she turned eighteen, she joined The Sword."

Though parts of this he knew from the various case files he'd had to read before beginning his undercover assignment, he'd only been given dry facts, not the complicated nuances from real life.

"So you moved here to this cabin to be near her?"

"I found this rental cabin, and it's close enough to the compound that if she'd wanted to leave, she'd have a place to go." He watched her struggle to maintain her composure. "But she never did. I don't know if she ever would have."

"Do you still live in Ohio?"

She nodded. "My parents left me the house. Lydia and I were happy, I thought. I worked and she attended school. I made sure she never wanted for anything."

"How'd she get involved with The Sword?" he asked. The FBI had suspected Pitts and his cronies used attractive young male members to recruit young women. He figured this had happened to Lydia.

Michelle shrugged. "She met a guy. Named Charles. Cute kid. I even liked him. Of course I had no idea he was part of The Sword. When Lydia ran off two days after graduation, I thought she'd gone off to get married. But no. They actually had her write me a letter renouncing our entire life together." This time she didn't even try to hide the hurt in her voice. "Even though it had no legal validity, it still felt like she'd ripped my heart out."

"I'm sorry."

She continued as if she hadn't heard him. "Once I learned where she was, I tried everything I could to get her out. But she was eighteen. An adult. And since she hadn't been taken forcibly, there was nothing I could do. Nothing at all."

Damn it all to hell. He went to her and pulled her into his arms and held her. Just held her. "You're a good woman, MM," he told her, his voice gruff.

"No. Don't say that, because I'm not." Surprising him, she pulled out of his arms. "I wasn't good enough to save my sister."

He had nothing to say to that, no comforting response, no soothing platitude. Because in the end, when it all came down to it, he hadn't been good enough to save her sister, either.

Michelle had never been so uncomfortable as she'd felt when Garrett had begun questioning her about her past. It was one thing to keep their time together on a casual basis, admitting they both felt the same wild pull of attraction, as long as it didn't go deeper than that.

Talking to him about her life after he'd left felt wrong. Too personal. And damn him, the way he tried to comfort her when her emotions brimmed too close over the edge made her want to accept his offer of solace.

Not again. Never again.

Because no matter what, in the end, once you got past all the "he saids" and "she saids," losing Garrett had hurt her more than she could bear to remember. Even now, so many years later, the anguish still felt fresh. She knew on the heels of losing her sister, she couldn't bear to experience such pain again.

All of a sudden, the quiet in the room was broken by a high-pitched whine and then the sound of the television playing the five o'clock news way too loud.

Stunned, they stared at each other for a moment.

"The power's back on," she said, even though pointing it out wasn't actually necessary. "I can't believe our luck."

"Don't get too excited yet." He didn't appear as overjoyed. "There's no telling how long it will last. West Virginia is a bit different than Ohio. Out here, every winter, the rural farms and homesteads lose power for days. Sometimes it comes and goes. That's why most of them have generators."

"Which this cabin does not."

"Exactly."

With all the lamps on, the room suddenly seemed overly bright, which made the ancient furniture appear even shabbier, the colors leached from cozy to dull.

"I think—" she began.

"Wait. Listen." Garrett pointed toward the TV.

"And the search continues for cult leader Kent Pitts. One of the guards injured in the crash remains in serious condition."

Michelle moved closer, eyeing the way the news showed a photo of the aerial search that had resumed.

"Law enforcement agencies all over the state are on alert," the newscaster continued. "So far, there has only been one sighting of the man. With the recent ice storm and blizzard, some speculate he might have frozen to death."

The anchorwoman managed to say this matter-of-factly, but with a hint of cheer. "And now on to various school and business closings, as well as streets and roads that are impassable," she continued. "As always, authorities are urging everyone who can stay at home to please do so."

Garrett swore softly under his breath and grabbed the remote, clicking the TV off. "I can't believe no progress has been made in locating either of them."

She exhaled. "I'm disappointed, too. Strange she didn't mention Kent's brother, Wayne, though...But at least we have electricity, no matter how temporary."

Though he gave a cursory nod, she could tell his thoughts were miles away.

She didn't blame him. She needed to clear her head as well. "Would you mind doing me a favor?" she asked. "Could you keep an eye on Caleb for a few minutes? I'd like to step outside and get some air."

"No." His sharp reply gave her pause. "It's too dangerous out there."

"I can handle it," she scoffed. "Remember, I've been here a couple months. I'm very familiar with the terrain."

"I wasn't talking about the snow and ice. What would you do if you encountered Pitts? You'd be alone and defenseless."

She shrugged and opened the end table drawer. "Then I guess I'd better bring my SIG Sauer."

Eyeing the gun, he appeared at a momentary loss for words. "I really wish you'd reconsider," he finally said. "I can't leave Caleb alone to come help you if you get in trouble."

"I won't." Eyeing his chiseled features and the coolness in his eyes when the familiar zing of attraction hit her, she also felt a hollow sense of emptiness. "Look, Garrett. I just lost my sister. Caleb has given me something to live for. I promise I'll be careful. I just need to get outside for a minute or two, take in some fresh air."

"Will you stay within eyesight of the cabin?" His clipped, professional tone worried her more than if he'd tried to cajole or tease her.

"I think so." She answered as honestly as she could. "But I'd really like to climb that hill out back and check out what's going on outside this little valley."

He jerked his head in a nod, the muscle working in his jaw telling her exactly how he felt about that.

The masculine beauty of his clear-cut profile made her long to trace her fingers across his skin. She'd loved him once, loved him so thoroughly and so deeply she'd never gotten over him. She loved him still. She guessed she'd always love him.

Yet another sense of loss swept over her, so profound she nearly went to her knees. How well she knew him, even now, even after being apart for so many years. He understood that losing Lydia had felt like losing her own child. That grief would overwhelm her if she let it. Which she would not.

She considered herself a strong woman, and knowing baby Caleb depended on her was the only thing that kept her from completely breaking down.

Inhaling deeply, she took stock. The past was the past, and she could do nothing to change it. She couldn't prevent Lydia from joining The Sword any more than she could have made Garrett stay. Even so, she wished Garrett had never come here, that the FBI had assigned some other agent instead. What right did he have to rip open old wounds? Her battered heart could hardly take any more. She hadn't even had much of a chance to properly grieve the loss of her sister.

Grabbing her down-filled jacket where it hung on the oak coat tree by the front door, she yanked it on and wound a scarf around her neck on the inside before zipping it up. Her gloves were in the pockets and she slipped them on.

"I'll be back," she said, turning to find him staring at her with an almost comical expression of dismay.

"Hot pink?" he asked. "You're going out there in a hot pink jacket?"

"Coral," she corrected automatically. "And this color is one of my favorites."

"It will make you an easy target."

"I'd think the opposite. Any hunter would see me, so I won't get accidentally shot."

He exhaled and shook his head. "If Pitts sees you, you'll lead him right here to this cabin."

That stopped her when nothing else could have. "You're right," she said, unzipping her jacket in defeat. "I can't go."

He must have taken pity when he saw her crestfallen expression. Or something. "You can use my parka," he said. "It'll be a little large, but if you don't stay out too long, it'll keep you warm enough."

She eyed his parka, the massive coat with FBI emblazoned on the back. "I—"

Caleb's cries saved her from deciding. She hurried over, scooping him up as he began wailing in earnest.

Without asking, Garrett went to the fridge and removed one of the bottles.

"Is it still cold enough?" she asked.

He nodded, heading toward the woodstove.

"Wait." She pointed. "Now that we have electricity, you can use the microwave. It's much easier."

"Got it." Jerking his head toward the door, he waved her away. "Go on, get your fresh air. I'll feed him, burp him and change him."

Still she hesitated, though she wasn't sure why. Clearly, Garrett had proven himself more than capable of caring for the baby.

Finally, she forced herself to turn and reach for his jacket. Of course, the arms hung down way past her hands. And she swore it carried his scent, an oddity considering he'd just been outside in the blistering wind and snow.

After rolling up the sleeves and tying the hood tight under her chin, she felt satisfied that she'd stay warm. "I'll be right back," she said without looking over at him, unsure what the sight of such a big, strong man cradling a tiny baby in his arms would do to her equilibrium.

The front door fought her as she struggled to push it open. Once she had, the wind nearly tore it out of her gloved hands. Somehow, she was able to grab it in time and force it back closed. Apparently, the brief lull was over.

Outside, conditions were worse than she'd even imagined. She immediately realized her idea of climbing the hill wasn't feasible—she could barely see her hands in front of her face.

Hunched over against the stinging ice of the storm, she forced herself to move forward, one struggling footstep at a time. She figured she'd barely moved ten feet when she decided to abandon her attempt. Who wanted to get fresh air in the middle of a blizzard anyway? Of course, snow had always exhilarated her, but this storm was more than just snow.

Turning slowly so she wouldn't lose her footing, she realized she couldn't even see the cabin. Luckily for her, the rapidly filling impressions her feet had made were still visible, so she made her way back.

By the time she reached the door, she felt like her feet and fingers had turned to ice. Fumbling with the latch, she managed to pull the door open and get inside.

Once closed, she turned the lock.

"That was quick," Garrett observed.

"I know." Pulling off her gloves, she went straight to the woodstove and held out her frozen hands. "It's crazy out there. I don't care what kind of help Kent Pitts has, there's no way he's going anywhere in this storm."

When Garrett didn't immediately answer, she swiveled her head to look at him. Still holding Caleb, he continued to rock the baby back and forth. She swore Caleb's sweet little face wore a blissful smile as he drank his bottle.

Garrett looked up and smiled. The power of that smile hit her low in her belly. "I changed him and he's just about done with his bottle. Then I'll burp him and see if I can get him to go back to sleep."

Struck dumb, she nodded. "I'll see about fixing us something for dinner."

That night, they ate well. With the electricity miraculously staying on, Michelle was able to cook pork chops with applesauce and red cabbage, along with a side of green beans.

The cabin smelled...like home. With the storm raging outside and them all warm and cozy inside, she felt peaceful. Happy, even. She wasn't sure how she felt about that.

Garrett offered to do the dishes since she'd cooked, and she let him.

They watched the late night news, both of them hoping for word of the Pitts brothers' capture, but all the newscaster did was repeat that the search was still ongoing, on a limited basis. They had no footage to show of it due to the extremely dangerous weather.

The area was also on a winter weather warning. "More on the way," a grim-faced meteorologist warned. Apparently, they were going to get slammed with another round of ice and snow, continuing for the next twelve to eighteen hours.

"Just what we need," Garrett said. "I was hoping we'd be able to get out of here soon."

She wouldn't allow herself to feel hurt that he couldn't wait to be rid of her. How silly was that anyway? She put more wood into the belly of the woodstove, planning to keep it going just in case the power went back out during the night. The constant scent of wood burning felt comforting.

And then, because looking at Garrett brought the past rushing back, she knew she had to attempt to find herself some sort of closure. Ever since the day Garrett had walked out of her life, she'd never gotten the chance to find out exactly why. All he'd said was that he didn't feel like their relationship was working out. He no longer wanted to get married. And then he'd gone. Just like that, without another word of explanation.

Maybe it was time she got one.

"Remember when…" she began.

"No." Garrett cut her off. "You were right. I don't want to talk about the past."

Trying not to feel hurt, she eyed him. "But I realized the past is all we have. There are a few questions I'd like answered."

His silence told her she might have wounded him. Or else he just didn't care.

"MM," he finally said. "Our breakup hurt me, too."

Chapter 6

Stunned, it was her turn to stare. "Then why did you end it? I would have followed you anywhere, done anything, as long as I could be with you."

He looked down, turning his hands over and studying his palms. When he finally raised his head and met her gaze, the pain in his blue eyes astonished her. "I broke up with you because you wanted more than I could give. Hell, you deserved more."

The fierceness in his voice told her he believed what he said. Confused and perplexed, she swallowed. "Garrett, all I ever wanted was you."

"That's not true. You wanted children, a family. And if anyone deserved to have those things, baby, you do."

"I wanted them, yes. But only with you."

He exhaled and looked away, the lines of his jaw rigid. "Don't you understand? You know where I came from. You've seen with your own eyes. I couldn't take the risk."

Disbelieving, she stood and crossed to him. "What risk? I saw how you were with Kayla and Chris. You even tried to be a father to Georgia, despite her being so much older than you. You gave them what they needed the most—love and a sense of family. I always used to marvel and think how you'd be the most amazing dad when you had children of your own."

"What?" He sounded so shocked she had to smile, just a little. "My father was an abusive alcoholic with an explosive temper. You were there. You saw."

"That was him." Aching, she reached out and lightly touched his face. "Not you. Never you."

He started to shake his head, but she stopped him by covering his mouth with hers. "You're great with children. You always have been."

To her dismay, he wrenched himself away. "Sorry, but I'm not. I tried my best with Georgia's kids. I tried to shield them from my father and later from their own mother. That wasn't enough to save them in the end. I don't know where they are, if they're safe, or even if they're alive." His voice vibrated with emotion. "Even now, after all these years, I lie awake at night and wonder about them."

"I'm sorry." She swallowed hard, aching to hold him and aware she shouldn't. "But the fact that their mother disappeared with them isn't your fault. How could it be?"

A muscle worked in his jaw. "I failed to protect them."

"You were wonderful with them," she countered stubbornly. "You're kind and responsible. You're a good man, Garrett Ware. You always have been."

One corner of his mouth twisted in what she thought

might have been the beginning of a smile. "Thanks. Though I guess you wouldn't have said that five years ago when we split."

The past. Somehow, she managed to shrug. "I've done a lot of healing in five years," she lied. "But I have to tell you, seeing how good you were with Georgia's kids was one of the reasons I was shocked when you said you didn't want any of your own."

His eyes narrowed; he studied her.

"I've spent my entire life working on not being a parent."

"But why? I really don't get it."

"Don't you understand, MM? I thought losing you was the worst thing that could possibly happen to me. I thought you'd ripped my soul in half. I was about to come after you, but then my sister took her kids and disappeared. When Georgia took off with Chris and Kayla, it felt like I'd lost the second half of my soul. I couldn't take that kind of pain again. I won't."

"Sometimes love is worth the pain. I wouldn't trade the time I spent with Lydia for the world." She took a deep, shuddering breath, realizing she was on the verge of tears and aware she had to soldier on. "Yes, she's gone and yes, I'll miss her until the day I die." She sniffed and mustered what she hoped was a brave smile. "But now there's Caleb. I would die for him, you know. Who knows what the future will hold?"

"Don't say that." He glanced at the door. "No one is going to die. This time, that egotistical maniac is going down."

"I know." She spoke with as much certainty as he had. "And no matter what you believe, you'll always be a good man."

And then, because she didn't dare say anything else, she got to her feet and went to check the baby's diaper.

They spent the rest of the evening in silence, letting the numbing sound of the television buffer their thoughts.

Before going to bed for the night, she again tended to Caleb, making sure he'd been fed and had his diaper freshly changed, before she put him down for the night. During this, Garrett seemed more and more distant, which part of her appreciated. Attempting to understand the past had given her nothing, nothing at all.

So distant was good, she told herself, trying to keep from looking at him as she readied herself for bed. Despite that, her body ached for his warmth beside her under the covers.

Resolutely pushing the thought away, she went to the tiny bathroom to change into her flannel pajamas. When she returned, Garett had already gotten into his sleeping bag on the couch and turned his face away.

"Night," she muttered as she walked past him.

He grunted something unintelligible in response.

Though her sheets were cool when she slid between them, she knew they'd warm up soon. Closing her eyes, she willed herself to drift off to sleep.

The first loud crack in the middle of the night woke her up out of a sound sleep. Momentarily disoriented, she sat up in bed and rubbed her eyes. Groggy, she reached for the lamp on her nightstand. One click and she realized the power had gone out again. Blinking as her eyes got used to the darkness, she went and checked on the baby. Caleb still slept, completely undisturbed.

And then she smelled it. Smoke. More than the usual ever-present odor of the woodstove.

But where?

"Did you hear that?" Garrett's low voice told her the sound had woken him, too.

"Yes." Pushing to her feet, she started toward him. "And there's smoke."

"It's pretty thick, even though I don't see a fire." He coughed, sounding worried. "I smell it. I'm trying to find out where it's coming from."

Out of habit, she fumbled for the closest light switch, but nothing happened when she flipped it. "The power is out again."

"I know." Garrett's tone was urgent. "MM, I need you to get your coat and bundle up Caleb as best as you can. This is dangerous. We've got to get out of here until I can find the source of the smoke."

Out of here? She remembered the ferocity of the storm and almost protested. But since she didn't want to take a chance of being trapped in a burning cabin, she immediately did as he'd requested.

Taking care of Caleb first, she wrapped him in his blanket, swaddling him like a burrito. He didn't have a winter coat, assuming there even existed such a thing for infants. Once she had him wrapped up tight, she went for her own jacket. "Is there any chance that maybe the woodstove chimney is clogged, and that could have caused the smoke?"

"It's possible," he said. "That's one of the things I'm going to check out. Are you ready?"

Blinking in the dim light, she nodded. "I don't have a coat for Caleb. Is it all right if I take your sleeping bag for him, just in case we have to be outside longer?"

"Grab it," he ordered. "And come on. The two of you can wait in my truck while I figure this out."

She grabbed a couple of pairs of diapers and two bottles of premixed formula and threw them in her diaper bag. "Let's do it."

As she moved toward him, there was another creak, one that seemed to shudder along the entire building.

"MM..." Garrett began. Before he could finish, part of the ceiling caved in, crashing down on the bed she'd just left and on her.

The snow and debris knocked her off her feet. The rush of cold air shocked her. Stunned, she shook her head, trying to clear it.

"The roof fell in." Garrett. Moving around her and trying to remove the debris with his bare hands. "We've got to get him out."

At first, she didn't understand. And then her heart stopped. Her arms were empty. Baby Caleb was somewhere under the fallen roof. Buried.

Heart pounding, she dug like a madwoman. If she got to him quickly enough, he might still be alive.

And then, miraculously, she heard him cry.

More than wonderful, the cry picked up in intensity, becoming a wail. She and Garrett exchanged a quick glance and begin working in unison.

"There," Garrett said, staying her hand. "Let me. Somehow, two pieces of lumber landed together, making a shelter above him." Gently, he brushed the remaining snow away. "The sleeping bag is still wrapped around him. He's not even wet."

Relief flooded through her, and she shuddered over the sheer strength of it. As soon as Garrett removed the two wooden boards, she scooped up the baby, more grateful than she could ever express.

"MM, listen to me." The urgency in Garrett's voice

made her raise her head from her inspection of the baby and look at him. "We've got to get out of here. We're still not safe. The smoke is getting worse and the rest of the roof could collapse at any time."

She nodded. "Let's go."

The instant he pulled open the front door, a frigid blast of swirling snow and ice pelted them.

"Damn," Garrett swore. "Looks like the storm is not getting any better."

Heads down, they fought their way in the howling wind to Garrett's truck. Once inside, at least they had a bit of a respite.

"You okay?" Garrett asked, putting one gloved finger under her chin.

She nodded, intent on inspecting Caleb to make sure no ice or snow had touched his perfect baby skin.

"Good. Wait here. I'm going to go see what I can find out about the smoke and why the roof caved in."

"Why?" she asked. "What's the point? Clearly we can't stay there any longer."

A muscle worked in his jaw as he considered his next words. "We might have to. I need to check out how bad the damage is."

"Can you start the engine before you leave?" she asked, shivering. "We can use the car heater to help keep us warm."

"Not yet," he told her, handing her the ignition key. "I only had a quarter of a tank of gas when I got here. I meant to fill up, but couldn't find an open gas station. Don't waste fuel unless you have to."

She nodded. "Hopefully if there is a fire, this blowing snow will put it out. And who knows, maybe just a small portion of the roof caved in and you can fix it."

Even though she doubted the rest of the cabin could be salvaged, she felt the need to say something positive.

Without answering, he reached past her and retrieved a flashlight from the glove box. He clicked it on and off, apparently to check the batteries, then pushed open the driver's side door and headed back out into the swirling storm. She locked the doors behind him as a precaution.

The bitterly cold wind must have shocked little Caleb into silence. But now, swaddled in the down sleeping bag, he began making the mewling little sounds she recognized as being a precursor to his hungry cries.

She fished in her bag for one of the premade bottles and judged it too cold. Praying this would work, she stuck it inside her jacket, under her arm, hoping the warmth from her body might help.

Caleb's snuffles morphed into cries. Once he got going like this, he wouldn't stop until he'd been fed.

Again she checked the bottle. Not as cold, but still not warm. Still better. Caleb had scrunched up his little face, which had turned red as he wailed.

She hesitated, not knowing enough about the care and feeding of infants to know if semi-cold formula would hurt them. She suspected Garrett would know, and she tried like heck to comfort the hungry baby until he returned.

Finally, she couldn't stand Caleb's hunger anymore. Again she pulled the bottle out from under her jacket, praying it would be slightly warmer. Removing the plastic protective cap from the nipple, she gingerly offered it to the baby.

He latched on, suckling greedily. He didn't appear to notice the temperature. Relieved, she watched him eat.

The wind buffeted the truck, shaking it from side to

side like a ferocious dog worrying a bone. She tried to look for Garrett, but the blizzard made it impossible to even see the cabin only twenty feet away.

Caleb finished the bottle. Trying not to give in to her growing worry, she lifted him up and burped him. Where was Garrett? Why was he taking so long?

What would she do if he didn't come back? She couldn't go looking for him, simply because she couldn't leave tiny Caleb alone here. Sure, he'd probably be fine and warm in the down sleeping bag, despite the fact that the temperature inside the truck was freakin' cold and growing colder, but she'd worry too much leaving him.

Garrett had to come back. He just had to.

Finally, Michelle saw the glow of the flashlight highlighting the blowing and swirling snow. Garrett appeared at the driver's side. Quickly, she pressed the unlock button. He yanked the door open and hopped inside, slamming the door to try and keep as much of the wind out as possible.

This startled Caleb, who began to cry. Over the next several minutes, while Michelle tried to soothe him, Garrett attempted to brush snow off his ice-covered parka.

"It's not good," he told her once Caleb had quieted. "Looks like the woodstove venting pipe might have been clogged with creosote and it caught on fire. Part of the roof is gone, as you know. The snowstorm kept it from being worse, but as a precaution I went back inside with a panful of snow and made sure the woodstove fire is completely out. But the roof isn't patchable. It's too unstable."

She stared as the ramifications of this hit her. "There's

a big hole in the roof, there's no electricity and now the woodstove is out and can't be relit?"

With his grim nod, the knot in her stomach grew larger. "That about sums it up."

"What are we going to do?" She continued the side-to-side motion that seemed to quiet Caleb and which she found strangely soothing, as well.

Garrett sat quietly for a moment. "I don't know. Normally I say we take the truck and try to make it out of here, but in addition to the snow and ice, visibility is barely five feet. We can't risk it, not with him." He jerked his chin toward the baby. "We don't even have an infant seat."

She lifted her head at that. "Yes, we do. I bought one when I got diapers and formula, but it's still in the box."

"I still don't think attempting to go anywhere on these roads in this storm is a good idea."

"I don't, either. But do we even have a choice?" she argued. "We'll freeze to death if we stay in the cabin." Thinking, she tried to come up with an alternative. "I saw a storage shed or smaller cabin in the woods, not too far away. I'm pretty sure it has a chimney, which means there's a fireplace. We can try to make it to that."

She watched as he stared straight ahead, clearly turning things over in his mind.

"You're right," he finally said. "Though I don't like this a bit, we've got to at least try. How far up the road is the shed?"

She exhaled. "I'm not sure. I found it while I was walking in the woods. It's a bit farther up the next hill."

"Up." Again he considered. "If the roads are ice, we'll never make it up that hill."

"Maybe we can try going into town? Once we get out of this valley, the roads heading that way are all down."

"Let's just see if we can get out of this drive." His grim tone did nothing to reassure her.

"Will you go get the infant carrier? I'd feel much better if Caleb is protected."

"Where is it?"

"On the right side of the couch, still in the box."

"What about other supplies?" he asked.

"I think we have enough for a few days. But if you can grab anything else, go for it."

Face expressionless, he left again. She watched the glow of the flashlight until it disappeared.

After what seemed another small eternity, he returned, carrying the infant seat, upside down and out of the box.

"I have no idea how to install this thing," he told her once he was inside the truck. He lifted it high, turning to peer into the small backseat area of his club cab. "I know it goes back there, facing backward."

"I wish I could help you," she told him, unable now to keep her teeth from chattering. "If you brought the instructions, I can try. I'm great at following directions."

Instead, he gave her a hard look. "You're freezing."

"Aren't you?" she challenged. "At least Caleb seems warm enough."

"Wrap the sleeping bag around you, too."

"I don't want to disturb the baby."

Shaking his head, he put the key in the ignition and started the truck. It took several attempts, but finally the engine roared to life.

She reached to turn the heater on, but he stopped her

with his hand. "Give it a bit. Nothing but cold air will blow now. It needs a minute or two to warm up."

She nodded, wondering why she felt so darn cold, still struggling to keep from showing her almost violent shivering. Luckily, Garrett was occupied with installing the infant seat, so he either didn't notice or chose not to comment.

"There." He sounded triumphant. "I think that'll do it."

Reluctant to part with the sleeping baby and his warmth, she didn't move. "I'm going to wait until it's a bit less chilly in here."

At her words, a huge gust of wind rocked the truck, as if nature mocked her.

Finally, he judged the engine had warmed up enough and turned on the heater. As soon as he did, warm air began blowing into the cab.

"Thank you," she exclaimed softly, breathing a sigh of relief. "It's getting hotter by the second."

Again they waited until it felt toasty. "Go ahead and put the baby in the carrier."

Moving stiffly, she did exactly that. To her relief, Caleb continued to sleep, even while Garrett buckled him in.

When he'd finished, he turned to her. "This is not going to be easy, you realize that, right?"

"I know," she replied, certainty growing within her. "But you know what? If there's anyone I can trust with Caleb and my life, it's you."

Garrett's expression went from worried to bleak. "Don't." He bit out the single word.

"Don't what?"

"Don't look at me like you think I hung the moon

and the stars. I'm not all that. I couldn't even save your sister, though I'll do my damndest not to let you and her baby down."

The bitterness and pain in his voice stunned her. She'd been so wrapped up in her own grief, she hadn't stopped to consider the effect the raid had had on Garrett.

She considered her next words carefully, while pellets of ice pelted the truck. "Lydia's death wasn't your fault," she began. "I know you tried to—"

"Enough." Waving her away, he shifted the truck into Drive. "You weren't there. I was. Hold on. And if you're the praying kind, then pray."

Chapter 7

Michelle held her breath as he slowly backed the truck around, managing to turn it so they could drive down the winding driveway that lead to the main road.

"There are some limbs blocking about midway up, but those were what your neighbor was trying to cut with that chain saw," he told her, his hands so tight on the steering wheel that his knuckles were white. "Hopefully, he was able to clear enough of the road for us to pass."

Assuming they made it that far. Barely had the thought occurred to her when they began to slide sideways.

"Sheet ice. I'm not even touching the gas or the brake," he said, sounding as though his teeth were clenched, as he managed to swing the steering wheel around to the direction of the skid. They slowed and then stopped.

Heart in her throat, she nodded, glancing back at the still—miraculously—sleeping infant. They were going to be okay, she told herself. They had to be. Anything else was simply unacceptable.

Garrett managed to keep the truck straight. They made it fifty more feet without incident, and Michelle finally relaxed a little.

Just as she exhaled, the rear truck tires started spinning and they fishtailed. "I've got this," Garrett muttered.

Despite her fear, she couldn't help but admire the determination and confidence with which he drove.

Again, he corrected the vehicle. However, this time, as the truck spun back toward the road, they hit something.

Just that—a log, a rock, whatever it was—sent them careening off the road, sliding out of control, heading toward a strand of snow-covered trees.

"Hold on," Garrett ordered, trying to control their direction, even though he had to know there was little he could do.

Everything seemed to happen in slow motion. They hit the trees with a sickening crunch of metal. At least, they weren't moving fast. The jolt sent both of them forward, but their seat belts held.

So did the infant car seat. Thank goodness.

The engine sputtered, still running, even though there was a big dent in the right side of the hood.

Garrett swore. He shifted into Reverse and gently pressed the accelerator.

The wheels spun, but they didn't move. At all.

"I don't believe this," Garrett said, trying again. "We appear to be stuck."

"Maybe we should—" she began. Before she could finish, the engine died.

She and Garrett exchanged incredulous looks. He turned the key to Off, and then tried to restart. Nothing, no engine turning over, just a series of clicks.

"It's dead," he said, stating the obvious.

"I know."

"Crashing into that tree probably pushed the radiator into the front part of the engine."

"Is that fixable?"

He gave a short laugh. "Not here, not in these conditions."

Outside, the snow and wind and ice continued to dance around them, wickedly brutal and intense. Without the heater, the cold seeped in again, too.

Garrett pulled out his cell phone, cursing yet again. "Still no signal."

"Doesn't your vehicle have some kind of radio, like a CB or something? All the law enforcement ones on TV do."

"This is my personal truck," he replied. "I took it instead of my bureau car because it has four-wheel drive. Which isn't doing a damn thing to help us on this ice."

"Oh." She eyed the somehow still-sleeping infant. She refused to panic, tried to remain levelheaded and calm. "Well, if this truck isn't going to make it, I know my little car doesn't stand a chance. What are we going to do?"

He winced, and she saw her question had managed to wound him. "I don't see that we have any choice but to try to get back to the cabin. Even with no woodstove and a hole in the roof, we stand a better chance there."

Again she turned to look at Caleb.

"If we keep him bundled up in the sleeping bag, he'll be okay." The certainty in Garrett's voice made her feel slightly better. But only slightly.

"I know it's terrifying." He squeezed her shoulder. "We don't have a choice. We can do it. We haven't gone all that far. I doubt we're even a third of the way down the driveway."

Though she remembered how hard it had been earlier to walk just a few feet, she managed a nod. "What about Caleb?"

"Keep him in the carrier. He'll be safer there if we fall. We'll just bundle him up in the sleeping bag."

She nodded, though the idea of trying to travel on foot with a tiny infant seemed impossible. She said so.

"Nothing's impossible if your survival is on the line. If we stay here, we'll freeze to death. If we can get to the cabin, maybe we can cordon part of it off and build a fire to keep warm. If not, we're going to have to try to find that shed you mentioned."

"I saw a chiminea out on the back porch," she said. "We can drag that inside and   "

"First things first." Leaning way into the backseat, he managed to unhook the infant car seat. Since they'd already loosely laid the down sleeping bag over him as a sort of blanket, Garrett simply wrapped it around several times, making sure to leave an opening they could cover loosely so Caleb could breathe.

"Are you ready?"

Words stuck in her throat, so she nodded instead.

"Let's go." As he opened his door, she did the same.

The icy wind and snow once again stung her face; the stark shock of cold made her gasp for breath. She managed to push her door closed behind her, watching as Garrett pulled Caleb from the backseat, making sure he was covered before straightening up.

"Follow me," he said, loud enough for his voice to

carry over the raging weather. She nodded, grabbed the back of his coat so they wouldn't be separated, and they were off, hunching over as they pushed back the way they'd come.

Already the snow had grown deeper, and she sank, struggling to walk, trying not to slip on the ice under the snow. She had the weird feeling that if she fell, she'd never get up again.

Terrified and determined, she kept hold of Garrett's parka, stepping where he stepped, letting him do the hard work for her. She prayed baby Caleb would be safe, covered in the down sleeping bag, protected from the furious elements.

Somehow, by some ethereal grace, they made it. When the cabin suddenly miraculously appeared through the swirling, blowing snow in front of them, Michelle felt like sobbing with relief. Garrett hustled her through the front door.

Inside, the place was cold and dark. The bitter scent of smoke still lingered.

"At least we have shelter from the storm," Garrett pointed out.

"Ever the optimist," she said, carefully unwrapping Caleb. To her surprise, the infant's bright blue eyes were wide-open. He blinked up at her and made a cooing sound.

Instantly, she knew everything was going to be all right.

With the situation this dire, Garrett knew he had to keep everyone's spirits up. Their survival could very well depend on it.

"First thing we need to do is figure out how to keep warm," he announced. "What kind of cabin doesn't even have a fireplace? You said there was a chiminea outside?"

"Yes. Around the back, near the bench." She shook her head. "Which is probably buried under the snow."

"I'll find it." Glancing at the pile of wood they'd planned to use for the woodstove, he realized all the wood in the world would be of no use to them without a way to vent it. "On second thought, I don't know if that's going to work." He explained why.

After she listened, she glanced from Garrett to Caleb and back again. "Then what are we going to do?"

"I think our best bet is to figure out a way to repair the woodstove."

She grimaced. "How can that be safe? If creosote buildup caused a fire, all that will happen is another one."

Which meant they could freeze to death or die from smoke inhalation. Since she had a point, he looked around the small cabin to see if he could come up with some other ideas.

There were none. Finally, he decided. "Where is this shed you saw?"

"Up that way," she pointed. "That's all I can tell you. Before all the bad weather, I walked all over these woods. I found the building—either a storage shed or another, smaller cabin about halfway to that hill. It's all boarded up, so clearly not being used, but I'm pretty sure it has a stone fireplace, so we could build a fire to keep us warm."

For the first time since the roof collapse, hope blossomed inside him. "How far?" he asked. "Is it walkable for the two of us carrying Caleb?"

"I think so." She lifted her chin. "If we made it here from your truck, we can certainly get there. The only problem will be getting in. You'd have to pull the boards off the door and windows."

"I can handle that. How about this. You two stay here and I'll go check it out. No sense in you and the baby waiting outside in this storm while I try to break in."

She only stared at him. Recognizing that glint in her eyes as the beginning of a protest, he held up a finger to forestall her. "This might be our only chance of surviving," he said. "Which way?"

Finally, she nodded. "Go around the cabin to the back. There's a path. Even though it's snowed over, you should see the gap in the trees. I'd say it's a couple hundred yards into the woods."

He nodded. "Thanks. Wish me luck."

Her green-eyed gaze locked on his. "Luck. Please. Stay safe."

"You, too. This door doesn't have a lock."

"I have my gun," she replied.

Turning, he braced himself. Though the damaged cabin had grown cold, at least here they were sheltered from that banshee wind.

"Wait," she said, unwinding a white piece of wool from around her neck. "Take my scarf. You'll need it."

Realizing she was right, he accepted it and wrapped it around his neck and the lower half of his face. Now he was ready.

He took a deep breath and opened the front door.

Wind-driven ice stung him on the exposed areas of his face, stealing his breath. He ducked his head down, managing to drag the door closed behind him before moving forward. He stayed close to the cabin and tried to hug the wall as he fought his way through crusty and icy snow. Twice, his feet slipped and he almost went down, but both times he managed to right himself.

Once he reached the backyard, he saw the rusty old chiminea poking a bit out of the snow. Continuing past, hunched over against the ceaseless buffeting of the wind, he drew his hood tighter around his face, glad for the scarf. He caught himself wishing he had ski goggles to protect his eyes, but he didn't have the luxury of fixating on things he lacked. He needed to find them shelter, or he was almost certain they wouldn't make it.

Though swirling, drifting snow had covered any path that might have existed, Michelle was right about the gap in the trees. Even better, once he got into the woods, the dense forest would provide him a bit of break from the relentless wind.

Trudging forward, he kept moving. He could feel his feet getting numb and knew he'd better hurry. Easier said than done, struggling in this snow, trying not to slip on the ice underneath.

How much farther? The cold was seeping through the soles of his boots, and it might not be too long before frostbite started to set in.

Still, because Michelle's and Caleb's lives depended on finding shelter, he had no choice. He continued to push forward. Just when he thought he couldn't make it too much longer, he caught a glimpse of it, a peeling wooden structure not much larger than a storage shed, shrouded in white. And Michelle had seen correctly— the tiny building had a stone chimney. As he drew closer, he saw that the door and single window had indeed been boarded up, though haphazardly.

Briefly, he wondered why, and then since it didn't matter, he looked around for a stick or something to help him pry the boards away from the door.

He found nothing, so he muttered a quick prayer and grabbed hold of the first board with both gloved hands. And pulled. The wood must have been old and rotten or hadn't been nailed properly, because immediately he felt some give.

Two more tugs, and he had it off.

The second board didn't remove that easily, but he kept after it and soon the door was free. He tried the handle, more relieved than he could say when it turned. No lock.

Inside, he saw that the small structure appeared empty except for the cobwebs and dust. No furniture, yet a tiny kitchen had been installed in one corner—or at least a sink and stove. If there'd once been a refrigerator, that appliance was long gone. In another corner, shielded by what clearly were hastily constructed plywood walls, he found a small toilet, and what appeared to be a stand-up shower, minus the curtain.

Clearly, at some point in the past, this shed had been used for a guesthouse. He couldn't imagine why it had been abandoned, but for now he'd chalk it up to their good fortune.

A stack of crumbling logs had been placed in the fireplace. A few more were piled next to it. Even better. Dry wood.

The little building appeared sound. At the very least, it offered protection from the storm and potential to keep warm until they could leave.

Now he just needed to make it back and get Michelle and Caleb here.

Before he did, he decided to build a fire. Might as well get some warmth started. He removed one of his gloves and fished a lighter from his pocket, wishing for some crumpled-up old newspaper. Which he didn't have, so he concentrated on seeing if he could get the wood to catch. To his gratification, it did.

Soon, he had a decent blaze going, well contained and warm.

Satisfied, he headed out again to retrieve Michelle and the baby.

Maybe relief fueled him, or possibly the wind speed had gone down a notch. For whatever reason, getting back to the damaged cabin seemed easier this time. A load had vanished and lightened his heart, enabling him to smile at a wan and worried Michelle as he stomped the snow off his boots and went inside.

"I found it," he said. "I managed to get in fairly easily. It's empty, but seems solid. Even better, there's a working fireplace. No furniture, but wood. I've already got a fire going. We should be able to stay warm there, at least long enough until the storm stops."

Weariness ringed her eyes in black as she nodded. "Sounds good. How far away is it?"

"You look exhausted," he told her instead of answering her question, keeping his voice gentle. "Let me carry the baby."

Instead of handing him over, her arms tightened around Caleb. "I've got him."

Her protectiveness made his throat ache. "MM, it's slow going and cold. The storm isn't showing any sign of letting up. If you stumble and go down, Caleb could get hurt. Please. Let me help."

She only considered a moment before nodding. Getting up slowly, she crossed to him and handed up the still-bundled baby.

"Thank you. I've thrown some drinks and canned goods into my backpack. Grab baby formula and diapers and whatever else you think you might need."

She did exactly that, stuffing enough formula and diapers to last a few days into a duffel bag.

"Are you ready?" he asked. At her nod, he turned to head back out. "Hold on to the back of my coat and don't let go. I don't want to lose you."

"You won't." With strength returning to her voice, she sounded confident. "I'll be right behind you. Just keep Caleb safe."

"I will."

Though the newly fallen snow had attempted to erase much of his footsteps, enough remained that he was able to use them as a sort of path. Back to the shed they went, him keeping the small baby close and grateful for the feel of Michelle's hanging on to the back of his coat.

Once there, as soon as he stepped inside, he uncovered Caleb's face. He'd made sure to leave a large enough space so the infant could breathe.

The instant he did, Caleb began to cry. "Looks like he wants you," he said, turning to hand the baby back to Michelle. Except she wasn't there.

His heart stopped. "MM?" After placing Caleb and his cushion of down sleeping bag on the floor near the fireplace, he rushed back to the still-open door and out into the storm. She had to be close; in fact, he didn't understand how she could have gotten lost. Especially since he could have sworn he'd felt her hand on his jacket the entire way.

Chapter 8

Cursing, Garrett hurriedly retraced his steps. His heart pounded, but he kept an iron grip on his control, aware if he gave in to panic, neither of them would survive. He found her a third of the way back, that bright pink parka like a beacon. She lay in a crumpled heap in the snow, so still she might have been dead or frozen.

He scooped her up—not an easy feat, but his adrenaline gave him strength. Half carrying, half dragging, he got her back inside the warm shed.

Caleb had fallen silent and appeared to be watching the fire, entranced.

"MM?" he said, leaning close enough to feel the rise and fall of her chest. The relief slammed into him then, so strong it crushed him. He felt along her face, her jaw and then her head. The egg-shaped bump near her temple gave him a clue as to what had happened.

Somehow she must have slipped and hit her head.

Praying she hadn't been seriously injured, he moved her closer to the fire, making sure her upper body was cushioned by the same sleeping bag Caleb used. He debated whether or not to remove her jacket but in the end left it on until she'd warmed up.

Darkness fell with the swiftness of a guillotine. Disoriented and cold, Kent lifted his head to the wind and smiled through chapped lips. Smoke. Which meant fire. And warmth. Of course. For one brief moment as he'd stumbled through the ever-deepening snow, he'd allowed himself to doubt he'd be able to complete his mission.

Now he knew he would. Of course.

Humming under his breath, he bent over and renewed his efforts to trudge toward the direction where he believed the cabin to be.

His will might be strong, but his body weakened, daring to attempt to fail him. Furious, he rallied, pushing forward by sheer strength of determination. He'd crawl if he had to, but he refused to allow himself to die until he'd taken care of his sacred duty.

Somehow, lifting one leg and then the other, he trudged forward. There. A glimpse of brown wood through the blowing snow.

The sight gave him renewed hope, a fresh spurt of energy. As he neared the doorway, he fingered the small knife in his pocket. Before he reached for the door handle, he removed his glove and gripped his small weapon with numb fingers. He had the element of surprise on his side. Envisioning his actions, he smiled. The cold no longer mattered. He'd rush in, eliminate the infant and then take on the woman, the foster mother.

Yanking the door open, he stepped inside.

And stopped, staring, so shocked that for a second, he forgot to breathe.

Empty. The freakin' place was empty.

Not only was this particular cabin unoccupied, but part of the roof had collapsed. The acrid stench of smoke permeated everything. Even worse, the inside of the place felt nearly as cold as outside.

Again he double-checked the address on the phone, stepping quickly outside to peer at the numbers painted in gold above the front door. Yep. He had the right place.

Then what had happened?

No matter. Outside, the blizzard continued to rage unabated. He had no choice but to take shelter here for the night. He could better assess the situation in the light of the morning.

Spying the woodstove—with a nice pile of wood heaped next to it—he rubbed his hands together with glee. He suspected the stove had something to do with the smoke smell, but he'd have to take a chance. He needed the warmth too badly if he was to survive.

He built a small fire and fell asleep curled up next to its warmth.

Her head hurt. Michelle opened her eyes and tried to sit up, which sent stabbing pains through her head. She moaned.

"There you are." Garrett's relieved voice made her wonder what had happened. "I need you to try and stay awake. I think you might have a concussion."

Licking her lips, she started to nod and winced instead. "Caleb?"

"He's all right. He's warm and asleep."

"The last thing I remember is trying to find the other cabin in the snow. What happened to me?"

He placed a gentle kiss on her forehead, making her smile. "You fell and hit your head. Luckily, I was able to get Caleb here and then go back for you. You would have frozen to death otherwise."

"Luckily," she repeated, unsure why everything seemed unreal, as if she was in the middle of a dream. Again, her eyes fluttered closed and again, Garrett woke her. This time, he stroked her hair. "Please. Stay awake.

His touch felt so good, she couldn't help but lean into it. "Don't stop." Her murmured plea surprised even her. Again she struggled to sit up. This time she succeeded, trying to think past the searing pain that nearly blinded her.

Garrett took her hand and guided her fingers to the walnut-sized knot just above her temple. "Do you remember what you hit it on?"

"No. But I feel like I have the mother of all hangovers."

He laughed at that.

"Thank you," she said. "Thank you for insisting you carry Caleb."

Garrett nodded. "We're all okay. We're going to survive. All we need to do is wait out the storm."

"And then what?" she asked. "Once the storm passes, what's the plan?"

"I'll go back up the ridge and call for help. The bureau will send someone to pick us up."

"As long as they get here before Pitts," she said, only half joking.

"Hopefully both Pitts brothers have already been apprehended." His reassuring tone managed to make that last niggling worry go away. "Now, do you think you can get up and move around?"

"Move around. Why? I'm warm and comfy here." *In your arms*, she almost added.

Instead of relenting, he stood and tugged her to her feet. "I just don't want you getting so comfortable that you fall asleep."

Blinking, she realized she did still feel kind of groggy. "I read somewhere that not letting someone sleep with a concussion is a myth."

He shrugged. "Maybe so. But better safe than sorry. After I'm sure you're all right, you can sleep all night."

"Night?" Since he'd left the one window still boarded up, she had no way of telling the time of day. "Is it still dark?"

He nodded. "Yes. And the blizzard hasn't let up at all."

Oddly enough, she found this reassuring. "That means if Kent Pitts is still hunting me, he won't be able to make it here."

"Exactly."

They ate an odd snack, sharing a couple of cans with pull tops, eating the contents cold and with their fingers and washing everything down with bottled water. Caleb woke and she changed and fed him, checking out every inch of him in the flickering firelight before letting him fall back asleep.

Only then did it occur to her to wonder about their sleeping arrangements.

"Where are we…?" she began. Garrett touched her arm lightly, interrupting her.

"You'll have to share the sleeping bag," he told her.

"What?" Eyeing him in disbelief, she shook her head. "There's no way we all three can fit in there."

"Not me." He pointed. "You and Caleb can have it. If I stay near the fire, my jacket should keep me warm enough."

"You won't be warm enough," she told him, refusing to examine the tangled emotions she experienced at the thought of sleeping cocooned up against his body.

"I'll be fine," he insisted. "You just worry about Caleb. My job is to look after you, not the other way around."

Remembering the obstinate tone, she shrugged and crawled inside the sleeping bag. But once there, she couldn't stop worrying. She feared she'd roll over on Caleb in her sleep. She'd heard or read stories somewhere of that happening to people.

"Lots of women sleep with their babies," Garrett said when she expressed her fear. "My sister used to do it all the time. Now go to sleep."

Intending to humor him, she closed her eyes. The next thing she knew, she woke to the sound of him adding more wood to the fire.

"Is it morning?" she asked groggily.

"No. Middle of the night. The fire was burning too low. Go back to sleep."

Something in his voice… "You sound cold."

"I'm fine." The curtness of his reply told her he was not.

She checked on Caleb. Still sound asleep and toasty warm. "Quit being stubborn. It's warm inside your sleeping bag and I think we can figure out a way to make room."

Silence. "You don't know how tempting that is." The

rawness in his tone shocked her. "But I'm only a man, MM. And I don't think I can withstand that much temptation."

Heat blazed through her at his words, his tone and the vivid, vibrant, sensual imagery as she imagined his body pressed close to hers. For a heartbeat, two, she couldn't get words out. When she finally replied, she trembled as she spoke her heart.

"I want you." Her voice wobbled. "I want you as much as I want the warmth of this fire. Garrett, we don't know when we're going to get out of here, or even if we will. There's a crazy killer looking for us. I see no reason not to celebrate us finding each other again." *Even if it is only temporary*, she added silently, pushing away the ache in her heart.

His silence felt like a knife.

"Are you sure?" he finally asked, the rough edge in his voice hinting at deep emotions of his own.

"Yes," she managed, meaning it with all of her heart. "Come here and stop being so stubborn. Caleb's asleep on my other side. There's still plenty of room—this sleeping bag could fit a grizzly bear."

The fire crackling was the only sound. Then...

She heard the rasp as he unzipped his jacket and took it off. The simple sound sent her heart racing. She struggled to calm herself, to act as if this situation was perfectly normal, when every inch of her skin had gone on high alert. She actually had to remind herself to breathe.

And then he lifted the edge of the sleeping bag and slid inside.

Already warm from the fire and the down sleeping bag, her body erupted with a blaze of heat. The welcome coolness of his skin made her sigh. "You're cold," she said, mentally grimacing at the cheesiness of what she was about to say next but said it anyway. "Come over here and let me warm you up."

He scooted over without a word, back to her. She snuggled up next to him, spooning him with her body as close as she could to his. The tingling low in her belly spread, tightening her nipples. She wondered if he'd turn around or if he meant to simply sleep.

"MM," he said. Then he shook his head. Taking her hand, he guided it to the substantial bulge in the front of his jeans. "I want you so badly I can hardly think. But—"

Whatever else he'd been about to say ended with a groan as she cupped her fingers around his arousal and gently squeezed. "No protests," she murmured. "Turn around. Please."

"Not here," he told her. "I don't want to take a chance of waking the baby. We can keep each other warm."

He helped her up. The instant they left the warmth of the sleeping bag, he hauled her up against him and kissed her. Instantly she forgot all her worries about the cold and the fact that there was nowhere else to lie down.

Once he'd helped her remove her clothes, he quickly divested himself of his. And then he kissed her again, long and deep and wonderful.

Body to body, standing up, she opened herself for him. When he slid into her, she held herself absolutely still, thrilling to the feel of him, so large, so hard, deep inside her.

"There's a point, you know," he told her, his voice husky. "A point beyond which there's no going back."

Unable to help herself, she moved. Slowly at first, and then gasping as he pressed back. "I think we've already passed that point," she managed, before losing herself to the feel of him.

Kent had never shivered so much in his life. He wasn't going to sugarcoat things, but that night was probably the longest he'd ever spent, including the time he'd done in jail for petty crimes when he'd been younger. He found himself wishing for his brother—at least the two of them could share body heat and keep each other warm.

Instead, Kent had to make do with a faulty wood-stove that kept going out. He'd fall asleep as close to the limited heat it gave off as he could get, only to wake an hour later shivering since the fire had gone out. He added wood, used his lighter until the thing would barely spark, but he couldn't keep a fire going. He wasn't sure why, but figured it had something to do with the collapsed roof and maybe a faulty pipe. Sure as hell, if he survived this night, he'd find out in the morning.

And he'd also learn where the cursed foster family had taken his son.

But as he expected, he managed to survive. A little cold would never be able to kill him.

The icy gray dawn revealed the storm's fury had vanished. Now, a steady, silent snow fell, with big, wet flakes, the kind depicted on Christmas cards. Eventually, he guessed this, too, would begin to taper off, and he could venture out and try to learn what had happened to his quarry.

For now, once he saw the precarious condition of the roof, he knew he had to find another place to stay. Better yet, steal another vehicle and track his son down.

Rummaging through the cabinets, he found a few cans of corn and beans. When he opened the fridge, the contents were beginning to smell. But he spied a container of sliced ham and judged it safe enough, so he scarfed it down, along with some still slightly cool apple juice.

Feeling fortified, Kent Pitts, Holder of The Sword, braced himself and headed out into the snow to locate his prey.

Chapter 9

Once again, the act of making love with Michelle deepened Garrett's conviction that he'd made a huge mistake ever letting her go. One he promised himself he would not make again.

After, he continued to hold her close, unwilling to release her just yet. But finally, some of the chill seeped through and she began to shiver.

"Come on." Hurriedly dressing, they rushed back to the warm sleeping bag. Caleb still slept, toasty and cozy. Michelle went first and Garrett waited until she was settled before joining her.

Holding her close as she drifted off to sleep, he marveled at how content he felt. More than that. He felt... happy. As if this was how his life should have been all along.

He wondered if, when this was all over, he'd even be

able to let her go if she didn't want him. Even the thought made his chest hurt.

Caleb's cries woke them. Instantly, Garrett sat up, watching as Michelle reached for the baby to try and soothe him. While she changed Caleb's diaper, Garrett went for the premixed bottles of formula they'd placed by the fireplace in the hopes of keeping them warm.

"They're not ice-cold," he told her. "Maybe a little chillier than lukewarm. And we have no way to heat them."

"I know. It's okay. He seems pretty hungry, so I'm sure he'll drink it."

She was right. Once Caleb had gone to work on his bottle, Garrett began looking around for something they could eat for breakfast. Among the jumble of stuff he'd tossed in the backpack, he took out some wheat crackers and a jar of peanut butter.

"Instant protein," he told her. "It's not traditional morning fare, but I think it will do nicely."

Without taking her gaze from the baby, she nodded. "Sounds great."

He frowned. "Are you okay?"

She raised her face to look at him. "I'm fine." Her green eyes, usually so expressive, contained not one hint of emotion.

He understood that eventually they would need to talk about the future. The MM he knew would never be frivolous with her love. He didn't expect that had changed. She would be beating herself up inside for giving in to their mutual attraction. Especially since she believed they'd go their separate ways after all of this had ended.

He had no intention of leaving her side again, ever.

They had a lot to discuss and work out. First and foremost, he intended to ask her to become his wife.

But now was not the right time nor the right circumstances. He'd messed up so many things in their past relationship and wanted to make sure and do it right this time. She deserved nothing less.

Once they'd eaten, he checked his watch. "I'm going to try and get up that hill again and make a call. I've got to find out the status of the case and whether or not the Pitts brothers are in custody. Will you be okay here by yourself?"

"Of course." Still watching the baby, she nodded. "If something happens, I've got my gun. I won't hesitate to use it if I have to protect Caleb."

"Good. I doubt there'll be trouble—even if they're still on the run, getting anywhere in this weather is damn near impossible. You should be safe. And I won't be gone long."

"Have you even checked outside to see what the weather's like?" she asked, finally raising her face and meeting his gaze. "It sure sounds like the storm has either died down or lessened."

Fighting the urge to kiss her, he smiled instead. "I'm about to find out. Lock up after me."

Once he'd put on all his winter gear, he yanked open the door. Snow still fell, but the lazy, fluffy kind that made for good skiing.

Except for the treacherous layers of ice underneath.

Moving carefully, he was pleased to see that the several inches of fresh powdery snow acted as a buffer to the ice. Since the shed they were using for shelter sat halfway between the first cabin and the hill, he didn't have as far to go before he started to climb.

Without the horrible wind buffeting him, he made it to the top much more quickly. Once there, the wind felt stronger.

Pulling out his cell, he checked the signal. Two bars. Not bad, but not good. He'd just have to cross his fingers he would be able to make the call.

Dunn answered on the second ring. "Where the hell are you?" he demanded, before Garrett could even get a word out. "I hope you're still staying put. We tried sending someone to retrieve you, but the roads are impassable."

Up here, the wind made it difficult to hear.

"I know. We tried." Briefly, Garrett outlined what had happened. "What about the Pitts brothers? Are they back in custody?" Instead of an answer, he only heard static. "Dunn?"

Nothing but silence. Garrett ended the call and tried again. This time the call wouldn't even go through. He shook his head and dropped the phone back in his pocket. Without an answer to his question, he needed to remain on his guard, weather or no weather.

Turning, he headed back down. A movement near the trees caught his attention. Deer? Shading his eyes with his hand, he focused as he tried to see through the falling snow. He cursed as he caught a glimpse of what appeared to be a man in a dark parka moving through the trees toward the old cabin. Was that writing on the back? Or a logo of some sort? Squinting, he tried to get a better view, but the forest swallowed the man up.

A neighbor? Someone who might have seen the smoke or noticed the collapsed roof and was worried people might be trapped inside?

Or Pitts? Garrett knew the cult leader had stolen one

of the guard's cell phones, which meant Pitts could easily locate the addresses where his children were being cared for.

Heart hammering, Garrett rushed to intercept him. But the deep snow hampered him. Sliding, fighting to keep his balance, he made it to the bottom of the hill by gliding as if he wore snowshoes. Which he really wished he had.

He couldn't see the man in the parka. Good. This meant if he took cover, he could track the stranger unobserved and unnoticed.

Withdrawing his weapon, he ducked into the trees, aware the stranger wouldn't have made it past his location. Except for animal tracks, the snow remained pristine.

Using the trees as cover, he headed in the direction where he'd last seen the man.

There. He stopped. Human footprints. Raising his head, he did a quick 360 scan. Nothing. But that didn't mean he hadn't been spotted. For all he knew, the intruder could have him in the sights of a rifle right at this moment. Or, he reminded himself, the possibility still remained that he could be a neighbor out checking the snowfall or the cabin.

Unfortunately, until he had reason to know better, Garrett had to proceed as this intruder was dangerous.

Tracking the footprints, he noted how they made a circle around the cabin, never directly approaching it. This could mean one of two things. Either Pitts had somehow managed to make his way here in the storm and now was scoping out the place before launching an attack, or the neighbor from across the way had seen the collapsed roof and figured no one was inside.

Garrett's money was on Pitts.

Every sense prickling an alert, Garrett continued to follow the trail. It lead right to the ruined cabin. Smoke from the faulty woodstove poured out the open door.

Damn. When Garrett and Michelle had fled with baby Caleb, they'd made sure the fire in the woodstove had been out.

This so alarmed him, he took a step back, instinctively moving away from the cabin and into the nearest group of trees, needing deeper cover.

Not good. Only a man on the run—or a complete idiot—would try to stay inside a cabin with a collapsed roof and ruined woodstove. Building a fire must have been the only way the intruder could keep warm.

It had to be Pitts. Moving as quickly as he could, using the trees for shelter, Garrett circled around and tried to spot the man again. He needed to keep Pitts away from the shed and Michelle. Hopefully, he could either capture the fugitive or take him down before he got anywhere near Michelle and Caleb.

For the first time, it seemed the weather might have been on his side. He hoped the elements had so weakened Pitts that he'd be easy to overcome. His predilection for swords and knives made him unpredictable, but worked in Garrett's favor. Pitts most likely wouldn't have a gun. And armed only with a knife, unless Pitts had deadly aim, using a blade to kill meant he'd have to be able to get close. No way was that happening, not on Garrett's watch.

The cold seeped through his already-wet clothing, chilling him all the way to his bones, yet Kent Pitts felt invincible. Zeal burned through him, heating his blood. He cared little for what happened to his physical body once he'd completed his task. And this close, no way a little ice and snow would stop him.

He continued on, confident his senses and the blade in his pocket would lead him to his offspring—blood to blood. Despite the icy wind attempting to strip flesh from his bones, he felt warmer with each step. In fact, the visions began to appear, and he knew as he had all along, that his path would be victorious.

Hot. So hot. He removed the coat first, dropping it carelessly into a heap onto the snow. Laughing out loud, he marveled at how wonderful he felt—strong and warm and now above the miserable cold and the storm.

The gloves, the hat, the shirt—they, too, had to go. He felt gloriously at one with the elements and welcomed the icy cold snow pelting his skin. He strode, he shimmied, he shouted with glee as he headed toward his destiny.

While Garrett was gone, Michelle used the time to take inventory of what they'd been able to salvage from the cabin. The acrid scent of smoke in her hair made her crave a shower. Exhausted and worried, she was ready for this all to be over. Surely, by now they'd captured the Pitts brothers. Soon, they'd send someone to collect Caleb and her. And then she and Garrett would part ways.

As soon as the weather cleared, she'd be packing up and heading home to Ohio. Since Garrett had said he worked out of Clarksburg, West Virginia, she couldn't help but wonder where he lived these days, trying to picture a house or an apartment. Then she decided it didn't matter. Once this was over, she'd never see Garrett again.

She would never forget the words he'd said right before they'd decided to split. *I didn't sign up for this, MM.*

Not a house and kids and life in boring suburbia. I can't do it. You need to find someone else, someone who can give you what you want.

Heartbroken, she'd been powerless to speak, unable to push words past the ache in her throat. Instead, she'd watched as he, back straight and head held high, walked away. Out of her life forever.

Or, she amended silently, for five long years. And proven once and for all she'd been wrong when she thought she'd gotten over him. His sudden appearance in the doorway of her rented cabin had been like a punch in the gut. She'd given in to temptation, she who'd trained herself to keep her desires under control. One mistake had turned into two, and now she felt as entangled with him as she'd ever been. His leaving would hurt just as badly.

His leaving…even the thought made her want to curl into a ball in pain. But she wouldn't. Just like last time, she'd manage to survive, even if all the color had been leached out of her world.

This time, she'd let him go with a smile, even if it killed her. They both had finally gotten what they wanted—he'd done well at his job and she had her family, sans husband.

Which was exactly as it should be. What mattered now was sweet Caleb, her sister's perfect baby. The instant he'd been placed in Michelle's arms, she'd made a silent vow to protect and love him the rest of her life.

A sound from outside made her shift nervously. A shiver of foreboding danced up her spine. Why wasn't Garrett back yet? What if something had happened to him?

Not a second after she'd had that troubling thought,

someone tapped lightly on the shed's door, which she'd bolted closed per Garrett's instructions.

"Garrett?" she asked quietly.

"Yes."

When she heard his voice, a ton of worry she hadn't even realized she was carrying slid off her shoulders.

Until she caught sight of his face.

"I saw someone," he told her. "It looks like he spent last night in the old cabin. His tracks led into the woods—luckily in the opposite direction from us. I think it's Pitts. I'm going to go back out and try to locate him before he finds us and Caleb."

Without hesitation, she immediately went for her pistol. "I'm ready," she declared, lifting her chin. "If he somehow makes it here, he's not getting anywhere near me or the baby. Especially the baby."

More than anything, he wanted to kiss her then. He'd never loved her more than that moment, standing so fierce and determined, looking like a mama bear protecting her cub.

Instead, he managed to nod. "Remember, he likes to use knives. He's good at throwing them, too. If he appears in the doorway, you can't hesitate. And don't shoot to wound. You'll have to take him out."

"I understand." She walked over to him and squeezed his arm. "Though I'd much prefer if you could get him first."

He had to smile at that. And then, unable to resist, he did what he'd been aching to do—swept her up against him and claimed her mouth with a kiss.

When he finally lifted his head, they were both breathless.

"You come back," she ordered, her fingers still clutching his jacket. "Find him and do what you have to do, but come back."

"I will," he answered. And turned to go before he did anything he might regret.

Back outside, the overcast sky had turned a lighter shade of gray. The huge, wet snowflakes from earlier had changed to tiny flurries. Which meant, he hoped, the storm was finally winding down. If they were lucky, tomorrow the sun would come out and the melt would begin.

Now to find his quarry. Stepping in his own footprints, he headed back toward the ruined cabin.

Tracking the man—whoever he was—turned out to be much easier than Garrett would have supposed. Judging by the tracks in the snow, his quarry had gone in a complete circle—twice. He'd simply gone around the cabin. And from seeing the second ring of footsteps, just a few feet from the first, the man had begun to stagger. Several impressions suggested he'd fallen and managed to get himself back up.

Hurt, wounded, or just nearly frozen? It didn't really matter. Either way, Garrett would soon catch up to him. And when he did, he needed to be prepared.

A flash of color in the snow gave him pause. As he drew closer, he realized what had happened. The intruder had begun to remove his clothing.

First, Garrett found a woolen stocking cap. Next, a winter parka with US Marshal on the back. A chill went up his spine. This had to be one of the Pitts. And if he was shedding his clothing, hypothermia had set in. Garrett needed to find him soon, or Pitts would freeze to death out in the snow.

Garrett wanted to arrest him alive. Not haul in a dead body, unless Pitts got close to Caleb and Michelle.

After the parka, which he scooped up, Garrett expected to find the rest of the clothing. Instead, he saw movement through the trees. He hurried as best he could through the thigh-deep snow. A shirt, shoes and socks were like trail markers directing him.

The instant he caught up with the shirtless and hallucinating man—Kent Pitts without a doubt—he knew what he had to do.

Chapter 10

Every sound had Michelle jumping out of her skin. Pacing—not an easy thing considering the room must have been ten by ten at the most—she must have checked on Caleb fifty times, even though he continued to sleep contentedly.

She told herself over and over that the odds of Pitts making it here without Garrett intercepting him were beyond astronomical.

Yet she couldn't shake the feeling that something bad—something awful—was about to happen. If not to her or Caleb, to the man she loved.

Loved. The certainty of this knowledge nearly had her doubling over. She loved Garrett. No matter their past, no matter that she knew they had no future, she loved him. Always had, always would.

Gazing at the still-slumbering baby, she knew her

life had become full beyond her wildest dreams. She'd lost her sister and she'd always carry that sorrow deep within her, but what better way to honor her memory than to love her sister's son? Her empty arms had been filled and she knew she should count her blessings. No way should she even think about wanting more. Especially since Garrett had long ago made clear that his idea of the perfect life was totally different than hers.

A loud bang from outside had her tensing up again. It had been close, close enough to shake the walls of the little shed. She lifted her pistol, thumbing the safety off. Her hand shook slightly, but she imagined she had steel in her spine. Pitts would have to go through her to get to Caleb, and she didn't intend to give him a chance to do that.

Another crash outside. She took a step closer to the door.

"MM." His voice sounded low, his tone urgent. "It's Garrett. Can you unlock the door and let me in, please."

For a second, she stood frozen. Something in his voice... Had something gone wrong? Was Pitts holding Garrett hostage and using him to try and get in?

The instant the scenario occurred to her, she knew it wasn't possible. Garrett would die before he'd let that monster near her or the baby.

She rushed to open the door, keeping her weapon ready just in case. Taking a deep breath, she pulled. And stared. Garrett half held, half dragged, an unconscious, nearly naked man.

"Is that...?"

"Yes. I've got to get him inside or he'll die."

She didn't move. "No. I can't let him anywhere near the baby. He could be faking."

"He's not." Garrett's words were clipped. "He has no weapon and on top of that, I've handcuffed him."

Reluctantly, she moved aside, still keeping herself between the cult leader and his son.

Garrett carried Pitts over to the fireplace and set him on the floor near the heat. "When he comes to, he might be kind of combative. Help me tie his ankles."

"With what?" Looking around, she saw nothing they could use. "I don't have any rope."

"There's some in my backpack."

She decided not to ask why he had rope and went and fetched it for him. While he worked, she watched with her arms crossed as he secured Pitt's ankles. "Make sure he can't move," she instructed, unable to help herself. The idea of having this man in the same room as Caleb terrified the hell out of her.

Once Garrett had finished, he went and got the armful of clothing he'd apparently dumped at the doorway. "This is the jacket he stole. I'm going to cover him with it and hope it warms him up. I don't know what else to do."

"Why are you helping him?" she asked.

He met her gaze. "I'm sworn to uphold the law. I couldn't just leave him to die in the snow. If I did, I'd be no better than he is."

Swallowing, she nodded. "I understand, but I make no promises. If he tries anything…"

"He won't." Garrett sounded certain. "If and when he wakes, he's going to be extremely weak."

"Then what are you going to do with him?"

"Take him into custody, of course," he replied. "Now that the storm has broken, it shouldn't be long until the bureau sends someone to retrieve us. I gave my boss our location when I called to check in."

Though she nodded, she wished she had his certainty. He'd always been like that—rock solid and confident in the things he believed in.

Pitts moaned. She expected him to begin thrashing around like a fish out of water as the feeling returned to his limbs, but he didn't move.

"We need to remove his wet clothing." Though Garrett sounded reluctant, he began doing exactly that. "Let me have that baby blanket."

Though the idea repulsed her on many levels, she handed it over without a word, looking away as Garrett stripped the cult leader down to nothing and then covered him with the blanket.

"At least you didn't use the sleeping bag," she said.

"Yeah. I can't risk losing that." Standing, he eyed the still-unconscious man. "I tried to move him as gently as possible. From what I remember about hypothermia, any sudden movements can trigger an irregular heartbeat. That in itself can be fatal."

"Part of me wants to shake him hard," she admitted. "For what he did to my sister."

"I understand. Believe me." The steel in his jaw told her he suppressed similar urges.

"If he—when he—wakes up, you're absolutely certain he can't get free and try to attack us?"

"Yes." The certainty in his voice reassured her.

They both stared at the motionless man in silence.

"I'll be glad when this is over," Garrett finally said. Though she couldn't help but agree with him, part of what she'd leave behind broke her heart. Again, and as equally painfully as it had been five years ago.

Just then, Pitts stirred. At first, he made a small tremor, but after that, he began thrashing violently.

"Settle down," Garrett ordered, his voice stern.

Immediately, the still-out-of-it man quieted.

"We need to get some sleep," Garrett told her.

"There's no way." Arms still crossed defensively, she jerked her chin toward where Kent Pitts sat, slumped over. "If you really think you can sleep, go for it. One of us needs to stand guard."

"He's securely tied," Garrett pointed out. "I promise you."

"That's good. Get some rest. I intend to watch him until reinforcements arrive and take him away."

Garrett exhaled, his gaze shifting to the still-unconscious man. "We don't even know if he'll survive this."

Since that had no bearing on her decision, she simply nodded.

"How about this?" Garrett finally asked. "You take first watch. I'll set my phone alarm to wake me in a couple of hours. Then I'll guard him while you sleep. Will that work for you?"

Slowly, she nodded. "Sounds like a plan."

"Good." Without another word, Garrett crawled into the sleeping bag, careful not to lie too close to Caleb. He closed his eyes and a few seconds later, his even breathing told her he'd fallen asleep.

Now she studied Kent Pitts. The only times she'd seen him had been on the television, not in person. In real life, he appeared much smaller than she'd supposed. Though short in stature, he appeared muscular, as though he worked out. The one time he'd opened his eyes, she thought they were a light blue, close to the color of steel. Even though his hair appeared to have turned prematurely gray, she couldn't judge his age with any real certainty. Her best guess would place him somewhere in his forties. Objectively, she supposed some would find him handsome, and no doubt his looks had helped him find all the young women willing to become his brides.

Like Lydia.

She shuddered. Though she knew hatred wasn't a healthy emotion, she burned with hate for this man. She couldn't forget what he'd done—and what he'd intended to do to helpless babies.

He moved again, the same restless, involuntary jerking of muscles. She continued to watch him, her pistol in her hand, just in case.

Caleb let out a cry, that first squeal that she'd begun to learn was a prelude to his hearty wail. He made a few, quieter snuffling sounds. It was getting close to time for his bottle.

At the sound, Kent Pitts opened his eyes. The vicious clarity as he turned toward them left no doubt he was fully conscious. Michelle froze.

"With The Sword I will fight for my right to live free, seek The Truth," he said. "And defend myself from The Enemy."

The strength in his voice surprised her. However, she didn't know how to respond to his rhetoric, so she kept silent.

"My son," he rasped, glaring at her. "Give him to me. I don't care what I have to do, but I refuse to let you corrupt him."

She knew better than to engage him, she truly did. Yet she couldn't seem to help herself. "Corrupt him? I heard you want to kill him. You murdered his mother in cold blood. She was barely eighteen. My baby sister." Her voice caught. "I loved her and never even got a chance to say goodbye."

Though he had closed his eyes, apparently tapped out of energy, he opened them again. They burned with a fanatical fierceness. "Lydia had no other family," he managed. "Only me and the people of The Sword."

"Yes. She did," she insisted. "She had me. I did my best to raise her after our parents died."

He'd let his head loll forward and she thought at first that he wouldn't respond. But he did, even though he spoke in a whisper so low she had to strain to hear it.

"She renounced you." His mouth curled with contempt as his voice appeared to gain a little strength. "On the day we wed."

She refused to let him rattle her. He was weak and restrained and she had a gun. "You killed her. Lydia was young and innocent and beautiful, and now she's dead. Why? Why did you do such a thing?"

His eyes had drifted closed again, and he didn't respond. Fine. She hadn't truly expected an answer anyway.

Just then, Caleb let out an ear-piercing wail. Pitts lurched up, not quite to his feet, but onto his knees. He then used the momentum to throw himself toward the baby.

Her heart stopped and after that, everything seemed to happen in slow motion. Not even pausing to think, Michelle launched herself at him, using her body to block Caleb. They collided and she knocked Pitts sideways, somehow managing to hold on to the gun.

She also screamed. The sound so startled Caleb that his wail cut off midcry and he fell silent.

Pitts fell, his legs at an awkward angle, thankfully far enough that he couldn't try the same stunt again. Though he didn't move, Michelle brought her pistol up and aimed it at his head. "Try that again," she said. "And I'll kill you." She meant every word.

Garrett must have jumped up at her scream. She saw him in her peripheral vision.

"MM," the soft command in Garrett's voice had her cutting her gaze to him, though she instantly returned it to her enemy. "Put the gun down. He isn't moving at all, look at him. I think he might have hit his head."

"No." The slightest tremble made her hand shake, but she still kept her weapon aimed at Pitts. "He tried to hurt Caleb. He killed my sister. He needs to pay."

"If you kill him like that, you'll be no better than he is. He's unarmed." Garrett took a step closer, holding out his hand. "You're not a murderer. Give me the gun."

Slowly, she shook her head. "No."

"What will happen to Caleb when you're sent to prison?" he asked. "Think about that."

That question, more than anything else, made her realize what she'd almost done. Hand shaking, she lowered her pistol and flipped on the safety. "Sorry," she mumbled. "All I could think about is how close he came to getting Caleb."

Garrett nodded before crossing to the downed man. He checked Pitts's pulse, both at his throat and again at his wrist. "He's dead," he said, his expression hard. "Looks like he hit his head or broke his neck when he fell."

Stunned, she took a step closer. "He's really dead?"

"Yes."

Now the shaking started in earnest. "I didn't mean for him to... I was only defending Caleb."

"Shhh." He got back to his feet, wrapping her in his

arms and holding her close. "It's okay. You acted in self-defense. There's a difference."

She let him comfort her, hoping like hell he didn't realize how much she needed him to keep her close. She promised herself she wouldn't cry, and she didn't, even though emotion clogged the back of her throat and her eyes filled with tears.

Caleb cried, reminding them he still needed to be changed or fed, and she exhaled. Stepping out of Garrett's arms, avoiding looking at the dead man on the floor, she went to Caleb and set about attending to his needs.

Garrett watched her fussing with Caleb. He'd never loved her more. Little MM, her green eyes wild, pistol in hand, so fiercely protecting her sister's baby. Her baby now, he corrected himself. She'd been terrified and trying to hide it, yet equally determined not to let any harm come to the infant.

Sure, he'd had to talk her down off the ledge, but he figured that was pretty normal for someone who'd an instant before considered herself and her child in imminent danger. From the way she trembled after learning Kent Pitts was dead, he knew she truly hadn't meant to kill the man.

Which was more than he could say for himself. If he'd been the one on guard and Pitts had made a move on the baby, he wasn't sure what he would have done.

In the end, all that mattered was that the ordeal was finally over. Unless…his heart stuttered in his chest. Unless Kent's brother, Wayne, had followed close on his older brother's heels.

No. He thought back. All he'd seen was one set of

footprints. The two men had split up, and no doubt Wayne had gone after Kent's other child, a daughter.

Still, he had to make sure.

Despite not wanting to alarm Michelle, he quickly outlined his thoughts. "I'm going to go check out the area and go back up on the hill and see if I can get a status update. Maybe Wayne's already been captured. I also need to see if anyone can give me an ETA for when they can get us out of here."

Busy taking care of Caleb, she nodded. "Okay. I've still got my pistol. I'll be fine."

He nodded and began suiting up. He hated the idea of leaving her alone with Pitts's body, but knew he had to make sure there wasn't another threat.

Once he stepped outside, he saw the clouds had begun to break up. Bits of blue and even spotty sunshine brightened the sky. The wind had died completely away and, even though the air still contained a bite of cold, the temperature had risen. Though he didn't have access to a weather forecast, it made sense that it would soon be above freezing. Which meant they wouldn't be there too much longer. If the weather continued to warm, the snow and ice would start melting. The roads would clear up and the bureau would send a team to retrieve them.

They'd be safe. Finally. As he trudged through the still-deep snow, continually searching for any signs of another intruder, he started planning. Once the FBI got here and transported them back to civilization, he knew what would happen after that. They'd be questioned separately. Medical doctors would examine all three of them, especially the infant, to make sure they were all healthy. Once the paperwork had been completed, it would be over.

And he and Michelle would go their separate ways. Even thinking about it made his chest hurt.

Shaking off the melancholy, he focused on the task at hand. Though he kept his eyes open, continually searching the tree line as well as the snow for tracks, he saw no signs that anyone else had been here. He felt even better after finding the tracks that he and Kent Pitts had left earlier had not been disturbed.

Some of the worry coiling inside him loosened up. He made it to the top of the hill much more quickly than either of his previous attempts, since the lack of wind and the melting snow made the hike much easier. As soon as he reached the top, he made a slow turn, surveying the area below. Not once, but twice, just to make sure. There were no signs of movement—not even wildlife.

Satisfied, he turned his cell phone back on and waited. As soon as he saw he had a signal, he punched the contact icon for his boss.

Max Dunn answered after three rings. "Ware, please tell me your charges are safe."

"They are." Tone clipped, Garrett recounted everything that had happened.

"He's dead?" Max sounded both relieved and disbelieving. "Kent Pitts is really dead?"

"Yes. And I assure you, it was both self-defense and purely accidental. Now please tell me you have his brother in custody."

"He's dead, too. Got in a shootout with one of the neighbors of the woman who was taking care of the other baby."

Silence while Garrett digested this. "Wow."

"Yeah, wow. Talk about a ton of paperwork."

Dunn's dry comment made Garrett smile. "Do you

have an ETA as to when you can send someone to get us out of here? My truck is out of commission." He knew his SAC would be highly amused if Garrett were to tell him exactly why the truck wasn't going anywhere.

"I'll have to get back to you on that."

Garret exhaled. "MM—the woman—has a car, but I'm not sure we'd be able to negotiate the roads with it. It's a four-cylinder, compact. I'm guessing Pitts had a vehicle. If you want, I can try to locate that."

"No. Stay put. I've got to coordinate a couple of things, but I'll let you know when I can send someone."

"I have no cell phone service in the cabin," Garrett reminded him. "Worse, we're holed up in what must have started out as a storage shed. There's no furniture, just a fireplace. Not a good place to stay in with an infant."

"Give me six hours," Dunn said. "I should be able to round somebody up and send them out your way by then. Will that work for you?"

After answering in the affirmative, Garrett ended the call. Six hours. He checked his watch. That meant they should be out of here before sundown.

He'd best get back to Michelle and let her know.

Chapter 11

Holding baby Caleb close, Michelle stood next to Garrett and watched as they put a motionless Kent Pitts's body on a stretcher and loaded him into an ambulance. Garrett kept his arms crossed and his jaw tight, not talking at all. She had to fight not to lean into him, to pretend for a few seconds that they were together, lovers, a family.

Instead, she held herself apart. Alone. Which she could accept. She had no choice. Aware that from now on, she would have to be stronger than she'd ever been. Caleb depended on her now. She couldn't afford to spend time wallowing in regret or pining after a man who clearly had his own life to live—one that didn't include her.

This chapter of her life was over. The time had come to start a new one. Kent Pitts was dead and his brother was, also. Neither of them were a threat any longer.

The ordeal was over. After the FBI had finished with her, she'd be free to take Caleb and go home.

She felt relief, of course. But the emotions swirling around inside her were more complicated than that. She could now envision a future. Her sister's supposed renunciation meant nothing outside of the cult and held no legal sway. After the necessary time had passed and she'd filed paperwork and had her home visit, she'd finalize the adoption and Caleb would become her son. Forever and always.

Whereas Garrett would become only a memory. As would Lydia. Thinking of her baby sister brought a fresh wave of grief. She swallowed hard, straightened her shoulders and told herself to remain strong. She'd do her mourning in private, at home in familiar surroundings.

Caleb cooed, reminding her of the bright spot in all of this. He was all that mattered now. She would learn to live with the constant ache in her heart, not just from the loss of her sister, but the constant longing for a man she would always want and could never have.

"Are you ready?" Garrett asked, his voice as impersonal as his expression.

She started to nod, but then she realized she had one thing left to do. "Just about. But now that it's daylight and the snow is melting, I need to go back to my rental cabin and see how many of my belongings I can salvage."

"I'll go with you," he offered immediately.

She forced herself to meet his gaze. "Thank you, but this is something I'd rather do alone. I'd appreciate it if you'd stay and keep an eye on Caleb for me."

Hurt flashed in his eyes, probably at her impersonal tone. Hurt, and maybe a hint of anger.

Since hurt would be inevitable on both sides by the time this was over, she pretended not to see. "Thanks," she said, grabbing her jacket and slipping out the door before he could protest.

Outside, she inhaled deeply. This time, the crisp air didn't hurt her lungs. Everything looked fresh and pristine in the layer of white. Like hope.

She straightened her shoulders, kept her head up and realized she needed to focus on the positive.

Despite the cold and the wet snow seeping through her boots, the walk in the snow through the woods to the rental cabin took her breath away. With all the tension she'd been under, she'd forgotten how gorgeous these hills were. Now that the danger had passed, she was free to let herself enjoy the unspoiled white landscape. Free to begin to plan a future, a life free of sorrow and pain and fear.

As long as she didn't think of saying goodbye to Garrett. Or maybe, she thought pensively, that was exactly what she needed to do today, the reason why she'd wanted to go to her rental cabin alone.

A few months ago, she'd come here and rented this place to be close to her sister and the cult. Michelle had never stopped hoping Lydia would reach out, ask for help and want to leave. Michelle would have moved heaven and earth to get her safe.

Instead, Lydia had married Kent Pitts—becoming one of many wives—carried and birthed Caleb and then in a horrible twist of fate, died at Kent's hand. All close to here. Michelle knew she needed to take a good look around and imbed the landscape into her memory. She didn't expect she'd ever be back. Too much grief would forever be tied up in these hills.

When she reached the cabin, it looked worse than she'd expected. What had once been a semi-picturesque cottage now looked like a shattered ruin from a recent war. Evidently, the weight of the snow had caused the damaged roof to collapse further. As she circled around to inspect all sides, she saw the structure appeared to have folded in upon itself. She'd need to be careful if she planned to go inside. It didn't look safe.

The crunch of boots on snow made her turn. Garrett, his tall form silhouetted against the sun, had followed her.

"Where's the baby?" she asked, more impatient than worried.

"I had one of the guys keep an eye on him," he answered.

"Why?" The sudden flash of anger surprised her.

He frowned. "Why what?"

"Why are you here? I clearly told you I needed to be alone."

He shifted his feet in the snow, apparently a little uncomfortable. Good.

"I wanted to make sure you're safe."

Once, she might have been touched. Now, each small kindness had the potential of deepening her pain. "While I appreciate that, again I have to ask you, why? Your assignment is over. You don't have to worry about me or Caleb ever again. Once you file your reports, I'm guessing you're free to go."

He stared at her. "MM, I—"

Grief mingled with fury clogged her throat. "Please don't call me that anymore. My name is Michelle. That old nickname is from the past. You know, the past that you said has no bearing on today." If she sounded bitter, so be it. Maybe she was.

"What's wrong?" he asked, clearly puzzled.

"I'm tired, Garrett." She shook her head. "So please move and let me get on with my life."

He started to speak and then closed his mouth, apparently thinking better of it. "I'll be waiting over here," he told her. "If you insist on going in that place, someone has to be around to dig you out if the roof collapses. And even if it doesn't, I need to walk you back to the others." He took a deep breath. "And then, after I do that, I promise to leave you alone, Michelle. If you're sure that's what you want."

She rounded on him, the urge to make him feel something, to hurt him as much as his indifference had hurt her. "What I want has never mattered to you," she said. "Why should that change now?"

And then, while he continued to stare, clearly at a loss for words, she turned back around and stomped through the snow to the doorway of the ruined structure.

Inside, the air of desolation and despair dissipated her anger. The small cabin had been, for all intents and purposes, completely destroyed. She spotted a few of her belongings: the diaper bag so new that the tag was still attached, the hardcover version of the latest infant care book and some of her hair products, all covered in a layer of soot. With a sigh, she brushed off what she could, shoving as much as would fit into the diaper bag.

Once she was satisfied she'd retrieved everything that mattered and started to lug the now heavy baby bag out, she realized she didn't care about any of it. They were just things. Easily replaceable. But they were hers, so she carried everything back outside, unable to keep from immediately looking for Garrett.

Despite everything, her heart skipped a beat when she saw him. He stood exactly where he'd said he'd be. She took in his big, broad-shouldered shape, aware she'd always find the sight of him reassuring. And sexy. That, too. Sexy as hell.

"I'm done," she said, lifting one foot after the other and attempting, despite the still-deep snow, to bulldoze right past him.

She might have pulled it off, if he hadn't reached out and grabbed her. "MM, wait—"

MM. Her silly, sentimental chest felt tight. Privately, she thought the anger was better. Safer, for sure.

"I told you not to call me that." She attempted to jerk out of his grip. Instead, he pulled her in closer, hauling her up against him.

"Michelle." His husky voice washed over her, tickling her nerve endings. To her consternation, she realized she was on the verge of tears. Panicked, she tried to find her earlier rage, but it had vanished like a puff of smoke.

He tipped her chin, forcing her to raise her gaze to his. "Garrett, I don't…" To her absolute horror, her voice broke. She cleared her throat and tried to forge on. "Whatever you're about to say, please don't. I don't need an apology, or a long, drawn-out goodbye. It is what it is, and you don't have to—"

"Hush," he interrupted. And then, before she could open her mouth to take a deep breath and finish, he bent his head and kissed her.

Heaven help her, her legs buckled. If not for his strong arms holding her against him, she might just have collapsed in a boneless puddle in the snow.

For one or two mindless seconds she gave herself over to the amazing, wonderful sexiness of his kiss. That, at least, hadn't changed. She'd never met another man who made her body come alive the way Garrett did.

To her stunned amazement, he was the one who broke it off. And then, while she panted for air and tried to make sense of what had just happened, he held her hand and her gaze and slowly lowered himself to one knee in the snow in front of her.

"MM—Michelle—will you marry me? Will you do me the honor of becoming my beloved wife?"

He'd said these exact words to her, in the same way, a little over five years ago. *Beloved.* Once, hearing his voice call her beloved had made every cell in her body sing. Of course, she'd accepted, and then right before their wedding, he'd proceeded to shatter her heart.

How could he? Hurt exploded inside her, nearly making her double over with pain. Only by gritting her teeth was she able to continue to stand upright. "Don't. Don't mock me like this. How can you not understand how much that hurts?"

Again she tried to pull away. And again he refused to release her.

"Is that really what you think this is?" The love and patience in his tone made her blink, even as she used the back of her hand to hurriedly wipe away tears she refused to shed.

"I mean every word, just as I did the first time. Michelle, I've been a fool," he continued. "I only thought I knew what I wanted."

Now she understood. This explanation had been long coming, but that didn't mean it would be any less painful.

"Closure?" she asked, her voice remarkably steady

considering she was dying inside. Wasn't this what she'd wanted all along? A way to tightly close the lid on their past, on them, so she could move on. "This is your way of trying to give me closure?"

As he opened his mouth to speak, she held up her hand. "You know what? I don't want it. I really don't need it. So just stop. Because what I want right now is to get back to Caleb. Then I'll do whatever it is that I have to do with the FBI and get on the road back to Ohio."

Having said that, she pulled herself away and marched back to the house to do exactly that. This time, he let her go.

Garrett didn't bother her again. She gave her report, twice, to two different law enforcement individuals. One FBI and one US Marshals, she thought. They interrogated Garrett as well, though separately from her. It was exhausting, but necessary, so she kept her answers concise and clear, and then they were finished with her. She left without even telling him goodbye.

Though it wasn't too long of a drive from West Virginia to her home near Columbus, a tangle of thoughts, recriminations and emotions plagued her. From experience, she knew the pain would lessen with time. Still, knowing this didn't make her hurt any less.

To distract herself, she turned on the radio, but since Caleb was asleep in the backseat, she couldn't crank it up as loud as she normally did when she drove.

She couldn't stop thinking about Garrett. Missing him, too. She knew she'd been a fool to let herself care about Garrett again. As if she'd ever stopped. But now, most of all, she wished she'd let him say whatever it was he'd been about to say. She knew better than to believe he'd meant it when he'd asked her to marry him, exactly the same way he'd asked her long ago. Once, she'd still believed in the possibility of a future with him by her side. Now, she wondered what he'd been trying to say.

The image of him kneeling in the snow, his brilliant blue eyes gazing so earnestly into hers, would be forever burned in her mind. Garrett wasn't the type to do anything halfway. What if he'd really... Hope briefly flared in her, until she quickly extinguished it.

No. Not just no. Hell no. A quick glance at the infant asleep in his car seat settled her uncertainty. Caleb needed stability, security. Not a woman who'd be a wreck once Garrett had let her down again.

Which he would, she had no doubt. As soon as the FBI called with some great assignment where he needed to be footloose and fancy-free, he'd tell her a fiancée and a baby were tying him down. And he'd be gone.

She knew she'd never survive that hurt a second time.

No, she'd done the right thing. And never seeing Garrett again would be all for the better in the end.

She only wished she could stop missing him so much.

As Michelle got closer and closer to her home, her excitement grew. The neat yards, the tidy row of neatly painted houses with their landscaped shrubs and flowers and trees felt like home.

When she finally turned onto her street, she felt a huge sense of relief. Her little house, white with green trim, looked exactly the way it had when she'd left it. Even after a couple of months away, seeing this place reminded her what it felt like to finally be home. Her neighbor had been checking on the house and kept the heat on.

Pulling into her driveway, she punched the garage door opener and parked inside the garage.

Finally, hopefully now she could breathe a sigh of relief. Once she settled back into the routine of normalcy, maybe she'd stop feeling as if she wanted to weep.

Taking care of the baby would go a long way toward helping her heal.

"Welcome home, little man," she murmured to Caleb as she removed him from his car seat. Then she carried him into the house on what would be the beginning of their new life together.

She'd just gotten Caleb down for the night, after giving him a warm bath and warm formula, when her doorbell rang.

Stifling a flash of alarm, she figured it was probably her neighbor, wanting to make sure she was really home.

But when she pulled open the door, she gasped out loud when she saw Garrett standing on her doorstep.

Her traitorous heart skipped a beat. "What do you want?" she asked, wincing inside at how rude she sounded.

"To kiss you again," he said, his smile sending flames licking at her insides. "But for now, I'd settle for finishing our conversation. You never did give me an answer."

"An answer?" She frowned as she realized he meant when he'd proposed. "But you weren't serious."

"Wasn't I?" Glancing over his shoulder, he dragged his hand across his chin. "Do you mind if I come in? It's been a long day, a long drive, and I really could use your bathroom."

This made her laugh, despite herself. "Come in then. Down the hall, first door on your left."

While he was gone, she paced, unable to help it. If she were a stronger woman, she'd send him packing. But she didn't have it in her. Plus she really wanted to hear whatever he had to say.

A minute later Garrett emerged. "Nice house," he said. "Warm and inviting. Exactly how I pictured your house would be."

She exhaled and nodded. "Thanks. Garrett, why are you really here?"

He came closer, stopping a few feet away from her. "Because I realized words are no longer enough. I have to prove myself to you. I'd like to stay—if you'll let me. I can sleep in your guest bedroom. I want to be with you—and Caleb—for however long it takes."

Now her heart hammered in her chest. "However long it takes for what?" she managed.

"To prove to you that I'm not going anywhere."

Dizzy, she looked away and tried to regain her equilibrium. "What about your job?"

"I've taken a leave of absence." He sounded proud. "They'd been bugging me to take a vacation," he admitted. "My unused days were piling up."

Though each word cut a chunk out of her already-bruised heart, she knew they had to be said. "But what about after? When your leave of absence or vacation is over, and they call you with an exciting undercover assignment that will take you away for months? What then?"

To his credit, he didn't try to sidestep the question. "I've already let them know I'd like to work out of the Columbus field office. It was either that, or I quit. They weren't too happy, but they've agreed."

Reeling, she wasn't sure what to say. Or think. Or do.

Garrett seemed to understand. "Is it okay with you if I stay?" he asked, his quiet voice husky.

Okay? Part of her wanted to launch herself at him and cover his face with kisses. The other part wanted to tell him no and send him immediately packing.

Torn, she decided she couldn't send him away. Not tonight. She didn't have the strength or the heart. And truth be told, she wanted him there.

Shaking her head at her own foolishness, she showed him the way to the guest bedroom, aware with him so close, he'd probably be spending more time in her bed than in his.

And she was right.

Epilogue

Two months later, Michelle marveled at her happiness. She loved her life. Garrett had been here, cleaning spit-up and dirty diapers, taking his turn at night feedings, and never once wavered from his apparent determination to prove how much he loved her.

Gradually, she began to believe he truly would stay. The iron grip she held on her emotions loosened—part of this might have been the crazy-hot sex they had just about every single night.

Over and over, he told her he loved her. She always thanked him, but finally she felt secure enough to open her heart and reveal her love to him.

This was how she'd always imagined their life together would have been. Partners, lovers and friends.

Signs of spring started to appear. Relieved, Michelle welcomed the return of the birds, the flowers attempting to poke their heads above the frozen ground. To her, the season of spring always signified renewal, rebirth. Particularly appropriate, since she and Garrett were starting over.

One night, after bouncing a grinning Caleb on his lap before bathing him and putting him down for a nap, Garrett dropped down to one knee, wincing as he landed on a baby toy, and proposed again. The hope and love shining in his bright blue eyes made Michelle's heart sing.

This time, she accepted.

They were married in the spring. Caleb's adoption paperwork came through a month later, right after Michelle took a home pregnancy test and learned she was pregnant.

She and Garrett included little Caleb in the celebration. "You're going to be a big brother," Michelle told him.

Garrett couldn't stop grinning from ear to ear. "Now," he told her, murmuring in her ear and sending chills up her spine. "If you have a girl, then I think our little family just became complete."

She smiled back, teasing him. "What if it's a boy?"

"Then…" He kissed the side of her neck, lingering. "We'll have to keep trying, won't we, Mrs. Ware?"

Her delighted laugh had Garrett grinning. "I guess we will, Mr. Ware. I guess we will."

* * * * *

REQUEST YOUR FREE BOOKS!
2 FREE NOVELS PLUS 2 FREE GIFTS!

H HARLEQUIN®

ROMANTIC suspense

Sparked by danger, fueled by passion

YES! Please send me 2 FREE Harlequin® Romantic Suspense novels and my 2 FREE gifts (gifts are worth about $10). After receiving them, if I don't wish to receive any more books, I can return the shipping statement marked "cancel." If I don't cancel, I will receive 4 brand-new novels every month and be billed just $4.74 per book in the U.S. or $5.49 per book in Canada. That's a savings of at least 12% off the cover price! It's quite a bargain! Shipping and handling is just 50¢ per book in the U.S. and 75¢ per book in Canada.* I understand that accepting the 2 free books and gifts places me under no obligation to buy anything. I can always return a shipment and cancel at any time. Even if I never buy another book, the two free books and gifts are mine to keep forever.

240/340 HDN GH3P

Name _____ (PLEASE PRINT) _____

Address _____ Apt. # _____

City _____ State/Prov. _____ Zip/Postal Code _____

Signature (if under 18, a parent or guardian must sign) _____

Mail to the **Reader Service:**
IN U.S.A.: P.O. Box 1867, Buffalo, NY 14240-1867
IN CANADA: P.O. Box 609, Fort Erie, Ontario L2A 5X3

Want to try two free books from another line?
Call 1-800-873-8635 or visit www.ReaderService.com.

* Terms and prices subject to change without notice. Prices do not include applicable taxes. Sales tax applicable in N.Y. Canadian residents will be charged applicable taxes. Offer not valid in Quebec. This offer is limited to one order per household. Not valid for current subscribers to Harlequin Romantic Suspense books. All orders subject to credit approval. Credit or debit balances in a customer's account(s) may be offset by any other outstanding balance owed by or to the customer. Please allow 4 to 6 weeks for delivery. Offer available while quantities last.

Your Privacy—The Reader Service is committed to protecting your privacy. Our Privacy Policy is available online at www.ReaderService.com or upon request from the Reader Service.

We make a portion of our mailing list available to reputable third parties that offer products we believe may interest you. If you prefer that we not exchange your name with third parties, or if you wish to clarify or modify your communication preferences, please visit us at www.ReaderService.com/consumerschoice or write to us at Reader Service Preference Service, P.O. Box 9062, Buffalo, NY 14240-9062. Include your complete name and address.

HRS15

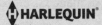
Her breath ghosted across his lips as she moved up onto her toes to get closer. His body tightened in anticipation of her touch, all too eager to resume where they'd left off last night. She placed her palm against his chest, the contact arcing through him like lightning. Did she feel the sparks, too, or was it all in his head?

He lifted his hand to trace the angle of her jaw with his fingertip and was rewarded with a small shudder. He smiled at her reaction. So she wasn't immune to him. That was good to know.

"Ridge," she murmured, her eyelids drifting down in preparation for his kiss.

I should stop this, he thought. *It's a mistake.* But no matter how many times he thought it, he still found himself leaning down, getting ever closer to Darcy's waiting mouth.

He had just brushed his lips across hers when Penny started to bark, a deep, frantic sound that made his blood run cold.

Darcy drew back, frowning. "What—?" she started, but Ridge took off for the house before she could get the rest of the question out.

Penny only made that sound when something was terribly wrong, which meant either she or the baby was in danger. He snagged a branch to use as a club, then ran as fast as he could in the mud, slipping and sliding as he moved. The dog kept barking, but now there was a new note in her voice: fear.

Oh God, he's back. The realization slammed into him, and Ridge kicked himself for having left the baby in the house. He'd never forgive himself if something happened to her. He took the porch steps two at a time and lunged for the back door, his heart in his throat.

Please, don't let me be too late.

Don't miss
COLTON BABY HOMECOMING by Lara Lacombe,
available March 2016 wherever
Harlequin® Romantic Suspense
books and ebooks are sold.

www.Harlequin.com

Turn your love of reading into rewards you'll love with

Harlequin My Rewards

**Join for FREE today at
www.HarlequinMyRewards.com**

Earn **FREE BOOKS** of your choice.

Experience **EXCLUSIVE OFFERS** and contests.

Enjoy **BOOK RECOMMENDATIONS**
selected just for you.

PLUS! Sign up now
and get **500** points
right away!

Earn
FREE
REWARDS
Join
Today!
HarlequinMyRewards.com

MYR16R